GRACE AND THE WIND

Kristina Dryža

GRACE AND THE WIND

Kristina Dryža

DoctorZed
Publishing
www.doctorzed.com

First published 2014 by DoctorZed Publishing.

DoctorZed Publishing books may be ordered through booksellers or by contacting:

DoctorZed Publishing
IDAHO
10 Vista Ave
Skye, South Australia 5072
www.doctorzed.com
61-(0)8 8431-4965

ISBN: 978-0-9924473-3-5 (sc)
ISBN: 978-0-9924473-4-2 (e)

A CIP number for this book is available at the National Library of Australia.

Cover image © Eugenia Tsimiklis

Printed in Australia
DoctorZed Publishing rev. date: 11/07/2014

I dedicate this book to my family; especially my late grandparents and father—Pranas, Elena and Saul, my mother—Emily, dearest friends and the provider of all life. This is as far as I can see at the moment.

ACKNOWLEDGMENTS

This book has had a long journey. To those that have been with me for the many steps: Dr Vik and Dr Milena Dryża, Gina and Natalia Kasprzyk, Helena Szewczyk, Aldona Pretty, Lina Verbyla, Sonya Lakes, Jeanette Casey, Patricia Comazzetto, Blair Thomson, Vida Gaižutis, Muntaha Bourke, Elsa D'Ercoli, Stephen Wasilewski, Dennis Muirhead, Maria Jones, Mojgan Khadem, Dr Reza Samvat, Vajiheh Vaezi, Jane Heard, Mary Roccisano, Melanie Osborne, Diane Bellchambers, Cinzia Vuat, Ian, Belinda, Rachel and Nick Hannaford, Sasha Sachs, Lisa Fry, Christie Laurie, Christos Christou, Nick Ashley, Michelle Ticknor, Mahesh Natrajan, David Skewes, Liz Page-Hanify, Dianne Rankine, Hiroko Oda, Rebecca Dettman, Christine Diamond, Marco Bonincontro, Sabine Toh, Megan Drechsler, Miriam Jacobson, Willy Banta, the late Charles Mardel, Alex McKie and all my fellow travellers from MoM and DYS—I humbly thank you all for contributing in your own unique way, whether it was offering an encouraging word, holding space or providing me with a quiet room to write.

To my publisher, Dr Scott Zarcinas, for helping me tether the Wind to earth, Marian Clift for her editing skills and making me read far more fluently than the initial manuscript presented, and Eugenia Tsimiklis, for the gorgeous cover design and always understanding my design aesthetic.

To the 15-year-old Grace that still lives inside me—I love you, and to the future Grace-in-becoming—I look forward to connecting with you and to the divine field of grace that surrounds us—I surrender.

To the Wind—stay close, to all the experiences that led me here—my deep appreciation and to my spiritual teachers in all realms—my eternal gratitude.

"To every thing there is a season, and a time to every purpose under the heaven." — Ecclesiastes 3:1

1 | Feeling Stuck

Grace Rose was in mathematics class. Pens, Post-it notes, compass, calculator, and other junk from her pencil case cluttered every inch of desk space. Her green blazer was wrapped awkwardly around the back of the chair, its buttons now uncomfortably pressing into her lower back. Not only did it pain her physically, the private school uniform was also an affront to any sense of feminine dignity. The green- and white-checked dress lacked shape, resembled an eight-person tent, and was useless against the elements; too sheer for the cool spring days and a portable sweat bath in the height of summer. The regulation black shoes ("Clodhoppers," her mother called them) completed the felony.

I should've sat closer to the window.

Grace thought this one action would change everything. The teacher was explaining trigonometric functions at the blackboard in his usual dry and dreary manner. She didn't know whether to cry out of boredom due to her complete incompetence with numbers, or her frustration at an education system that forced students to memorise facts instead of learning through direct engagement with the world.

Grace never really absorbed the foundational skills of any subject; she just wanted to get to the fun stuff without learning the basics. As such, she'd passively read horoscopes instead of actively learning about the planetary positions and their effects. Likewise, she couldn't be bothered learning about tides or weather patterns when she just wanted to be out in the water surfing the waves. Grace knew why she never made much progress with any subject—it was the refusal to put the time and effort in to lay a solid foundation from which to build.

I can't wait to escape this stupid school.

While Grace very much wanted out, she was most definitely trapped in, like the reflection she caught of herself in the window, an image imprisoned in glass.

She thought of herself as having no noticeable or obvious talents, yet she craved to be anything but ordinary. Naturally dark blonde, she bleached her hair a couple of shades lighter in an attempt to brighten her face and lighten her mood. Little more than average height and build, the only not-so-average part of her was the size of her pupils—they were always dilated, the size of flying saucers— although she considered her eyes anything but special. They weren't the crystal blue eyes of a swimsuit model's, which bewitch teenage boys and older men, but rather subpar. Green, but not a sparkling green. More a dirty-suburban-pool-with-algae-at-the-bottom green.

A black fleck dominated the lower right hand corner of her right eye, which she liked to think of as a beauty spot. Her grandfather (who she called Kosmos) once commented that she had perfectly proportioned almond-shaped eyes, which she later confirmed by removing an almond from a jar of unsalted mixed nuts in the pantry and holding it over her left eye. It was a perfect fit.

Grace glanced up at the clock, willing it to go faster. She dreamt of the day when the unrelenting pressures of school life and stupid extra-curricular activities would come to an end. If it wasn't homework, it was compulsory basketball practice or piano lessons, which she despised. She hated practicing scales and couldn't see their point; they were deathly boring and useless.

Finally, the classroom bell rang, forcing her out of her reverie and into action. With her left arm she swept everything off her desk back into the pencil case and walked to her next lesson.

"Grace, hey, wait up!" yelled a female voice down the corridor.

Madison Bailey, a fellow ostracised student living on the fringes of school life, bounded up to her. While Grace desperately sought companionship, it wasn't exactly Madison's company she was after. Though Madison was her closest ally at school, she never completely trusted her. As much as the popular girls at school dismissed Grace, Madison intimidated them, but if they were to actually include her one day, she'd sell Grace down the river for less than small change.

"There's a pool party Saturday night at Amber-Jane's," she said. With her older-than-her-years personality—not in the wise, but rather confidence sense—Madison's husky tone of voice had the raspy character of a hard-drinking jazz singer.

"I don't want to hear about it. As if I'd be invited anyway."

"It's okay, I've spoken with her."

Grace's nose twitched with intrigue. Amber-Jane Collins was the doyenne of the popular clique of girls. Tall and athletic with shiny, dark chestnut hair, she never suffered the routine of pimple popping that for Grace was as frequent as hand washing.

"Why would she say it's okay for me to come?"

Madison was deadpan. "Well, she said anybody can come."

Grace threw both her arms above her head and with great theatrics replied, "Oh, of course, silly me, I forgot. I'm Anybody. Grace Anybody Rose. Daughter of Dylan and Carla Rose, sister of Abel, fifteen-years-old and in tenth grade at Hamilton High, but just Anybody to my nearest and dearest."

She figured the only reason she'd been granted permission to attend the pool party was that quantity mattered more than quality.

Why is it the fickle in high school only care for head counts?

She suddenly yearned for the company of her two closest friends, Juliet King and Ruby Cameron. They were trustworthy anchors in the sea of superficial teenage friendships, not adversaries trapping her in the continuous swell of judgment. Their mothers met at a North Gateshead mother and baby group, and the three were raised in each other's shadows. Now the families lived in other parts of town and the girls went to different high schools.

They love me, quirks and all. I'm Somebody to them.

"Are you going to come or not?" Madison asked.

"All right, fine. Nothing to lose and only social humiliation to gain."

"Great! Let's tell our parents we're sleeping at each other's houses and then we can stay out all night," Madison replied.

Grace knew in the grander scheme of life staying out late wasn't a big deal, but with the limited freedom she had, it equalled a passport with all the visas stamped.

Throughout the week, Grace learned more about the pool party. She discovered that kids from other private schools in the city would also be attending. She didn't care so long as Gabriel Thomas, the boy she had a mad crush on, was there.

Every night, with a mixture of fear and conviction, Grace tried on possible outfits for the party. All went from wardrobe to floor until the closet was bare and the carpet full. She experimented with different makeup looks too. Grace knew she wore too much blusher, but didn't care, as she'd read that during the Second World War women in concentration camps pinpricked their index fingers and rubbed the blood on their cheeks to give them a healthy glow. She wanted to give the same appearance of health.

The party day finally rolled around and Grace headed downstairs, just as her brother was getting ready to leave for soccer practice. Four years older, Abel was everything Grace wasn't—laid-back, easy going and popular.

"Gonna bother gettin' dressed today?"

"If I feel like it," she shot back.

Grace wished for a more meaningful relationship with her brother. Six-foot-four with dark brown hair and piercing, azure blue eyes, Abel was the guy everyone wanted around at parties.

So what went wrong with me?

With that depressing thought, Grace prayed that her parents had left for the day.

I know they mean well with all their questions, but please, not today.

2 | Indulging in Fantasies

Getting ready for the party wasn't nearly as much fun as Grace had anticipated. She stared at her messy dresser. All the eye shadow powders and lip pencils were missing their lids.

Ugh, I hate doing my makeup alone.

There was no one to share lipsticks with, to question whether to go sparkly on the eyes or play up the lips. She held her hair up in a bun and then let it fall below her shoulders and mouthed, "What do you think? Up or down?" to the mirror.

For the party Grace had decided to wear a vintage pair of acid-wash jeans that had a lime swirl on the front left thigh and back right calf. They were a touch too tight, so when she sat down the excess fat got trapped at the top of her thighs like sausages trying to escape their casing.

Why am I so fat and ugly? Why?

Grace barely noticed her words. She uttered something similar a hundred times a day.

She chose a purple satin negligee to go with the jeans and tied a navy cardigan around her shoulders to temper any unnecessary 'sultriness'. She had so much mousse in her hair that it looked—and felt—like straw.

For a teenager, she had a modicum of insight into herself. Lack of exertion with her personal presentation was a form of protection. People might say she was unattractive, but Grace could argue that it was because she didn't try. Obviously she'd look totally different if she made an effort; therefore people weren't making a fair (if such a thing existed) judgment of her. She dreaded making a concerted effort with anything, as it meant deliberately putting her best foot forward and exposing herself to criticism.

If I spent three hours doing my hair and makeup, I could look as good as the models in the magazines. I just choose to spend my time more wisely.

Unfortunately, spending her time more wisely didn't mean reading classical literature (she preferred young-adult fiction) or listening to Debussy, but running hours of repetitive self-loathing affirmations in her head.

***

Grace walked to the train station down Atkinson Drive, barely noticing the panoramic view overlooking the city and the sea beyond. Nine kilometres from the city centre in the foothills, Grace thought the location of her house a little like her life—undefined: not the city, not the hills proper and definitely not the beach.

On the express train from Hillside to West Beach, Grace indulged her Gabriel fantasies. Mostly they involved him seeing the light and deciding that Grace was the one for him. Ignoring her became code for "I'm mad about you." She envisaged reaching for some chips at the party and their hands touching or, even more daring, him asking for her number under the guise of studying together. Delusional thoughts, yes, she was completely aware of that, but necessary to keep her dreams alive. Like oxygen.

At that moment Grace spotted Madison waiting at the station. Dressed from head to toe in black, a silver stud glistened out of the left side of her nose, her hair was straightened, and she held a canvas satchel that contained all her prized possessions—cigarettes, patchouli body spray and blotting papers for oily skin.

They were an hour late for the 3 p.m. start, and the sun's ferocity had muted slightly. The girls instantly knew which house it was by the shrieks from the back garden and the blaring of music over the fence. Grace self-consciously tugged at the amethyst pendant around her neck and felt a fluttery feeling in her stomach.

She sensed it was a mistake to come, but pushed past the feeling.

3 | Crushed Dreams

Amber-Jane's house was a Victorian double-fronted two-storey. The wooden gate leading to the back of the house was open, and as Madison and Grace walked around, they saw Amber-Jane flicking her mane of silky hair from side to side as if in a hair conditioner commercial. A skimpy, white Lycra dress flaunted ill-advised time spent on a tanning bed. Quickly glaring at them, she returned to reminding her coterie of sycophants exactly how fabulous she was.

The new arrivals placed their bags under one of the many cream cotton and cane umbrellas and surveyed the landscape. The social groups were clearly defined, as was typical at these parties: sports jocks, fashionistas, surfers, the graphic design students, a handful of trendy individuals from the year below, and kids from other private schools in Gateshead. Though they went to other schools in the city, these kids had the same style and demeanour of Hamilton's popular crowd.

I'm sure they've never broken a skirt's zipper trying to wiggle it over their thighs.

Oliver, who also existed on the fringes of high school life, rushed over with some beers for them like a man who'd struck gold and couldn't believe his luck.

Grace sculled the strong dark ale from the long neck of the bottle and asked Oliver to get her another one. Her parents would kill her if they knew she drank alcohol, though what frightened her more was how senseless it made her—it wasn't a comatose state; she could still talk and carry on, but with no real awareness of her words or actions. It was as if somebody else invaded her body and carried on being Grace, while she herself was nowhere to be found.

And so she couldn't remember how the scene exactly happened, but there she was at last, alone with Gabriel in the house's formal dining room. Gabriel's rolled-up t-shirt sleeves sat on top of his broad shoulders to emphasise the firm lines of his biceps, and the white hibiscus print on his blue board shorts only enhanced his robust masculinity.

In Grace's eyes Gabriel's face was a study in symmetry that could launch a million aftershave ads. His nose appeared cut by a surgeon, the line was that sharp and clean; his eyes were the green Grace wished hers were—sparkling emerald—his eyebrows perfectly framing them. His tan shaped his cheekbones the way beauty companies promised customers that their bronzer products would.

Grace didn't know much about Gabriel's personality given that he'd barely spoken more than twenty words to her. Ever. Most often it was, "here," when forced to pass some class handouts to her. What Grace knew of him was second-hand through gossip. She imagined him as a secretive painter/musician/wordsmith who'd serenade her with personally penned lullabies when she couldn't sleep. A passionate pursuer of the creative arts and an accomplished athlete on the sports field, he'd be her ticket to social acceptance. Well, in her mind anyway.

Grace would later come to know this current state as 'alcohol-related amnesia', and as a result she didn't remember the conditions under which she told Gabriel that he was the love of her life and how he inspired her to write poetry. With all the pent-up intensity that frightens guys and makes them run a kilometre in the other direction, she declared that they belong together, that this was their destiny. Gabriel's only response (with all the emotional maturity a sixteen-year-old guy could possibly muster) was that he hated poetry and made a mad dash for the nearest exit.

Years later, Grace still cringed at this evening; how quickly dreams could smash into little pieces at your feet. No matter what she had imagined in her head, the ghastly truth that was actually playing out in front of her was what she needed to deal with.

Grace had dreamed of a chance like this for well over a year, and in less than thirty seconds it was gone, her hopes snuffed out at the click of a finger. She was left on her own, swaying from the compounding influences of alcohol and utter embarrassment.

The residual part of Grace that wasn't subject to the alcohol induced mental blackout went to find Madison. Outside, the cool air returned fragments of consciousness to her. She saw Gabriel join Amber-Jane and whisper in her ear. Both turned in Grace's direction and sniggered uncontrollably. She felt all the humiliation of the world rain down on her.

Drenched in a wave of complete indignity, Grace barged through the partygoers and bolted out the wooden gate onto the street, the shame too much for her to bear. It was impossible to leave the party with her head held high; her dignity was beyond repair. She wanted to simply disappear without a trace, to be swallowed up by the earth.

She started to run, first through the streets near the beach, then jogging, then power walking, followed by aggravated pacing back and forth. Two steps this way, two that way.

Why did you do that, you idiot? You had the perfect opportunity to become friends with him and you blew it. I mean G, try to be his friend first; not his girlfriend. You had an 'in' and now you've messed it all up. You absolute moron! You should've taken it slow not, "Tada, here I am, the soul mate who was under your nose the whole time." Don't you think if he even slightly liked you, he would've tried to talk to you at least once during the three years you've been at the same school together? How can you be so utterly retarded? You always do the wrong thing. Always! Why did you go so lovey-dovey over the top mentioning poetry, you idiot? I mean G, why oh why couldn't you have acted cool?

In her head she ran through at least seven different scenarios of what she should've said to Gabriel. By this stage Grace had no idea where she was, but knew she was no longer near the ocean as the salty sea air had vanished. She got a shock when she caught her reflection in a shop window. She looked deranged, like a crazy person, with lots of muttering under her breath interchanged with deep sighs.

A car horn beeped and made her jump in fright. Without thinking, she had almost walked straight into oncoming traffic. Not even acknowledging the frightened, bedazzled face of the young female driver, Grace stepped back on the footpath to continue passing unrelenting judgment on herself.

4 | The Wind Enters

"How can you not value your own life?"

Vitriolic thoughts still pumped through her mind, and it took Grace a while to realise that the words didn't actually come from her.

"How can you not value your own life, Grace?"

She almost snapped her neck trying to see where the voice came from. Grace even peered into the garden of the single-fronted cottage next to her to make sure no one was hiding in the metre-high hedges playing some sort of sick, practical joke. She couldn't see anyone.

"How can you be so preoccupied with what others think of you that you walk into oncoming traffic and put your own life at risk?"

Where is this voice coming from?

"Why does their opinion matter more than your own?"

Grace screamed back, "Because it matters! Don't you get how publicly humiliated I am?"

There was nobody around her, only the houses and night sky, and everyone in the neighbourhood was peacefully asleep.

"No, I don't. Only your personality cares that it's been humiliated. Grace, your soul is always intact. Why do you let these harmful thoughts control your life?"

Whoever she was speaking to obviously wasn't from this planet. *I'm going crazy, I'm hallucinating.*

But then for good measure she shouted back, "Because that's what people here on earth do!"

The Wind hadn't planned on entering Grace's life so abruptly. It had hoped to enter subtly, with more gentle murmurs and hints of its coming, but the current situation called for immediate action.

11

"No need to shout, Grace, I'm right here. You're far more than just your thoughts, emotions and actions; you're also the awareness of them."

"Huh? What? Who are you?" Grace barked back. "And how do you know my name?"

She felt stuck in quicksand—absolutely paralysed—with her feet sinking deeper and deeper into the asphalt.

"I'm that which can't be put into words, but that in the deepest part of your heart you know to be real."

Words tumbled out as her fear began to diminish and annoyance crept in. "Whatever! Whoever you are, leave me alone! Can't you see I'm busy?" With her remaining mental strength, Grace made her leaden legs walk forward, even though she felt a piercing chill travel through her bones.

"Stop confusing who you really are with these harmful thoughts."

Grace recalled the last time she was an emotional mess. It was a few weeks back after a massive row with her father. She had been grounded for staying out later than an agreed-upon time at the underage disco in Franklin. She had stormed out of the house to pace the streets, and the perceptible presence of a gentle wind had soothed her. She had felt a remarkable sense of calm, but tonight the wind stirred her emotions into a blizzard.

"You are the awareness, not merely your thoughts."

"What?"

"You are choosing to dwell on the very thoughts that destroy you."

A charge electrified her body. Disbelief swept through her.

Was it even possible? No, it couldn't be. Was it . . . was it the wind speaking to her? Was she having a conversation with the wind? No, impossible. It couldn't be.

She definitely heard a voice, and there was nothing else other than the breeze making the hairs on her arms stand on end. She looked around again. Streetlights shone, cars sat quietly in parking bays and security lights turned on and off with each gust of wind.

I'm losing my mind. I'm talking to thin air.

Grace pinched her cheeks and clapped her hands in an attempt to ground herself.

Oh no! I'm going to end up in the funny farm. Am I schizophrenic? I can't be. But I'm hearing voices. I'm hearing voices!

A wave of icy panic flooded her.

I'll be committed.

She stomped her feet as if she were squishing ants.

But if it is the wind, how does it know my name?

"Grace, your deluded thinking is making you feel even worse. You become powerless if you internalise your negative thoughts without examining the essence behind them."

I'm literally going mad. I'm hallucinating. Somebody help me, please. Please . . . somebody . . . anybody . . . help? Please help me?

The words were all in her mind. She dropped down on the footpath and pulled the cardigan over her head.

"Grace, you can't hide from me. I've let you run away from me countless times before, but now you must allow me to help. I love you too much to leave you curled up and alone on this sidewalk."

The party felt a lifetime ago. It would've been far easier to stay and deal with the fallout from her misguided interaction with Gabriel. If this was madness, Grace understood why people spent their entire lives fearing it.

"Who are you?" Her voice displayed the tiniest bit of courage.

"For now, know me as the Wind, but you will in time come to know me as yourself."

"Look, I don't have time for games," she replied.

"I am the you that you haven't grown into yet."

"What? Are you mad? You're the wind, but you're also me? You're insane! I can't deal with this right now. Just go away!"

"Know that I am the Wind, Grace. I am the breeze cooling sun-bathers on a diabolically hot summer's day, scattering leaves to the great annoyance of street sweepers, blowing air into children's kites and windsurfers' sails. I can make my presence felt, but if you bottle me up, my essence gets contained."

"I can't be dealing with riddles at the moment. Really, I can't. I don't bloody care! For the final time, leave me alone!" Grace thought she let out a deadening scream, but no sound escaped from her mouth. The gravel of the footpath dug into her forehead and the tops of her feet.

"Come, there are a few things I want to share with you. Let me be a strong hand to guide you through the dark."

She thought about this for a second. Maybe the only way up was to take the Wind's hand? But did the Wind actually have a hand to hold?

5 | Rejection

Why doesn't anybody like me?
Pins and needles had formed in the arch of her right foot. Grace sobbed as she bent down to brush away the tiny bits of gravel that left lingering red grooves on the tops of her feet.

"That's merely a thought."

All this talk of thoughts and thinking strained her ears, let alone her mind.

"Your thoughts can bind or release you, Grace," the Wind said. "There is a way through your suffering, though. Ask yourself, 'What's the thought triggering this feeling? Why does it have so much control over me?'"

It was as if someone had uttered something in a foreign language, when she'd never heard of the country, much less stepped foot on the soil. The words didn't compute, no frame of reference existed and she was engaging in conversation with thin air. It was sheer madness, yet she kept the lines of communication open.

"Didn't you see how they all laughed at me?" she said.

What a dumb question! The Wind obviously wasn't at the party.

"That's your interpretation of the event."

She was indignant as her volume increased. "You didn't see it. How would you know?"

"I did witness it, Grace. The more important question to ask is, did you? Did you hear the exact words Gabriel said to Amber-Jane? Are you sure they were even talking about you?"

She sat on the kerbside and hugged her knees.

How did the Wind know Gabriel and Amber-Jane's names?

15

"I know what I felt."

"Grace, I doubt it. You don't know your real feelings, as you're too busy pushing them away, denying them right of entry. You don't know what Gabriel whispered to Amber-Jane; he could've been speaking about anyone or anything."

How did the Wind know any of this?

"Or cracking a joke, or relaying gossip completely unrelated to you. You presumed his words—fiction not fact—and this imagined story is bringing you to your knees. Literally."

Silence.

"Grace, when you mistake your thoughts for who you really are—rightly or wrongly—they will have an impact on you."

Grace shrieked. "This is all your fault! Why did you let this happen to me? I was honest, I spoke from my heart. I told Gabriel what I truly felt." She jumped up with a jolt and lashed out at the brush fence behind her.

"No, Grace, you spoke out of fear and neediness. You don't even know your heart yet."

She turned to punch the air in front of her. Her hands red, Grace shouted, "I hate you! I hate you!"

"Okay," said the Wind calmly. "I'll let you throw your tantrum, and while you do, let me remind you of some home truths. Are you ready, Grace? One, take responsibility for your own life; stop blaming others. Two, accept the situation as it is; don't wish it to be any different. Three, realise that acceptance is the path of least resistance. Four, get out of your head and into your heart. Five, know this moment will never come again; make peace with it. You could even try to enjoy it."

Hearing the word 'enjoy' ignited her fury. "Are you insane? I'm supposed to enjoy the guy of my dreams laughing in my face? I'm to enjoy the rejection?" Her voice rose to a shrill tone again. "I ought to revel in the unworthiness that is my constant shadow? I should treasure being a social pariah? All of this is to be enjoyed?"

The Wind was unperturbed. "Witness the perfection of this moment. Accept how it is, not what you wish it to be."

Grace was incensed. "So not only must I take pleasure in the rejection, I also need to see it as perfect?"

She had to get home, but how? She started jogging again and her handbag kept slipping off her shoulder. Eventually she came to Tower Road and knew where she was. How could she kill the Wind? She couldn't strangle it, shoot a bullet through it or stab it to death. Fuming, she kicked the closest thing, the traffic light's concrete base.

The Wind stayed constant. "Grace, everything about this situation is ideal. It's not your personality's view of perfect, but it is the universe's. It's creating these situations to help open your heart."

"Oh great! So now the universe is involved too."

"Stop trying to control each and every aspect of your life. You can't micromanage all the details, otherwise what else is there left for the universe to do?"

With no traffic passing on the roads, Grace didn't bother waiting by the traffic lights for the flashing green man to indicate it was safe to cross.

"Painful situations are mostly of your own making Grace."

How could a night so eagerly anticipated degenerate into a complete and utter farce?

"Grace, you focus too much energy on wanting to be liked and attach yourself to people too quickly in your need for approval. You have to learn to love yourself first. Only when you approve of yourself, will others."

The fight left her. Her ire abated.

"Grace, there's a park two streets west from here. Compose yourself and calmly walk there."

She did as instructed. The absurdity of the situation warranted it.

"You're still too absorbed in your thoughts to appreciate the magic of this evening's events. They conspired to bring you here to claim your sovereignty. There will never be another Grace Rose."

"Thank goodness," her father would've joked.

"Realising on your deathbed that you didn't live the life divinely chosen for you because you never thought you were good enough, can you imagine the pain, Grace? Realising that you wasted your life coveting everyone else's, never blissfully engaging in your own existence. Can you imagine the sorrow?"

By a cluster of birch trees, Grace lay down on the flattened grass. It was too cold to take her cardigan off and make it into a pillow.

"Grace, accept that there's hurt inside you, but don't think that the real you has been damaged. Your true self, your soul, is indestructible. You will rest here tonight, and I will watch over you."

Resigned, she curled herself into a ball and hugged her knees to her chest as the agitation in the air settled.

6 | Dealing with the Fallout

Grace woke suddenly, feeling the grass of the park on her cheek. Before the usual recriminations kicked in, she took a slow breath and filled herself with the warm summer air that ensured she didn't freeze last night. Sitting up she remembered the Wind's words, "Get out of your head and into your heart." She focused on this moment, on the air entering her abdomen until the fear hit.

What am I going to tell Mum and Papa?

Pulling out the mobile phone from the squashed vinyl handbag, she saw that there were nineteen missed calls from Madison. Grace hit the call button, and Madison answered after only one ring.

Upon seeing Grace's avatar, words tumbled from Madison's mouth. "Where are you? You just bolted. I had no idea where you were. I had to tell my parents you decided to sleep over at Amber-Jane's."

Not aware of the ins and outs of school politics, Madison's parents obviously didn't know what a preposterous lie this was.

"What happened, Grace? You were out of there like a shot."

"I don't want to talk about it."

But she really did want to talk about it. She wanted to tell her story to a sympathetic listener who'd be willing to rehash every minute of each scene over and over again.

"Where are you now?"

Grace couldn't tell Madison she slept in a park that, until last night, she didn't even know existed. "I'm at home."

"Want to see a movie later?"

"Can't. Having dinner with my grandparents."

"Okay. You sure you're fine? You know I'm here if you want to talk. And if not today, then at school tomorrow."

The word 'school' made Grace shiver. "I'm totally fine. I'll see you in the morning." She put the phone back in her bag and the panic started.

How to get home?

Her mother gave her some extra money for the weekend, so a taxi home wasn't a problem. Getting into the house without detection, that was the issue.

She called Abel. "Are Mum and Papa home?"

"Yep. Want me to get 'em?"

She never thought it rude that there was no greeting between them, a bit like writing emails with no formal salutation, just launching straight into what you want to say.

"No, no, no," she rattled out. Grace calmed her voice. "I mean, do you know if they're going out today?"

"I think they're going to the Conley's for lunch."

"Hilarious! Papa can't stand the Conley's."

Grace used to call her father 'Dad', but around about her thirteenth birthday he became 'Papa' (pronounced with a French accent crossed with an Irish lilt). Her father, never quite sure how to deal with his daughter's quirks, thought it best not to question them and now answered to 'Papa' without fail.

"Where are ya? What's shakin'?"

"Just call me when they leave for lunch. I'll explain when I get home."

She never really considered it before, but in this instance she felt blessed to have Abel in her life. Her gratitude disappeared the minute she remembered Amber-Jane and Gabriel laughing at her.

The Wind was back. "Everything in life happens exactly the way it's supposed to. Don't play the scene over and over in your mind, thinking about what you should or shouldn't have said or done."

Grace brought herself back from wherever her mind wandered and answered, "Oh, it's you." She got up to stretch her legs and forced her mind back to last night's events.

"Grace, this process is futile and will only cause you more pain. Don't attempt to rationalise the situation, for it will be in vain. The past has passed, so let yesterday go. Be in tune with what's happening around you now."

Grace replied with the word that drives parents around the world insane, "Whatever."

7 | Numbing the Pain

Monday morning came, and Grace knew she couldn't go to school. She frequently got tonsillitis, but there was no way to fake it this morning. Getting the temperature of the thermometer to increase by artificial means, like running it under hot water, would be difficult without anyone noticing, but if she were vomiting, she'd have to stay home. Grace decided to mix lemon juice with milk, but after downing the dreadful concoction there was no evidence of illness, only slight nausea.

She returned to bed and half an hour later her mother entered her room and placed some school books on the chair by the door. Crumpled clothes lay scattered on the bedroom floor amongst half-read books, while large pin boards on the wall balanced the weight of countless photos, magazine articles and concert ticket stubs.

"Morning, sweetie, how was the party? You were fast asleep by the time we got in. Our lunch turned into dinner and drinks."

"Fine."

As a sullen teenager, Grace found her mother more annoying than helpful. If Carla asked questions about her day, Grace felt it a violation of privacy, and her mother's questions were met with monosyllabic responses. But given some space, and in her own good time, Grace would often venture forth with details.

With maternal sense, Carla knew not to press too hard so she kept their conversations as light and general as possible until Grace volunteered further information. Grace often thought her mother engaged with her in the same way the Japanese did business with foreigners. They used the soundless gaps in negotiations to be still with their thoughts, while the Westerners filled the nerve-wracking silence with words, showing their hand and spilling trade secrets in the process.

Today was no different. Carla knew from experience how the rest of the conversation would go with her daughter:

"Who else was there?"

"The usual people."

"What did you do?"

"Talk."

"What did you eat?"

"Food."

It would be worse than pulling teeth.

"Mum, I'm not feeling well."

Carla sat on the pink and white batik bedspread and touched Grace's forehead, neither clammy nor hot. Dylan had already left for work. "What's wrong, sweetie?"

Grace propped herself up in bed to turn and face her mother. "My tummy hurts."

"Well, take some painkillers and go back to sleep."

What! It's never this easy.

Grace couldn't believe her luck. She usually needed a fever plus at least two other symptoms before her mother allowed her to miss a day of school.

"Grace, I'm running late for a meeting, so stay in bed and try to sleep it off. I'll be back in the afternoon to check up on you." With a quick kiss of the forehead, she headed for the door.

Carla worked at the local library's information desk, and as a rule she never seemed hurried. "A lady never rushes, Grace," she repeatedly declared. Carla kept astute sayings like this on systematic recall and knew the maxims backwards, though only a few were implemented. Most were recited as airy-fairy phrases and not put into practice.

Grace often thought her mother's behaviour childish—following only those rules of society she wanted to—but since most people absolutely adored her, she got away with it. Carla was a ball of contradictions: inconsistent in her life philosophies, sayings and actions.

She was also a gracious hostess and competent cook, but Carla's organisational skills were sorely lacking. Five minutes before guests arrived for a dinner party she still wouldn't be dressed and would ask Dylan to hold the fort—which he hated—or worse, ask Grace and Abel to go mingle with the guests while she got ready.

After hearing her mother's car engine start, she headed to the kitchen and sat down on the breakfast bar stool.

I wonder where she's off to?

But before pursuing this train of thought, Grace threw her hands up in the air and shouted, "Awesome!"

She found a slab of praline milk chocolate in the pantry to devour for breakfast. Praline was her utmost favourite flavour. She peered into the freezer's top drawer looking for some Turkish Delight ice cream (another top-five flavour on par with salted caramel). Ice cream was her father's weakness too, so he turned their freezer into an Italian gelateria.

Seventh heaven!

She lifted the spoon greedily to her mouth and some ice cream fell on her pyjama pants. She scooped it up, ate it and unconsciously rubbed the stain into her pants.

If only every day could be like this!

Next, Grace opened a packet of sour cream and onion chips, moved to the family room and grabbed the TV remote control. Within the next hour, the harsh rebuke would begin, but in this second, junk food represented freedom and a moment to transcend the laws of cause and effect, choice and consequence.

Grace collapsed onto the caramel leather sofa and channel-surfed the TV stations. She planned to maximise the morning's laziness before hopping back into bed with a school-prescribed novel in hand.

Playing truant meant time travels faster than the speed of light. Upon hearing her mother's car in the driveway, Grace switched the TV off, sprinted up the stairs, jumped into bed, placed *Tess of the*

d'Urbervilles on her stomach and closed her eyes so that it'd look as if she fell asleep while reading.

Carla entered the house, placed her keys and handbag on the kitchen bench, walked through to the family room and touched the TV. Feeling its warmth, she smiled and climbed the spiral staircase up to Grace's room.

"There you are, sweetie. How are you feeling?" Carla sat on the corner of the bed and gently stroked Grace's unwashed hair.

"Oh, hi, Mum. What time is it?" Grace asked as she pushed her knuckles into her eyes. "I must've fallen asleep."

"It's almost 2 p.m. Have you been sleeping all day?"

"Aha," she replied in her best fake sleepy voice.

"Do you think you feel well enough to go to Kosmos and Veronika's for dinner?"

"I think so."

"And your tummy's okay?"

"Aha."

"Okay, well Abel will be home at 5 p.m., and then we can go. Your father will meet us there."

Her grandparents were her idols. She adored Veronika's appearance, especially how she wore her black hair (with hardly a hint of grey) like Jackie Kennedy did in the White House. With her deteriorating eyesight, her grandmother wore glasses with lenses as thick as double glazing, and the black spectacles dominated her face and sunken cheekbones. To complete her distinctive look, she painted her lips orange vermilion.

Veronika always appeared serene and appreciative of the beauty surrounding her. She honoured the beauty of every living thing and circumstance, even though most of the people around her chose to focus on the problems of living in this world. She also never seemed to get flustered when people mistakenly spelled her name with a 'c', not a 'k', and gently enunciated the correct spelling in countless telephone conversations with administrative staff.

Although only five-foot-three, family and strangers alike were

influenced by Veronika's glow. Their home in Hunter Park was burg-
led twelve years ago, and the same policeman who dealt with the
case still popped in for regular cups of tea. Veronika had a magnetic
attraction; people felt worthy in her presence, not through anything
special they did, but by the very act of their breathing.

As Juliet's mother once said, "She approaches life's challenges with
such dignity and it inspires others to do the same. What an amazing
woman you have for a grandmother."

Of this Grace was sure.

Kosmos perfectly complemented his wife's charisma. A stroke six
years ago left him paralysed down the entire left side of his body,
but he was still the backbone of the family. His loss of mobility only
increased his stature. A retired violinist for the symphony orchestra,
Kosmos told Grace that while he was suffering the stroke, he had a
vision of himself playing the violin. Not to an audience of strangers
that applauded his talent, but to his two grandchildren who couldn't
yet value his musical genius.

Kosmos thought holistically, acted honourably and enjoyed
telling a dirty joke or two. Like everyone else older than Grace in
the family, he loved dispensing wisdom as throwaway comments
that could easily be found in a Chinese fortune cookie, such as, "It's
expensive to buy cheap." Or, "Choose quality, and quality will choose
you."

Their mahogany front door was unlocked when Carla, Abel and
Grace walked in. Kosmos was sitting in his usual seat at the dining
room table, the bay window highlighting the rose garden behind
him. His lacquered wooden cane hung on the back of his chair, and
the day's financial newspaper was open in front of him. Kosmos
always stood up when the family entered the house, but could never
move fast enough to meet them at the door, so the greetings took
place between the French country dining chairs.

8 | Family Bonds

Grace knew she was a sloppy dresser, but didn't care. Tonight she wore faded black jeans that were a touch too long, and over her tatty t-shirt a shapeless, purple acrylic cardigan.

Veronika, on the other hand, was the epitome of class, yet she never once said a word to Grace about her grooming habits, believing it a pilgrimage that Grace had to make on her own when she was ready.

Standing at the stove, Veronika made crepes that they would wrap around Frankfurter sausages and eat with their hands, exactly as she had done for them as young children. She transferred a crepe to some paper towels to drain the excess butter and poured the batter for the next one into the frying pan.

"How are you, my cherubs?" she said as they entered.

"Grace stayed home from school today," Carla said as she kissed her mother on the cheek, leaving a hint of her own pink lipstick.

"Really, Grace, my swan. What's wrong?" She left the stove to give her two grandchildren a hug.

"Oh, I'm okay now. I had a kind of tummy ache."

"Well, you do look rather pale," Veronika said, stroking Grace's cheeks. Staring up at Abel, she said, "And you, young man? Are you sure you've stopped growing?"

"Yep, I've stopped growin'. Had a biochemistry test and biology practical in the mornin', then an earth science and physics lecture in the afternoon."

"Well, there you go, Mother, that's more than I know about what's going on with Abel," Carla said. Her mobile phone then rang and she answered, "Okay, well, good luck. We'll see you later. Tell them you're blessed with an understanding wife." She put the phone back in her handbag, and said, "Dylan's still in the office and can't make it, so let's begin." She pulled the cling wrap off the potato salad (with the extra spicy honey mustard sauce) and placed the bowl, in the shape of a lettuce leaf, in the centre of the table. "Children, drinks?"

Abel and Grace poured themselves ginger beer and sat in their regular seats. Veronika brought the crepes and sausages to the table separately. Grace reckoned there was something about rolling the crepes with your hands that added to the deliciousness of the taste.

But it wasn't food the family ingested at Kosmos and Veronika's, it was love. The meals they ate as children (and now teenagers) continuously had the same effect—they felt doted upon, even though the meals were uncomplicated and basic.

Simplicity ruled with Veronika, and she tried to pass this no-fuss attitude on to Grace, who still believed complexity was the height of sophistication. She knew her granddaughter was too young to grasp the vast difference between 'simplicity' and 'simple' and that 'multiplicity' weakens the soul.

9 | Feeling Unworthy

Grace summoned the energy from somewhere to go to school the next day. Sitting on her own surrounded by the steel grey walls of the canteen, Grace saw Gabriel lining up for lunch. He glanced in her direction and looked at her as people do when the first mosquito arrives at a barbecue—with annoyance. The humiliating events of the party didn't diminish her desire for him, and she slipped back into her usual daydream where he tells her that she is the most beautiful girl in school.

Amber-Jane and the rest of her gang huddled by the canteen's entrance. Amber-Jane raised her voice so everyone within earshot could hear. "Look at her. She's pathetic. She actually thinks she has a chance with Gabriel. What a dreamer! She obviously hasn't looked in the mirror lately."

Grace picked herself up, put her tray away and dragged herself to the library. She didn't know whether to bury herself in the world history or science and astronomy titles.

Science. No one will find me there.

When the tears started, and she knew they would, she wouldn't be so exposed.

Why won't they accept me? Why am I always left outside the circle?

Her mind kept ringing with misgivings like a phone that nobody's in a hurry to pick up.

Why am I so fat? So ugly? So despised?

At first she was so absorbed in her misery that she didn't hear the Wind.

"Grace, why are you speaking to yourself like that?"

Grace didn't answer.

"Grace?"

"Because it's true," she finally said.

"Says who?"

"Says everyone."

"I question your judgment, but let's explore why other people's opinions mean more to you than your own?"

Grace wanted to end the conversation. Conversing with thin air was an outlandish proposition, but no one else remotely cared about her bleeding heart, so Grace relented and let the Wind in.

"Because they're the most popular crowd at school and they dictate my life. What they say goes. They think I suck, so I must." She continued, "I'm not popular, I'm not admired, I'm nothing. Everything they say about me is true."

Then the tears started.

"They react to the insecure and needy self that you display to the world. They sense that you desperately want to fit in. Your self-doubt makes you a victim," the Wind explained.

"So this is all my fault, you're saying?" She wiped the angry tears away with the hem of her dress.

"Why are you wasting your time trying to capture Gabriel's attention?" the Wind wanted to know.

"Because if he liked me, if he chose me, it would mean that I must be okay. Then all the other kids would have to accept me because I'm this cool guy's girlfriend. I'd finally have peace in my life. Him choosing me would validate me as a person."

"Another cannot validate us if we don't believe in our own worth first."

Grace doubled over, hugging her knees in tight. The library carpet smelled revolting, like mildew.

"Grace, you don't understand your true worth yet. Soon you will understand how valuable you are to the world exactly as you are. You do not need to be thinner with fewer pimples and a good-looking boyfriend. As you are, in this moment, you are absolutely perfect."

"Oh yeah, how could I forget, I'm on the cover of next month's *Teen Vogue*." Grace used her jumper sleeve to wipe her runny nose. The Wind ignored the sarcasm. "You are right. In this moment you're not thinking, feeling or acting like a cover girl. You're acting as if you're undeserving of anything in life, so how can anyone possibly value you if you refuse to value yourself? You set the bar for how people will treat you. People will only interact with you as you see yourself."

Grace was not ready to hear this and wanted to shut down.

"Grace, all change has to begin with you. What's going on inside you reflects externally. If you think you're ugly, defective and unpopular, the world will also view you that way."

"I don't want to hear anymore."

Curling up like a baby, Grace knew no one would find her here until the bell rang.

10 | The Rhythm of Life

The bell rang soon enough, and it took Grace five long minutes to pick herself up off the floor. She knew she'd be late for class, but instead of proudly marching into the room she slunk into the classroom ashamed. One day she'd come to learn that appearing confident at times—no, always—was more important than the actual situation or circumstance. But that day seemed a long way off.

"Miss Rose, you are forever marching to the beat of your own drum," the English teacher said. His crew cut gave him the appearance of a stranded marine. "You will soon realise the lone drummer gets nowhere. Now sit!"

Who is the lone drummer and what does he even mean?

Those in authority admonished Grace for not following the rules of society, and whatever she did—the way she held her cutlery, executed exam revision plans, introduced herself to strangers—was always wrong.

"Miss Rose, please save your daydreaming for the park. Now everyone, page fifty-three of *The Hobbit*."

For the rest of the day she dwelt on the phrase, "You are forever marching to the beat of your own drum," but by day's end she was none the wiser. Was it that she was offbeat? Or there was a band playing and she wasn't in tune with them?

She got off the bus resigned to the fact school was a non-negotiable combat zone and that grades and homework were her tour of duty. Walking home she accepted that it was easier to listen to the Wind than to venture into the rugged wilderness of her own mind. Her level of resistance to its presence dropped.

"Marching to the beat of your own drum means having the conviction to listen and move to a different beat than the one society is tuning in to," the Wind said. "If the beat that your friends and peers are marching to isn't to your liking, have the courage to choose a different rhythm to move in sync with."

Grace was now walking in a zig-zag pattern. "What's so wrong with that?"

"Because they, the wider society, can't influence the vibrations of this rhythm. You move independently."

Grace held the thought a while, then said, "Oh, okay. I kinda get that. My teacher can't control me then?"

"Precisely. It's vital for you to step in time to the music inside of you. Your heartbeat is the original beat, and love is the supreme universal rhythm flowing through you. Connect with this inner drummer."

"Huh? You've lost me. You're speaking gobbledygook."

Grace communicated with the Wind through thought, rather than actually mouthing her words. It was one way to make her situation appear less crazy. She tried to keep her animosity at bay, but if the Wind dared to mention Gabriel's rejection of her as a mirror representation of the disdain she felt towards her own self, she was out of there.

"Explain it to me simply."

"Okay, clear your mind and let's start at the beginning. Everyone has a unique heartbeat, right?"

"Right."

"A heartbeat that is theirs alone."

"Aha."

"Well, that heartbeat belongs to your body, but it also belongs to the universe."

Grace stopped underneath an ageing oak tree in the park, closed her eyes, placed both hands on her heart and tried to feel its beat and message. Feeling like a fool, she said, "It's telling me to fly free." She forced her eyes open. "What does that even mean?"

"Maybe not to constrain yourself with chains of your own making?" the Wind replied.

To Grace a lot of the Wind's advice was incomprehensible, so it took a few minutes before she could respond, and only then with the scantest of words.

"Maybe?" she replied and looked to the sky for confirmation.

"Check-in on your heartbeat often, Grace. It will always guide you correctly. Don't disconnect from the music."

More minutes passed.

"Each time you tune into the inner music, it grows easier to hear. Feel this music in your body, not the mental noise that gets piled up on top, and soon your actions will be informed by the universe's melody."

She left the park and continued home.

"You're too young to appreciate this advice now, but never give the beating of your heart to a less-than-worthy other."

The advice went over Grace's head, as she was too preoccupied with formulating her next question. "Is this why it's important to know what makes your heart sing?"

"Yes."

For Grace, there was never an easier answer. "Well, I love to swim at the beach and, of course, to spend time with my grandparents, Veronika and Kosmos."

"Feel the beat these activities inspire in your heart. As you progress through life, Grace, you'll meet many people who can't hear any music inside of them."

"Why?"

"Because they don't know the correct frequency to tune into."

Grace's initial hostility to the Wind's presence diminished as she began to understand what it was trying to do, to lead her to worlds of consciousness at present unknown to her. "Which is?"

"The frequency is joy."

"What do you mean? Like contentment or something? It can't be that simple, can it?"

"I hate to give this away so early in the game, Grace, but the solution is often very simple. Go have fun, be childlike. When you play and laugh your heart sings and you become the drummer who marches to her own unique beat."

11 | The Sound of Silence

Grace pulled on the security door. It was locked, meaning no one was home. "Yippee!" she cried out. She searched for the house keys, which she found in a different part of her bag each day, and recalled one of her mother's favourite mantras: a place for everything and everything in its place.

Grace abhorred the disciplined routine of leaving her keys in the same spot day in, day out. As a result it was always a drama to remember where she left them. She was famished, so headed straight to the pantry.

The Wind said, "The other frequency to tune into is silence."

"You mean nothing?"

"Not analytical or reflective quiet, but pure stillness."

"Got it! Fruit and nut chocolate will hit the spot." She ripped off the foil and tore off two whole rows. "Okay, so pure silence. How do I do this?" she asked between gobbling squares of chocolate and flicking through the newspaper left on the kitchen bench.

"Go to the sitting room and sit in the chair by the window. Feel the sun on your face and fold yourself into the embrace of the chair. Become still and listen to the beat that drives your body."

Grace climbed onto her father's recliner where strips of leather were missing from daily wear and tear. Her mother hated the chair—it didn't go with anything else in the room—and kept at Dylan to (at the very least) have the chair reupholstered, but Grace liked the feel of its worn contours and its faded 70s sage green colour.

"I can only feel the beat when I try to find my pulse, like after sports practice," Grace said in frustration.

"But you felt your heartbeat earlier, yes?"

"Well, I thought I did."

"Grace, you need to feel the central life force—your essence—that drives the undulating of your body's cells as you breathe. Try to sense this cosmic life energy pulsing through your veins. To do this your analytical mind must be switched off. It can't always be the dominant beat; it can't navigate 24/7."

Grace didn't understand. "Why?"

"Because the rhythm of your heartbeat is tied to the greater universal rhythms. The reordering of 'master and servant' has yet to occur."

No pause, just, "Huh?"

"The mind as servant needs to answer to the master, your soul, the eternal part of you. Grace, remember that it's the universe that determines how long our hearts beat for. You don't yet spend enough time in your soul to put the mind back in its rightful place," the Wind said.

Grace looked out the window where a yellow and black butterfly caught her eye. She wanted to bail out of this conversation. She didn't sign up for this, whatever these obscure exchanges with the Wind were. She was just a girl trapped in the throes of adolescence, not an adult seeking the meaning of life, yet she kept her side of the dialogue going. "So let me get this straight, the soul should lead with the personality following, not vice versa?"

"Correct. It's essential to surrender control to the very essence that gives you life."

By now three rows of chocolate were demolished.

"But what exactly is my soul?" Grace asked as she flipped up the recliner's leg rest.

"Think of the soul as the master DJ. This DJ spins the beats, which all the other songs mix from to create the soundscape."

Although Grace found this analogy difficult to understand, she related to it because she loved watching the DJs mash up tracks at the underage nightclubs in town to represent myths, symbols and concepts through the selected beats.

12 | Breaking Hearts

G race loved to dance. Swaying and moving to songs revitalised her and instantly lifted her mood. A catchy pop song on the radio lifted her spirits no end, and an 80s song played at the gym could inspire multiple sets of lunges (her most hated exercise). Even when dancing around the bedroom with her iPod, currents of energy sparked through her veins as heart and body united.

"You're right, Grace, dance can change your mood, so look for opportunities to move rhythmically. Observe how couples walk when holding hands and how the act of moving together establishes an emotional connection."

"That's all well and good," Grace said, "but in case you forgot—hello!—I'm single."

"So take pleasure in your own movements. Subtly swing your hips as you walk. Move free of tension."

On reflection, Grace observed how she felt when moving with the beat of the music. Dancing was a vehicle to another world, a place to feel whole. In rhythmic movement insecurity and fear stopped being her constant companions, allowing bliss and exuberance to step in and lead. Nothing could touch her when her favourite song was playing; life both sped up and slowed down as the music moved her at a tempo she couldn't naturally rouse within herself.

When dancing, Grace connected with the ground beneath her feet and the sky above. One step fluidly led into the next. Her body felt malleable, like water. Yet, when she wasn't dancing, she felt the complete opposite.

Weird, I'm so uncoordinated otherwise.

"Grace, the aim is to become the music instead of just reacting to the beats. Beats of all kinds, from the sound of hands clapping to metronomes, are integral in helping us move through life. As a foetus, the first beat we hear is our mother's heart, the quintessential experience of life. When you reconnect to any beat, you're reliving the time in your mother's womb. Your mother's heartbeat first comforted you, which is why you feel such inner peace when dancing," the Wind explained.

A few years ago, Grace looked at her mother across the kitchen bench as they ate banana bread with dollops of lemon curd and whipped cream and, like a magic trick, tried to feel her mother's heartbeat. She sensed its pounding.

The Wind chimed in. "You directly experienced the sacrosanct exquisiteness of another's life force."

On the many occasions that her mother infuriated her, she would go back to that fleeting moment of conscious connection. Grace became less irritated when she acknowledged it was Carla's heartbeat that kept her going for those first nine months of life.

13 | The Interior Life

"Grace, why are you carrying the weight of the world on your shoulders? You don't have to do it all on your own, you know." The Wind was questioning Grace on why she constantly felt she should be doing more. "Why is nothing ever enough? And do you ever feel satisfied?"

The questions startled Grace. Not because of their intrusiveness, but because she struggled to recall a time when she was truly satisfied with a piece of work that she had produced.

"You believe you haven't done enough because you feel you aren't enough. You think that you have to prove your worth. Peace will forever be elusive if you are always striving to do more. I'm asking you to just be."

Grace was sitting at her desk littered with candy wrappers, picking at her face and feeling anxious about her geography homework, the most useless subject ever.

Why do I need to know about different levels of soil salinity? How will this information help me get a job in the real world anyway?

"Grace, will you ever be enough? Can you even envisage a life without endless worry?"

"Look, leave me alone. I'm just trying to do my homework."

"Your life is a constant work in progress," the Wind explained. "You don't have to finish your homework—or anything in life for that matter—to be whole. Your need for certainty and control wants all the loose ends in life tied up in pretty bows, but life doesn't work that way. Some strings remain untied. I hate to be the one to tell you this, Grace, but you'll never finish every book you want to read, watch all the movies you want to see or travel to each and every country that you dream of."

Well, that was a reality check. Grace moved her laptop out of the way and rested her head on the daily planner that covered the majority of the desk. Coffee stains and cookie crumbs smudged the days of February.

"I know you feel besieged by all the half-read books in your bookshelf, but you have to let the guilt go."

Out the words rolled. "I can't. I'll feel like a failure."

"Why do you feel that you must read all these books, Grace?"

There's nothing as frustrating as being asked an obvious question and not knowing the answer. Then it came to her. "If I have all this information then no one can hurt me."

"So, you're telling me you read out of fear, not love? Do you think that knowledge from books can protect you from life?"

And there's nothing more annoying than being told something about yourself that appears so noticeable to strangers, but completely unfamiliar to you. Grace was humbled.

What's the reason behind my relationship with the Wind? And why are we in dialogue? And what did it mean by 'I am the you that you haven't discovered yet?'

"This will become clearer over time, Grace. For the moment these half-read books drain your energy, so close them in your mind. Choose to consciously seal the open-ended loops that bleed you dry."

Grace didn't realise how much these gaping holes of uncompleted projects played on her mind. "I'm not a closer."

"Everything unfinished, abandoned and incomplete will taunt you, Grace, but it's you who keeps sending out the invitation to be castigated. Choose what to finish in life. Don't let the things you really wish to do suffer at the expense of that which does not matter. Trust me; little satisfaction comes from closing loops under force or duress."

"But if I don't finish things, am I a failure?"

"The real failure is not that you can't finish the piles of books by your bed, but that you're not reading the ones you really want to read. Grace, focus your attention on what you do want, otherwise the inconsequential stuff, like books you feel you ought to read, will suck up your time, energy and space. Your real dreams will die under the weight of these meaningless obligations."

"But why do I have all these gaping energy loops in my life? Why do I struggle to finish books?" Grace remembered her mother saying that she never knew when to leave a topic alone.

"Because of unrealistic expectations," the Wind replied. "Grace, you somehow think you can read a book a week. With your current schedule that's close to impossible. Don't overload yourself by actively inviting things you don't really care for into your life. Be selective about who or what you bring close to you."

Grace knew that the Wind was right, but didn't yet want to accept it. Who wants to know that they're the ones bringing their own pain and suffering onto themselves?

"And anyway, more reading won't get you to your destination any quicker. Be, Grace, be."

She lifted her head. "Wind, why are you here?"

"I'm guiding you how to live. I'm teaching you the secret of living life in rhythm with the universe. I'm here to mentor you on circadian and tidal rhythms, the significance of lunar cycles and the changing seasons. However, I know in your current state it will be difficult to harness these patterns of energy. Therefore we must bide our time and use your immediate daily dilemmas to sow seeds of wisdom for the future. Because there are never any accidents or mistakes in the universe, we will be guided by the present moment."

"Oh." She traced the coffee rings on the planner with her fingers.

"So if you see a magazine you're half-interested in, don't buy it. If people want to give you flyers on the street, hand them back. Grace, why read things you're not even interested in as they bring undue stress to your life? Choose which information to internalise—that which serves the highest good—and let the rest go."

"How do I know what's for the highest good anyway?"

"When you're acting from your most loving self for the greatest good for the greatest number of souls, the non-essential falls away.

Until it becomes automatic, you have to actively choose the most loving thought or action available to you. You can decide what you invite into your life and how you manage it, Grace. You really can. Don't allow all this excess information in that overwhelms you. Hone your powers of discrimination. Always ask your soul, 'Is this essential or non-essential?'"

"My soul?"

"The essence of you that has no beginning or end. Your unique connection to the divine."

Grace pictured herself at a spa resort wearing a white, fluffy robe with cooling cucumber rounds on her eyes as the Wind spoke in the tones of panpipe spa music, beseeching her to explore her interior life.

14 | Loving the Unknown

In close to two decades from now Grace would ask her husband why he wasn't aligning the conditions in his life with the desires unfolding inside of him. With French manicured hands she'd cup his stubbled chin and say, "Work with this seed that wants to be born in a state of flow. Don't get frustrated, regretting and resisting everything. Be in reverence of the invisible, and there'll be no struggle, pain or discomfort in birthing this new idea into being."

Her future husband would say he couldn't imagine the teenager his wife once was. He only knew Grace as dedicated to serving the callings of her soul, family and humanity at large. He didn't see the long and windy road that had led her into his life.

The Wind explained to the teenage Grace the sense of comfort that comes from embracing the unknown. "You witness the magic of time working things out—without your involvement. You surrender to a timing and force greater than your personality and get out of your own way. You trust the celestial clockwork, and the unity of all life, and become an unobstructed conduit for the divine to flow through you."

"But I want a crystal ball," Grace demanded. "I hate not knowing what life has in store for me."

The Wind answered, "No, and here's why. Remember how Abel told you the end of *The Lens Cleaner* when you hadn't seen the film yet and how furious you were with him?"

"He took that film away from me."

"Right, well, knowing how the film ended before having a chance to view it yourself is the same as the universe taking your life away from you."

The Wind's logic did and didn't compute.

"Grace, if you knew in precise detail how your life would unfold it'd be deathly dull. If you knew your school exam results, which university you'll go to, what city you'll live in and how many children you'll have in advance, all the excitement of possibility would be taken from you. Where's the adventure? Your life's journey would be one straight line to Boredomville."

"But it'd save me a whole lot of anguish if I knew that things would turn out okay," she pleaded.

"Except that that's not the point of life, Grace. We have to come into contact with all the emotions under the sun, from the so-called 'good' to the unbearably 'bad'. Pain is one of those emotions, but then so is ecstasy. By trying to protect yourself from life, you're rejecting the very gift life is giving you—the gift of experience."

This was a present Grace didn't appreciate. She despised making mistakes and couldn't yet accept them as an inevitable part of travelling the path to wisdom.

"You're the one who brings untold anguish to your life by refusing to view uncertainty as the great and wonderful teacher it is. Pain also lets us know that something is wrong in our lives—it inspires transformation. You're consistently subjected to pain, which is one of the main motivators for change, yet you're unwilling to find new ways to approach old problems and you turn your back on the great learning experience that sorrow brings."

Grace felt apprehensive.

"Grace, you will fall, you will fail. You must! There's no other way. The more you attempt to avoid uncertainty in the future, the more uncertainty will chase you today; it'll hunt you down in your thoughts and make you doubt everything."

This was too much to take in. "So what you're saying is that life is not to be lived by never making mistakes, by not having bad things happen to you?"

"That's right, Grace. Life is lived by bringing the light of the soul to what is happening to you now. If you can perceive what appears to be an adverse situation through the lens of the soul, you'll grow and prosper through these experiences. Life will keep pushing you until you bring your soul into each passing moment."

Grace rolled her eyes at the Wind.

15 | The Gift of Friendship

Juliet and Ruby were as dissimilar in their character traits as Grace was to each of them, but it didn't affect their lifelong friendship and they spent most weekends hanging out together.

Every now and then Juliet was hard work. A total perfectionist rather than a lazy perfectionist like Grace, she never rebelled against her parents and was the quintessential 'good girl'. Grace's father on more than one occasion despaired, "Why can't you be more like Juliet? She doesn't give her parents half of the grief that you give us."

Juliet had yet to find her own voice. Petite with long black hair, she plucked her eyebrows to within an inch of their lives. Juliet had no desire to stretch the boundaries and was satisfied exploring the cultural landscape her parents defined for her. She'd only climb a mountain with a detailed map. Uncharted territory didn't appeal. She interpreted the world through logic and the only place where Juliet took risks was in her charcoal drawings, because the work remained self-contained on the page. When Grace mentioned that her sketches would work great as storyboards for a film script Juliet freaked out; it'd mean the drawings might come to life, a frightening proposition.

Juliet was the only one to have a boyfriend, James Hird. He went to the same school and was one of the state's top rowers. He was nice enough but that was it, nice enough. James was beige. He never caused affront to anyone, except to those with a deep dislike of beige, and that included Grace. Beige was just so bland and characterless.

Ruby, on the other hand, was more adventurous, yet practical, with a tinge of obsessive-compulsive behaviour that often drove Grace up the wall. Her ash blonde hair (which came from a packet) was habitually curled in ringlets just below her ears. Out of the three, Ruby was the one with the social conscience, giving money to charities as an alternative to Christmas presents, or planting a tree to honour a friend's birthday instead of buying a gift. Both minor and major levels of injustice fired her up. She had a strong affinity for the underdog and loved a good 'rags to riches' story.

This Saturday, the three girls were going to the movies and then out to dinner. Grace enjoyed these conventional movie nights, but hungered for parties where you couldn't predict the night's outcome (Amber-Jane's party excluded). These movie nights were formulaic to a fault: catch the bus into the city centre, meet in front of the lion water fountain in the main pedestrian street mall, head to the cinema, then afterwards to a nearby restaurant for dinner.

After watching a rom-com that was miraculously both romantic and comedic, Juliet ran into two friends from her school outside the cinema and all five of them went out for dinner, courtesy of the cash handouts from their parents.

16 | Trapped in Thought

Grace woke at 5:55 a.m. the next morning filled with regret and self-loathing. The red lines against the black backdrop of the alarm glared at her as last night's memories aggressively forced themselves on her.

Why did I eat all those croquettes? What must they have thought about me pigging out like that? Why can't I control my appetite? Why didn't I order a salad? Why can't I eat like a sparrow? I should've caught the bus home before we ordered dessert. Actually, I shouldn't have gone at all. I'm so ugly and fat. I've got no discipline whatsoever.

No spaces existed between her hostile, critical thoughts. This morning even the sheets on her bed contorted around her body and drained the very life out of her.

"I can't bear to hear you talk to yourself this way," the Wind said.

For Grace beating up on herself was so automatic that she never gave it a second thought. She once read in a magazine to think of everything you say to yourself as going out via a public broadcaster and to question if you'd really want the world to hear how you address yourself.

The Wind quietly asked, "If you ignore scoffing down those seven croquettes, do you think everything else about the evening was perfect?"

Without even having to think Grace replied, "No, because I would've worn a different dress and sat next to Ruby instead of Juliet and . . ."

"There's always more with you, Grace, isn't there? Where does this insatiable need to control and micromanage every moment come from? And what or whose version of 'perfect' are you trying to create?"

Berating herself yet again, she didn't even hear the Wind.

How could I be so greedy? Why can't I restrain myself?

She threw the quilt off the bed and kept only the cotton sheet on top of her. No wonder she felt so exhausted the majority of the time; all her energy went into worrying about other people's perception of her.

"Okay, let's look at this. You feel that you shouldn't have eaten so much food?" Grace nodded and the Wind continued. "And you're completely over-thinking and over-analysing something that happened in the past?"

"I guess."

"Grace, please remember that you're not your thoughts. Your personality has usurped control of the soul. This happens when you let these obsessive, ruminative thoughts of a time you can't change run rampant in your head."

All the Wind's mumbo jumbo hurt her brain far more than the thoughts that initially woke her.

But what did it mean by 'personality'?

"Your personality is a construct you use to experience the world, but it's not the whole of you. It's just the clothing your soul wears and is transitory."

"Oh."

"Whereas the soul has an eternal perspective."

"Double oh."

"Grace, if you don't reclaim your divine sovereignty, then that one thought, 'I shouldn't have eaten so much' will lead to 'I'm hideous' to 'I'm completely repulsive' to 'I never do anything right' to 'everyone is better off without me' to, you tell me what's next, Grace?"

Grace didn't want to carry that thought through to its natural conclusion.

"You are picturing the personality's view of 'perfect'. You feel bad about yourself, which leads you to separate and disconnect from your soul. Your personality will eventually die, but your soul is eternal. Doesn't it make more sense to side with your soul?"

Grace felt another lecture approaching.

"These disparaging remarks you replay over and over in your head are your downfall, never your saviour, and the more you keep this mental commentary running, the more you'll suffer."

"Enough!" Grace shouted. "Enough is enough is enough!" She pulled the sheet off, sat up and rested her hands on her knees. "I don't understand what you mean by personality or what separateness you're referring to."

"That's because you've yet to awaken your higher consciousness."

"Well, just add that to the list of words I'm not au fait with."

"But Grace, do you want to know? Are you ready to take the next step?"

She turned on the main bedroom light and pulled the stool out from under the weathered vanity dresser. She stared at the mirror with a bemused look on her face. The few freckles on her nose appeared more noticeable under the artificial light. Her gaze moved to her eyes, principally the puffiness below the lower lids. Viewing her worn reflection sapped any get-up-and-go in her. Grace knew the Wind was offering a helping hand, but out of childish spite she wanted to reject it. She recalled the phrasing in a song lyric: I'm so sick and tired of being sick and tired.

"Okay Wind, I surrender, I surrender," and drew a tissue out of the box and waved it for good effect.

The Wind said quickly, "I accept your surrender, Grace. All I ask is that you don't ignore me when I make contact, and we'll go from there."

Grace laid her left cheek on some rare space on the dresser. Her hair, which desperately needed a wash, fell across her face, and her arms flopped to her sides. It appeared like a forced surrender, but it was entirely voluntary.

17 | Acceptance

"The personality fears that if you start listening to your soul, it will no longer have a role to play. It fears it will fade away and die, so it's fighting for its very survival with all guns blazing."

Grace lifted her head off the dresser, swapped cheeks and fell back into the same position.

"Its survival depends on you believing that you are only the sum total of your age, gender, nationality, social class, occupation, likes, dislikes and nothing else. It's your personality that thinks life would be better if only you were Gabriel's girlfriend and ten kilos lighter. It keeps fuelling this feeling of unworthiness in you. Grace, if you could witness your divine completeness right now, all your imagined problems would disappear."

Staying in her rag doll position, Grace found the strength to squeak out, "I'm not perfect."

"That's right, you're not."

The affront went straight to her heart.

"Because you're not perceiving yourself through my eyes, Grace. Through the lens of the soul you're perfect, complete and whole. Your personality unfortunately wants you to believe otherwise. It plants false assumptions that make you think there's something wrong with you, that you're faulty and broken; a mistake, not a gift. It wants you to feel separate from the divine, so it claims dominion over you, and your critical self-talk only strengthens its authority."

Grace wanted to raise her head, but decided against it. The defenceless alignment of her body soothed her.

"The frailness you're presently exhibiting is absolutely flawless.

You don't need to be anything other than who you are right now; collapsed in a heap on your dresser. That's why I'm here, Grace, to help you grow into your divine essence so that you can view life from my perspective."

Grace was defiant in her response. "I'm not so sure I trust your eyes, they see things that definitely aren't real."

"In time you'll learn to view all things from the vantage point of eternity because that, Grace, is who you are—eternal. This personality you're so attached to is finite and will die at the end of this life, so again, why give so much power to something temporary when your soul is immortal?"

She wanted to go back to bed, crawl under the covers and crash out.

"Grace, from the heightened perspective of eternity, how does eating seven large potato croquettes even register as an event?"

Grace knew the Wind was right, but struggled with its point of view.

Eternity? Eternity? What does eternity have to do with anything? With school? With not having a boyfriend? With tomorrow? Or for that matter, today? Eternity doesn't exist here.

"The physical world responds to each thought, feeling and belief you hold, Grace, and you're constantly sending the message that it's okay to disrespect you, as it's how you treat yourself—with contempt and loathing. Have some self-respect. Stand up for your soul. Don't allow these obsessive replays of past events to disempower you."

"Here comes the rallying cry."

"Grace, your wings aren't clipped by others, only by your own misperceptions. Accept that at this moment you're consumed by regret, recrimination, frustration, and anger. Really experience these emotions. What do they feel like in your body? Denying these sensations playing out inside you means they'll only stalk you more. Don't push these physical impressions into the secret recesses of your mind. Become conscious of them, feel how they're playing out in your body and bring them to the light so that they can integrate with the truth of your being."

"I am conscious of them. If I wasn't, do you think I'd be this messed up?"

"Wanting these hurts expelled from your body and mind is not the solution, Grace," the Wind said. "The heartaches have served a purpose; to bring you to this moment."

"How?" she croaked. "How can they possibly be of use?"

"Remember that pain is not something to avoid, Grace. It's when we don't know how to deal with our pain that it turns into suffering."

"So how do I stop the suffering?"

"You reunite your individual mind with the universal heart."

Grace was tiring of her limitations.

"Accept all of yourself, especially the parts you're not so keen on. The universe adores everything about you: your mistakes, your courage, it even accepts your self-hatred, so stop labelling parts of yourself as good and bad."

"I don't," she snapped.

"You do, Grace, I see you do it every day. You help an elderly gentleman cross the street and think yourself good, then accidentally stand in front of someone in the supermarket queue and immediately judge yourself to be bad and ill-mannered—all within the same hour. Stop fragmenting yourself—remember your wholeness."

Grace felt a nerve being hit. "I don't think I know how to feel my emotions."

"Finally, some real honesty from you, Grace. I know you don't, but you're very good at thinking about your emotions, aren't you?"

It was all too much. She pulled her Strawberry Shortcake doll from the bottom drawer of the tallboy and hugged her. The strawberry scent from the doll's decade-long lifespan had long since evaporated.

"When you're so busy judging yourself, love can't enter either your heart or mind."

"Life is all about judging. You're judged at school, by your parents, their friends, shopkeepers, everyone."

The Wind paid no heed. "But you're the one who keeps putting yourself on the pageant stage for assessment, Grace. The judges only form a panel when a contestant voluntarily places herself before a council of critics."

She hugged Strawberry Shortcake tighter, not wanting to admit the glaring truth in the Wind's words.

"Grace, whatever issue you try to escape from must return. You only momentarily left it, you didn't resolve it. A temporary escape does nothing about a permanent problem. Can you turn and look at this pain gently? Can you consider the possibility of it being an ally?"

Grace dropped the doll and knew there was no way to get out of this moment. She had to stay present with her feelings. She sat on the bed and asked the Wind to show her the way.

"Be with the sensations and feelings in your body. Don't resist them and run away by hiding up in your mind. Also, be less self-absorbed and stop viewing yourself through the eyes of others. Emotional sustenance comes from within, not without."

She stayed silent.

"Grace, your neediness does nothing to enhance your skin tone, your chronic fretfulness in no way accentuates your figure and taking yourself and your dramas so seriously will not fix a bad hair day. Ever."

"Don't mock me!"

"It seems the only way for you to grasp how self-involved you are. Your desperate need for attention means that you're too wrapped up in serving your own personality, not serving the souls of others. If only you knew the joy that comes from humility and a life devoted to selfless service."

Grace instinctively tried to smooth her tresses into shape. The last remark infuriated her.

Doesn't the Wind get that celebrity is the currency of the twenty-first century?

18 | Being the Witness

It was Sunday morning, a moment in time for the Roses to gather as a family. Their Sunday breakfasts were a physiological act of sustenance, as much as a psychological ritual of familial bonding. Abel and Grace rotated shifts each weekend to prepare the meal. After breakfast the sibling who didn't cook had to clear the table, load the dishwasher and tidy up. This morning it was Grace's turn.

Grace wiped down the granite countertops with heavy 'woe is me' sighs. More sighs accompanied the rinsing of dishes, utensils and the stacking of plates in the never-quite-enough-room-for-all-the-cups-and-saucers dishwasher. Grace wanted to finish quickly so that she could reconnect with the Wind.

With the dishwasher on, she bounded up the stairs two at a time and closed her bedroom door behind her. She made her bed and lay down on top, resting the back of her head on the red, heart-shaped cushion with the words AMAZING GRACE stitched in yellow. Abel gave it to her one Christmas in jest, and it quickly became one of Grace's prized possessions, though she'd never admit it to him.

"Witness and accept your thoughts and bring them to the light, so that you can inspect them through the lens of love."

"Huh? What am I supposed to accept?"

"Grace, when you use the word 'accept', it's as if you're talking about a bitter pill I'm forcing you to swallow."

Her mind wandered to what the rest of the world thought about on a day-to-day basis.

What even constitutes 'normal' thoughts? Perhaps everybody else is equally obsessed about stuff that doesn't matter? Or scarily, possibly only me? Maybe

everyone else is just getting on with the business of living, never seeking uncon-
ditional love, as they already know that's who they are at their very core so
there's no need to chase it?

"Grace, stop obsessing over what you imagine everybody else is thinking. You invest so much of yourself in your thoughts that you're beginning to believe that's who you are."

Grace snapped back, "Well, if I'm not my thoughts, who and what am I then?"

"You're the awareness of your thoughts."

"Huh?"

"Quick, think of something."

When Grace felt beleaguered, she became scornful. "I can't believe I'm having this conversation. I'm too old to invent an imaginary friend. I'd rather have a security blanket," she said with utter disdain.

"So we agree you thought about something."

"Um, yeah, I guess."

"But as you were thinking, were you aware of the process of yourself thinking?"

"Well, I know I thought something."

"Did you observe the thought forming in your mind and then choose to follow this train of thought?"

"You're hurting my head," Grace said. She felt she'd been pushed as far as she could go, but something deep inside her knew that to broaden her limited perception of the world—despite the emotional pain and anguish—she had to keep moving forward.

The Wind sensed her discomfort. "Grace, please stick with me. I hold the key, but it's you that holds the lock, and we must work together to open the treasure within."

19 | Humanity

"Let's get to work. When you have a limiting belief or disempowering thought, it's important that you become aware of it as it arises in your mind. Grace, you are the watcher," the Wind explained. "You are not the belief or thought itself; you are the awareness, so shine an eternal light on any darkness you witness within."

Grace bit on her lower lip. "Okay, I get the light part; not so sure about the other stuff, though."

"Your thoughts construct illusions; don't succumb to them. Thinking how things should be, rather than how they are, never works. Things are as they are."

"Yeah, that's all well and good, Wind, but none of what you're saying deals with why I feel so guilty about consistently making poor decisions and habitually doing dumb things."

"Grace, release the resistance to the feelings of guilt you're experiencing and instead drop into them. Pay attention to the actual sensations in your body. What does guilt feel like? Don't do anything to change it, just let the sensations within your body transform on their own accord."

"So starve the thought and feed this state of awareness?"

"Yes, perceive the feeling and how it's translated as a sensation through the sensory organs and emotions. Grace, thinking that everything you do is a mistake is the food that powers the feelings of guilt you carry. This in turn will only attract more to your life to feel guilty about. Why not focus on your love of humanity, instead of on your perceived individual failings?"

Grace hadn't thought about humanity much before. She only loved a select few close to her, not humanity as a whole.

"Grace, I'm attempting to expand your vision so that you'll soon see yourself in everyone, enabling you to love wider. Only loving your limited circle of family and friends restricts the magnitude of your love to a tiny sphere of influence."

Born and raised in the same city, the world 'out there' was something Grace mostly interacted with through her laptop screen.

"Do you mean people in Africa? Or the ancient tribes of South America? Or villagers in India?"

"Grace, I mean everybody, including the shopkeeper down the road," the Wind said.

She didn't have enough love for herself, let alone any extra left over to give to the whole world. Grace couldn't imagine a love this vast.

"What we think about we feed on. And you, my love, are consuming a diet of guilt and misery. How can you expect to grow if that's how you're nourishing yourself?"

"Um, weren't we discussing humanity?" She'd never heard any of this information before; there was nowhere for it to be filed in her head. She needed time to process all this information.

"Grace, I'm planting the seeds to awaken your soul. You're exactly where you need to be. Your reality right now contains the very essence of your soul's purpose. You needed to play the regret tape about over-indulging in some fat-laden croquettes for us to have this particular conversation right now. What you perceive as a shaming experience actually led you to a vulnerable and honourable moment of awareness. Grace, we are always creating consequences. Cause and effect with one step leading to another."

"So my binge and consequent freak out forged the path for this current exchange to occur?"

"Precisely. By denying the present, you deny life. Your soul doesn't enjoy going back in time, it feels incredibly uncomfortable and out of place there. Look around you. Where are you now, Grace? I know where you are. You're in your head, lost in your thoughts and not appreciating the exquisite splendour of this moment."

Grace stared out the window and smiled.

"Live less in your head and more in your heart and when you take up residence here, you'll find the peace you're seeking."

Her father had emerged from the garage with the pruning shears to trim the overgrown branches by the side of the house.

"I obsess about past events so much that fresh, new moments can't even enter. That's it! I'm done!"

"When thoughts of regret enter your mind ask for grace to carry you through."

"Ask who?"

"Grace, have you ever acknowledged your soul in the mirror?"

She shrugged her shoulders.

"Being in touch with your soul gets you out of your intellect and into the vibrations of grace."

"Why would I do that?"

"Because we dwell in an environment created by the degree of harmonious thoughts, feelings and beliefs we hold and actions we take. Though with you, Grace, there's a constant battle of discordant vibrations."

"Battle?"

"Inner conflict, disempowering thoughts and endless declarations of war on the present moment. It would be to your benefit to stop fighting yourself and the world. If you made peace within your interior landscape, can you even begin to imagine the peace that would greet you in your external environment?"

Grace couldn't imagine it. Worse, the Wind was sounding like a broken record, skipping back again and again to the start of the same old song.

"You're blocking life's flow. I want you to surrender to a divine plan bigger than the frivolous needs of your personality so the thoughts of a denser vibration fall away."

"How?" she interrupted, still transfixed on the steel garage doors.

"Accepting my words is the easy part; applying them is where the challenge lies. I need you to live, experience and breathe my words. As dance teachers tell their students, 'Thinking the movement is not becoming the movement.'"

"But I never have peace of mind; I constantly think everything can be better than it is."

"Stop judging everything so harshly! The criteria you use is flawed. You can never win. You think one day you'll master the rules your inner critic applies, but the minute you do, the rules will change. Grace, your version of peace is unattainable."

She was tired of her room, of the Wind, of her own maddening thoughts.

"You believe an existence without slip-ups will bring something to your life that you don't already possess. Nothing is missing from your life, other than you not showing up for it! Stop this constant undermining of yourself. Stop viewing yourself as incomplete. The ideal you seek isn't found in others, or in a future version of yourself. It lies in the highest conscious expression of your soul within each situation you find yourself in. Choosing the most loving response available to you—moment to moment—is all you can do. Wanting to be someone else or somewhere else, well Grace, you're just wishing your life away."

It was true. She did want to be someone else, but not another person completely. She wanted part of one person's looks, another's family lineage, bits and pieces of another's social skills, somebody else's artistic talent, and blend them into a better version of herself. Grace now understood that no seeds of acceptance existed in these thoughts and wondered if she'd ever feel comfortable in her own skin.

"Be more compassionate towards yourself, and the universe will respond in turn."

"I need the world to be nicer to me first," she said, pouting like a second-grader.

"Grace, it can only be kinder to you once you're less cruel to yourself."

20 | Mindfulness

"Gosh, that Leona in the administration office drives me up the wall. She constantly has to be doing something, be on the go, maximising every second. She says if she does nothing she feels guilty. I mean, can you believe this?"

Grace hated being trapped in the car with her mother. She had to listen to her rants about her job, her friends and every man and his dog. Carla had an opinion on everything.

On this cloudy Sunday afternoon, Grace tried to offer a softer approach to her mother's harshness. "Well, it's hard for some people to relax, Mum. Perhaps she's being pulled in too many directions and being busy is the only way she knows how to cope?"

Grace also thought it hilarious that her mother phrased her observations as dialogue, when it was always a soliloquy to a trapped audience of one.

Grace needed to research her paper on the catalysts of World War One for history class and the State Library couldn't arrive fast enough. Finally, the car approached the building's grand entrance, and she quickly kissed her mother goodbye, ran up the stairs and pushed through the main doors of the library. The antique oil paintings and antiquated paper encyclopaedias beckoned.

She loved this place, a cathedral of the mind, where only serious study should occur. It was as if the walls knew if you partook in a lesser thinking activity. Grace loved working in the Renaissance-style reading room with its gilded ceiling and friezes and tried to raise her level of consciousness to match the stately ambience of the room.

No sooner had Grace sat down at an old-style school desk, which had a hole for an ink well and a groove for pencils, that the Wind said, "People often confuse themselves with the actions they perform. They forget their soul when carrying out these acts. They lose who they are in a long list of things they need to do. They lose their entire being."

Her chair screeched across the marble floor as she pulled it closer to the desk. On the one hand she wanted to tell the Wind to butt out, that she didn't ask for its opinion, but then she was also curious to learn more. "Well, that's understandable. People are fathers and mothers, bosses and employees, friends and lovers."

"Yes, but these are just roles people play, Grace. They're not our totality; we are far more than these mere titles."

Grace wanted to immerse herself in her research. History was one of the few subjects she was good at, and this conversation with the Wind was a distraction.

"All I'm saying, Grace, is that the majority of people try to prove their worth through their busyness."

"I concur." Well, she wasn't sure if she agreed, but did so on her mother's behalf given their earlier conversation.

"It's about bringing your being to everything you do, and this requires silence."

Grace had thought that she was in a quiet zone, until the Wind interrupted her.

"Bring stillness into your life on a regular basis, even when you're studying, shopping with friends, watching TV and eating dinner. Don't fill that golden silence with thoughts."

"Well, what else would I fill it with?"

"Awareness."

"Awareness! Oh, is that all?" she joked, chewing on a 6B pencil.

"Be the watcher; aware of the rhythm behind each action, as you pull a book from the shelf, or copy some notes into your journal, or compose your essay's framework."

"Easier said than done."

"This goes for everything, Grace. Be aware in all situations. Observe when you need to rest, when it's time to renew yourself and when in the midst of the game you really need to kick it up a gear. Flow into each activity from a state of mindfulness. Remember when you're resting, Grace, that I'm with you and when you're out and about, make space for me to join you too. When you connect with me you'll create space in your mind to observe yourself. I can then guide you and help make life's burdens that touch lighter."

Grace felt okay when she entered the library, but now felt amazing. She effortlessly began working on her paper, scribbling down the key points she remembered from class. She pulled five books from both the highest and lowest shelves and checked she had the correct titles. She imagined the books balancing on her head, keeping her posture straight, as she softly walked back to the row of desks and began to pen her hypothesis. She needed no encouragement to complete this assignment. She worked in delight, memorising dates, comparing opinions, happily researching the cultures of every nation involved in the war. She could hear the Wind, but let it play as background music to her study.

Grace tuned in and out to the Wind's musings throughout the afternoon. One point the Wind particularly emphasised was that living in rhythm was a series of steps—a progression of layers—that can't always be observed by the naked eye and that nuances can only be appreciated in retrospect.

"Grace, ask yourself what the rhythm of handwritten lines in a letter should be?"

Grace laughed. She couldn't remember the last time she wrote a letter but conceded she did indeed write birthday cards. The Wind suggested spacing the lines and paragraphs to correlate to the emotional sentiment of the card.

"The intention behind your message should dictate the rhythmic spacing of your words."

Grace was tuning in more than out, especially as the Wind described how crucial pace was to reading.

"Do you read in a hurry? Or do you let the author's construction of language settle at a deeper, more profound level?" The Wind said that it was crucial to know why one was reading. "It's all about intention. Are you speed-reading for a deadline the next day or leisurely flicking through a fashion magazine while on vacation? Let the context dictate the rhythm at which you read, as only then will reading suit your purpose."

Time flew, but made no difference to Grace. The Wind was with her, passing on wisdom like a tap of constantly flowing water. She once heard that children learn to read with their ears, not eyes—so true for her now—while beliefs are absorbed through the eyes, which is especially why the Wind wanted Grace to make peace with the mirror.

When she finished her essay, Grace made a point to leave the desk the way she found it and returned the books to the shelves. She sat back in her chair and glanced up at the indecipherable Latin inscriptions on the ceiling, acknowledging all the help she received from above.

21 | Flow

Grace was getting ready for bed when she felt the Wind close. "When you tell yourself you shouldn't have said this or done that, you weaken your instinct. If you chastise yourself, you're both judge and defendant. Do you understand, Grace?"

She did, but didn't yet want to raise her standards and up her game.

"What memories do you want to have?"

Grace knew the Wind was only trying to help, but the intensity of their chats could be so overwhelming at times. She just wanted to go to bed.

"Look at the memories you're creating through your judgments."

Grace didn't want to. She thought of the disappointing salad she had last night with the unripe avocado. That was her dominant memory of the evening.

"The salad wasn't the problem, Grace, it's your thoughts about it that caused the anguish. The salad is neutral. Look what meaning you attached to the condition of a mere avocado and the toxic charge you created around the meal."

Could Grace laugh at the absurdity of it all?

"The only way to turn your judgment around is through forgiveness and compassion."

She got ready for bed. Smoothing out her candy-striped pyjamas against her body, she tried to feel the vigour of life flowing through her. It wasn't happening; the only thing flowing was sheer weariness.

"It's not about controlling every little detail of your life, Grace. The natural rhythms of existence can only touch you if you allow life's patterns in. You can't stage-manage and direct this. You can't conquer and bring nature under your control. You can't impose your will on nature's fragile web of relationships to serve your own needs so learn to coexist with life's ebbs and flows."

Grace nodded in agreement.

"When you wish a circumstance happened in a different way and fight the reality of it, you've lost your link to the celestial. The way the situation played out was heavenly. Some results will be to your personality's liking, others not. The underlying perfection never changes, only your attitude to it does. All is always in cosmic divine order. Grace, you can't control a wave, demanding how and when it should break, so you let it be and accept its rhythm—whether it's a ripple or a large wave—the same with life."

Grace mostly read in her bedroom. She believed that the more she read, the more she'd understand about life. The knowledge the Wind passed on hadn't yet drastically changed her comprehension of the world or her behaviour. It only left her feeling more confused.

"You are confused because you are not yet feeling the dynamic that drives all of life and aligning yourself to it. The rhythm of life comes from within and enters into the constitution of all things. You believe that books hold all the answers, but they mean nothing unless the knowledge atlas is lived."

The Wind ruffled the pages of *Views of New York*, the coffee table book that lay open on her desk.

"There's a natural rhythm to life. Don't fight it, Grace. You can't jump ahead until you've experienced the knowledge you already possess. You must lay a strong foundation before adding a new layer. And another thing," the Wind said, "I don't want you conceptualising rhythm and making it a mere mental concept. Don't intellectualise it—live it. Tap into the rhythm underpinning each moment—action and reaction, trial and error, the heartbeat that pulses through each of us, the pendulum swing of the rise and fall. Honour the measured motion of the in and out movement of all things as you go about your life, or should I say, flow through your life."

"Flow?"

"Flow is the opposite of the one-dimensionality and angularity of modern life. Flow means perceiving yourself as a dynamic entity that fluidly responds to life's influences—swinging to and fro, backward and forward, an advance and a retreat, an out breath and an in breath. This power manifests in the creation and destruction of worlds as much as it does within your own mental state. Rhythm pervades the universe."

The Wind sensed Grace's confusion and changed tack. "Your adverse thoughts make you unable to see the million and one amazing things happening underneath your nose. Honing in on your failings means all you experience in life is a litany of letdowns. Where are your successes, Grace? The times you took a risk and didn't let fear take hold? When you've been the supportive shoulder to cry on? Where are those moments?"

"They're few and far between, I guess."

"Not really. They've occurred, Grace, but were lost on you as you chose to focus on what wasn't right or on aspects that didn't meet your expectations. Your entire thought process concentrates on what's lacking from moments, making your life so trivial that you forget the universe entirely."

Grace yawned and switched the bedside lamp off.

"If your perceptions are narrow, you allow your weaknesses to consume and suck the very life out of you."

"Alright, I'll give you that, Wind. I can see how small I'm playing."

The Wind whispered, "Good night," and Grace fell straight to sleep.

22 | Soul Truth

It was a lovely morning. The gathering sun warmed Grace's disposition as she pulled her new cobalt blue sundress out of the wardrobe. Still on its coat hanger, she hung the dress over her neck and thought to go for a walk on the beach next weekend to catch the last few rays of the departing summer.

The Wind entered with a new missive. "You're a microcosm that doesn't believe it's part of the macrocosm—like a limb that refuses to accept that it belongs to a body."

"What?" Grace was lost.

"Grace, this is serious. People kill themselves because they can't live with their thoughts."

"If they give us so much grief and sorrow, why do we need them? Why even have a personality if it only causes us pain?"

"Because the personality is the vehicle for the soul to express itself here on earth."

That seemed too neat an answer to such a big question, but Grace didn't query any further.

"Let the personality know that from now on the soul is in charge; it's taking orders from a new captain. Focus every day on making sure the soul leads and that there's no mutiny on board. The personality wants to rule as it's been barking orders your whole life, but Grace, instruct this attention-seeking persona that things are changing from this moment on."

She didn't know to whom she was speaking but mouthed, "Personality, you no longer reign over this ship. My soul is now in charge, and that's who you will take orders from. My soul is the truth and that's who you're answerable to." For added effect she added, "Capiche?" and twirled around her bedroom like a whirling dervish, the dress still hanging around her neck.

"Grace, your soul will enter everything you do once you allow it to be the captain. The mutiny is in your hands."

On some subtle level she felt there'd been a reshuffling of the board. She sat down on her bed, astonished.

"It's this ridiculous dissecting of irrelevant details which makes your personality think it's the centre of the world. The personality can't see the soul's journey. When it's in charge, do you even notice anyone else out there in the 'World of Grace'? Can you feel the love of humanity? Of nature? Does anybody else even exist?"

Embarrassed, Grace stared off into the distance.

"You know you can't see anyone but yourself and your problems, which are all of your own making. The minute you personalise your issues instead of viewing them through the lens of the soul, your suffering begins. And when you're that self-involved, you can't access a higher state of consciousness, or do what your soul most wants you to do."

"Which is?"

"To use your life to serve."

A certain lucidness flowed through her. "When I had that 'I shouldn't have eaten all those croquettes' meltdown, I went way further than normal self-absorption allows," she admitted.

"Ditch the shame, Grace; it's a waste of time. Next time know that you can substitute the word croquettes for donuts, potato chips or any 'I shouldn't have said this or done that' phrase uttered from your mouth. While the content may change, with this attitude you're always dealing with the same structure."

Grace suddenly glimpsed a pattern previously invisible to her and knew she'd only be able to break her thought patterns through increasing awareness, neutrality and viewing life symbolically. This, however, would take time to unfold.

23 | Letting Go

Two days and two nights later, the Wind was again engaging Grace through her present level of consciousness. "Grace, you must believe that you belong to the world."

She meditated on humanity but was finding it extremely difficult.

"What goes on in your energetic realm reflects out into the wider physical world. The solar system lives within you, Grace. A physical earthquake on the other side of the world can simulate an emotional earthquake within you, leading you to question what ground is shaking beneath your feet? Which mental and emotional foundations are being rattled?"

Grace felt besieged and inundated with concepts she didn't understand.

"Your selfish thoughts lead to the selfishness you experience in the world. Your hostile, attacking thoughts maintain a hostile, attacking world. Do you understand this? If you don't speak lovingly to yourself, how can you bring love into this world, let alone give it to others? Grace, self-hatred pollutes the world as much as smog."

With her self-loathing triggered, she got up to raid the kitchen for a post-supper snack. Before opening her bedroom door, Grace realised that she was reacting to an impulse, not watching it. Holding the urge in non-judgmental awareness, it dawned on her that she wasn't really hungry. She simply wanted to consume something other than the Wind's candid words.

"Watching you hate and despise yourself is like watching you hate and despise me. I am in you and you are in me. We reflect one another. Don't deny me and wish me to be other than I am. Just love me, Grace, and love others just because they are."

Grace crawled under the covers and felt her throat choke up. The naked sincerity of the Wind's appeal terrified her. "Of course I accept you as you are," she replied. It was easy to accept the Wind and its invisibleness; herself and her denseness another matter entirely.

"If you can love me as I am, you can love yourself just as you are," answered the Wind.

"I think you might be pushing it a tad too far there."

"Don't deny your unique quirks and traits, Grace. You love food, it's an integral part of how you make sense of the world, so don't reject yourself for this. You're a bookworm, relish it! You think in tangents, what a skill! Don't flush these valuable gifts down the drain because you've not yet grown into their priceless, eternal value. Now go stand by the window."

Grace opened the wooden Venetian blind and gazed at the moonlit garden. She knew her mother's pink petunias were blooming; she had noticed them earlier in the day. The crescent moon and the stars glistened in the ebony sky.

"Tomorrow when you wake, look at the garden again and appreciate it as an evolving structure. Notice how it lets itself be influenced. It doesn't contest the changes; the garden lets change guide and transform it."

Grace nodded in acknowledgement.

"Allow things to happen in the order they're meant to."

Instinctively she knew that change led to growth; the trick was not engaging in a futile battle fighting the process.

"Now look up. Listen to the night. Can all that mental stress you hold inside even begin to compare to the beauty of the stars? Your frustrations can't match the resplendent vastness of the night sky, can they? Grace, you believe that your self-made problems are as big as the universe, but take a step back and remember who you are."

"What does recalling who I am have to do with what's outside the window?"

"Once you start living as a soul, you'll recognise the soul in others. Remember, you're made from the very same fabric as the stars, Grace, and the light you shine into the world will be reflected back to you."

That line would make a cool bookmark.

"Disempowering thoughts will still come though, so don't fight them. Watch them from the position of an observer exactly as you're now looking onto the garden and the thoughts will neutralise themselves."

All Grace could do was nod. Her head felt swollen and heavy, like a wrecking ball sitting on her shoulders. Criticism was her default lens viewer, not observation.

"As you witnessed earlier, hunger may not always be for food. You had the good sense to pause and ask yourself what exactly you were hungry for. You're starving for acceptance and you try to satisfy that feeling with food. Grace, you don't yet know how to fill yourself up from the inside, which is why you believe that more food, or some other external substance, will make you happy. Know this, and know it well; food will never fill that part in your heart that's ravenous. With every unnecessary eating-for-the-sake-of-eating episode, you're making yourself believe that love exists outside of you and not within. As we progress together you'll experience the veracity of this."

She felt a soft breeze hit her face though the window was closed.

"And while you're gazing out into space; stop replaying the past; it can't be rewritten. I know you think that with enough mental effort it can, and by jeez, I've seen you try—but know it can't be done. Grace, can you hear me?"

"Yes."

"The only time you can ever rewrite is this moment. So tell me, what will you write?"

"Let go and trust in the flow of life." Were they really her words? The next words certainly came from the Wind. "And so it is."

24 | Money Matters

Juliet, Ruby and Grace spent their first day of school holidays at the local mall. The day started with the girls taking the escalator up to the second floor of the Minx department store.

The Wind took this opportunity to share some thoughts about money and material possessions with Grace. "What gives money its value is not how much of it you have, but how you feel about it. Money is neutral, it's an exchange of energy—it only starts meaning something when you do things with it."

"Well, if it doesn't have any power on its own, why do people think having a lot of money will make them happy?" The other girls couldn't hear Grace's telepathic dialogue with the Wind.

The Wind replied, "People believe money will grant them happiness, prestige, freedom, and a guarantee that bad things won't ever happen to them, but the attachment to money is the very thing that causes their suffering. Grasping onto money means gripping onto fear." It added for good measure, "Holding onto money that tightly reveals something other than the present moment has control over you."

"If the present moment is the only time that matters, why can't I take Papa's credit card and go on a massive spending spree? I mean, you said it's only the now that matters."

"Oh, this old question," the Wind replied. "I don't mean living in the now by running up unnecessary debt for your poor father. I mean the now in context to your present circumstances."

"Can you speak in English please?"

The Wind used an analogy to explain. "If you never spend more than $10 at lunch, it'd be ridiculous to suddenly spend $100 on today's lunch, correct?"

"But what if it's a special occasion?"

"Then it's a special occasion, but you can't spend $100 on lunch every day if it's not within your resources to do so. Living in the present means living within your means."

The girls were at the makeup counters. The products appeared shiny and new and more aspirational than anything any of them currently owned or could afford.

"I want the lifestyle where this is normal," Juliet said as she fingered a $450 moisturiser in a tiny, blue glass jar with a chrome lid. "And I want a chauffeur, cook, personal trainer, and multiple homes around the world too," she added. It was part fantasy, part goal setting.

Grace chipped in that she wished she had a supermodel's life. "That way men would desire me, women would envy me, and I'd be famous, with an awesome wardrobe and I'd travel the world in first class." Actually, her greatest dream was to have children, but that aspiration wasn't glamorous enough within the mass consumerism of the mall.

"I won't even comment on the current conversation between you girls," the Wind interjected, "so I'll shift it to something more to my liking."

The Wind can be such a boring know-it-all at times.

"Grace, money is energy; it has its own vibration. It can vibrate at a high or low frequency. The frequency is determined by the feelings you have about it and the ensuing actions you take. If you spend money on sweets that make you fat, your money drains you, it dwindles your reserves, but spend money cooking a lovely meal that comforts and nourishes a friend going through a rough time, and you've shifted the frequency up several notches."

Grace ambled over to the perfume counter.

The Wind continued, "Money shouldn't stagnate. It's an energy that needs circulating. I don't mean spending it to accumulate more for yourself; but passing on its benefits to others."

"All our problems would disappear if we had more money," said

Juliet. She was scrutinising eye creams with extracts of caviar and gold in them.

"I know," Ruby concurred.

"The dreary and the mundane wouldn't touch us. We'd take taxis everywhere and do whatever we wanted," Grace added.

"You'll never have enough money, Grace," the Wind whispered in her ear, "because until you learn to have enough, you'll never experience having more."

At her present level of immaturity, Grace was pretty annoyed to hear this.

25 | You Are Enough

L ater that afternoon, Grace decided to head to the beach on her own. The bus dropped her off near the Parves jetty, and she slipped her pointed-toe flats off and rolled her green corduroys above her knees. She didn't want to run through the morning in the department store again in her mind. All she wanted was to feel her feet sink into the cool, wet sand and listen to the ocean's reassuring waves.

"If you were granted everything you asked for, you wouldn't be happy because you'd still want more," the Wind said. "If you had three houses, you'd want four. Your desires balloon if you don't know how to be content with what you already have. Learn to stop seeking material comfort and allow spiritual reassurance to clothe you. The saying 'less is more' holds great truth."

Grace knew the Wind's words were partly true—okay, mostly true—but didn't want to believe them. She had never experienced enough, so how could she settle for it?

And if I've never known more, how am I supposed to lose my desire for it?

"Grace, you do know more. With every desperate, grasping plea for attention, every second and third helping of food, every mini-drama that creates more maxi-dramas, you and 'More' are best friends. Who you don't know is 'Enough'!"

"Alright, I get it!"

"I don't know if you do, Grace. If you have an intense connection with a stranger . . ."

"I feel it should go somewhere, develop into something more."

"And it shouldn't necessarily," the Wind said. "If the relationship progresses, the initial intensity may fizzle out, and you'd kick yourself for not keeping the encounter as an electric, one-off event. Relish what you experienced and let it be. By wanting more you cling to the unnecessary. What you have in the moment is all you need. Stop craving more than what the present moment is capable of giving you. Trust that you have enough and that you yourself are enough. New moments can only enter your consciousness when you release your grip on the past. Know when it's time to move on."

Her mind kept drifting back to the morning at the mall. Shopping was a form of escape, a chance to buy her way into a new life.

The Wind continued, "We can't take our possessions with us when we die, but we can take the memories that heightened our awareness. No growth in consciousness is ever lost."

"English is the lingua franca, Wind. Break it down."

"When we die, people won't remember the designer kitchen we had, but how we acted in it. Did we regularly invite people over to share meals and celebrate good times? Did we create an environment where guests felt comfortable? Were we genuine in our hospitality? As you mature, Grace, don't hold on to the possessions money gives you, but to the growth and lessons it provides."

The annual high school dance was happening in three weeks and Grace wanted a new dress.

"You don't need a new outfit. You have enough clothes in your wardrobe to dress for the ball right now."

"But it won't be new," Grace protested.

"Not everything needs to be new. People don't react to a dress, but to the attitude of the person wearing the dress—new or not."

Near the surf lifesaving club Grace allowed her feet to again sink into the sand's grittiness. The water lapped at her shins as the sand clamped around her ankles. She felt free, not constrained.

"In time you'll experience that there's nothing more beautiful than a life filled with reflection, study and service."

This was way too much for her consumer mindset to digest.

"You are enough, Grace; from this moment on you must stop thinking and acting like you're not. You'll never experience your desires if you can't express gratitude for all the blessings you already have."

26 | Personal Power

The autumn dance was in a week and Grace—of her own accord—told her mother she was willing to create a new look from what already existed in her wardrobe.

"I'm dying of shock. Did I hear you correctly?" her mother said, feigning surprise.

"You heard correctly."

"You'll work with what you've got? Well, I never believed that'll be the day."

"And today is that day," Grace replied without a hint of irony.

"Well, do you want some help?"

"That'd be great," and there was no sarcasm in Grace's voice, only genuine appreciation for her mother's offer of assistance.

Grace and Carla stood in front of the open wardrobe.

"I've never worn this top with this skirt before so that could be nice?" Both were a shade of purple, her favourite colour.

"At one of your father's work dinner dances years ago I dressed up a plain, black turtleneck by tying three differently coloured scarves around it: one around the breasts, another the ribs, one on the tummy and tied each in beautiful bows at the back. You wouldn't believe the number of compliments I received."

"Okay, so let's give it a shot, Mum."

Her mother tied a yellow scarf first, then orange and chestnut around the black tank top Grace was wearing. "Et voila! The last scarf will blend in perfectly with that caramel silk skirt I brought back for you from Thailand."

"Perfect!"

"It's all about the fit. Shoulders exposed, tummy tucked in, an elegant line. You'll look absolutely gorgeous on the night."

Grace gave her a kiss on the cheek. "Thanks, Mum."

"Remember, a genuine smile, a kind heart and good posture are your best fashion accessories," smiled Carla.

The Monday morning after the dance, Grace was sitting in mathematics class reminiscing about the evening. It wasn't the best night out ever, but Grace enjoyed who she was that evening—a young woman playful and confident in her own skin. She focused on being with the people who wanted her around—even if they were nerds—rather than chasing after people who weren't interested in her. Grace enjoyed the presence of each person before her, instead of wishing she were part of a conversation happening on the other side of the room. She was well and truly over putting herself at the mercy of those who rejected her. She spent her time with the people who did find her funny and genuinely valued her company.

Why was I so blind to them before?

As she began to answer the algorithm puzzle on the blackboard, Grace instinctively put her hand over her workbook so that Bessie, sitting behind her, couldn't copy her work. Her answers (though probably wrong) were hers and hers alone.

Grace's attention drifted back to the dance again and she was proud of how she implemented the Wind's advice. She didn't beg for attention, so didn't hand her power over.

"Stand tall in your magnificence, so that the universe can respond in kind—it mirrors your consciousness," the Wind added. "It can only act in response to someone faithfully in charge of his or her own personal power. Show that you can command this vital energy that's been bestowed on you, Grace. Don't fritter it away like a drunk at a bar."

27 | Living Light

G race was sitting in the corner behind the library eating her egg and watercress sandwich in peace. The cool air gently shook the silver birch trees.

"Education is to be shared with others, not something you hoard for yourself. Knowledge is a form of energy and it's to be passed on—it needs to keep moving. Sharing is the only way to retain knowledge and strengthen its power. Think of knowledge like the sun. You should have so much light inside you, Grace, that you can't help but give it away."

"Oh joy! Precisely what the doctor ordered, another call to be more than I currently am."

"Grace, I am giving you the tools to experience a lighter, joy-filled life, and you view these tricks of the trade as twenty times heavier than the burdens you're currently lugging around."

She was snooty. "It's tough unlearning a lifetime's worth of faulty thinking, okay?"

"Learn from the experience of others. It's not necessary to make every mistake yourself. Others have made far more mistakes at a far grander level from which you can learn. Instead of this wishy-washy 'life is too hard' attitude, be receptive to my teachings. Don't you want to be as light as I am, Grace?"

"Don't really think that's possible, Wind. It sounds a little like the myth of losing a dress size in a week."

"Grace, you have the capacity to think, feel and act light, but you weigh yourself down. I can only point the way; you're the one who needs to take the steps to weightlessness. If you choose to embroil yourself in stuff that doesn't matter; you're the one dragging yourself down."

"Now cue the self-responsibility lecture."

"Remember that you are the one allowing me to speak. You are instigating our conversations. I'm only responding to your requests."

"And I bring our dialogues about by the situations I create?"

"Yes."

"Okay, okay." Grace took a moment to absorb the enormity of what she said. "Okay, just so I'm clear, I'm the one who instigates our chats?"

"Yes, and I respond to your feelings, behaviours, beliefs and memories. Comprende?"

"Si."

Hearing Spanish made her crave her favourite tapas dish—chickpeas, spinach and bacon.

"Grace, remember what I said about concentration."

"Something about how it's essential to develop the power to harness your mind, that it's crucial for success, blah, blah, blah."

"If it's all 'blah, blah, blah' to you then why did you call me here? What is it you wish to know?"

Grace wasn't prepared to take responsibility for her reaction to every thought and choice yet, so she scrambled for something half-decent and intelligent to say. "Er, knowledge?"

The Wind let her fake it. "Well, knowledge doesn't really belong to anyone. It's used to facilitate life—not only for you—but for everybody. Hoarding knowledge prevents any new intelligence from coming in, as you've erected barricades around static energy. Did Bessie trying to copy your answer take anything away from you earlier today?"

Grace felt threatened. "Yes, because if she gets a higher mark than I do, I'll be in a lower percentile rating."

"Really?"

"Yes. You know we get class positions along with our grades." It felt fantastic to know something definitively and to put her point across authoritatively, no matter how trivial.

"And you're willing to accept that this class position reflects your actual knowledge?"

Man, the Wind was dumb sometimes. How can it be so clever, yet awfully dim-witted at the same time?

She laughed and recalled Abel's favourite episode of *The Simpsons* where Bart said to Milhouse, "How can someone with glasses that thick be so stupid?"

"Grace, you forget I can read your thoughts."

"Woops! I mean, I have to accept it as it's the way the school system works."

"But Grace, that's not the correct way to interact with the world, by letting a system judge you. Find another way."

"I have no idea what you're banging on about."

"Don't let the school system be the judge of you."

Grace's mind focused on devouring tens of tapas; she was really hungry.

"Grace, please be aware of your thoughts."

She was caught out.

"Your future employers, the woman you sit next to on a plane in thirteen years' time, your father-in-law right through to your daughter's preschool teacher, none of them will care about your percentile in tenth grade, second semester mathematics class. They won't even care about the ranking in eleventh or twelfth grade. They won't define you as a person by this percentage. It's only you who's limiting and defining yourself by this judgment."

"Excuse me. I have to explain my report card to Mum and Papa."

"Again, Grace, that's because you're living in the details and unable to grasp the bigger picture. You're not witnessing the wholeness of life. Don't lose touch with the only pulse of time that counts."

"Huh?"

"The eternal."

"I thought the only time that mattered was now?"

"The eternal expressed through the now."

She was perplexed and furrowed her eyebrows. "You're not living in the real world," she said, and sighed.

The bell rang and the lunch break was over.

"Grace, my world is as real as yours. I just create my own rules in alignment with the universal laws, while you choose to follow restrictive ideals imposed on you by others."

"Whatever. I don't have time for this. I've got to get to class."

The Wind kept talking to her as she started toward her classroom on the second floor.

"There's knowledge that enables you to make money in this world, but that's not the only intelligence I'm talking about. Academic knowledge is bound by time and space and is situation dependent. Many people pursue this learning, but have no universal or self-knowledge. They understand nothing of the cosmology that governs our lives from the influence of tidal, lunar and circadian patterns to the seasonal and annual rhythms that operate in and around us. They have no idea how divorced they are from true wisdom."

"Well, you certainly haven't taught me much about these rhythms," Grace said. She caught her reflection in the canteen window and saw that her French braid wasn't straight.

"Indeed I have, but not in the way you'd learn at school."

Grace had a quick sip of water at the fountain and bounded up the stairs.

"For one thing, Grace, it's difficult when you're not spending nearly enough time in nature, and so have minimal connection to the ecosystem. Knowledge of the earth is to be one with the world, but too often today people gather around the TV to watch sport instead of congregating outside to play in nature's kingdom."

"Alright, that bit I get," she said. "Knowledge of the earth is to be experienced."

At the top of the stairs Grace spied Madison. She smiled and waved as she headed into the classroom.

"Just as you'll never observe the stars having a nervous breakdown, you'll never witness an oak tree wishing it were a maple tree, or a red rose regretting what it did that day or pining to be yellow in colour."

"Each aspect of nature is just perfect, because all things in nature exist in their own strength and bring an irreplaceable essence to the world. Each element is in harmony with the moment." Her own response shocked her; she actually sounded wise.

Maybe the Wind's whispering is starting to have an effect?

"Grace, remember, you cannot break the rhythms of nature, only yourself against them."

She sat down with poise and grace, bringing her presence to the geography class. It was her soul that explored the dynamics between people, their environment and the phenomena on the earth's surface for the next hour.

28 | The Moon's Cycles

In the car on the way back from basketball practice, a recent conversation with the Wind replayed in her mind.

"Grace, you get exhausted so easily; you run yourself completely ragged. You're burning out, not burning bright. When you're that worn out, what I've taught you flies out the window and you fall back into your old ways, choosing candy over fruit, TV over exercise, rejection over acceptance, and fear over love."

As she climbed out of the car, Grace remarked with wonder to her mother that it was a full moon. Carla, preoccupied with her own thoughts, replied, "Yes, dear," and continued into the house.

Grace stayed behind staring at the moon; it called to her. In history class she learned that in ancient times people counted time by using the moon's phases, not calendars, and that these cultures let the moon's cycles dictate to them when to plant, harvest, hunt and gather. After some time she followed her mother inside.

"It's a shame that most of us don't know where the moon is in its cycle. Most of us barely make time to gaze up at the sky each evening."

Grace almost fell off the kitchen stool. It was her mother speaking while making a cup of tea, not the Wind.

"In our modern day Western world we've lost the ritual of self-reflection in tandem with each of the moon's phases." Carla stared at Grace with the quiet intensity of a yogi. "Do you know that on our third date your father picked me up from your grandparents' old home in the hills, drove us to an open field and proceeded to lay a tartan blanket on the grass and prepare a picnic?"

Grace's face reflected her disbelief. She knew her father loved Carla and the children in his own peculiar way, but not in a cuddly, romantic manner.

Her mother continued her trip down memory lane. "He had bought a baguette, some goat's cheese, a French Neufchâtel, that heart-shaped cheese which way back then was terribly exclusive, and some grapes and almonds. He said that the cost of the food bankrupted him, so he could only afford a cheap wine."

Papa buying cheese in the shape of a heart? Well, I never.

"And some milk chocolate."

They burst into laughter. Dylan now didn't touch any chocolate with less than 80% cocoa content.

"Let's go outside and appreciate the moon," Grace suggested.

They walked outside and Carla continued, "We sat on the blanket amongst the food, cradled the plastic cups of wine in our hands and watched the stars. It was a new moon, and your father explained its influence on the tides, and since humans are composed of more than 75% water, that our relationship to the moon is one of the most significant connections we'll ever form in our lives. He then declared that he wanted to have a significant relationship with me."

Standing outside, chilled to the bone in her sweaty sports gear, Grace felt that she could withstand the cold for hours listening to her mother evoke a time alien to her. "Wow! Papa was a completely different person back then."

Carla's blonde bob accentuated her high cheekbones as she shook her head. "He's still the same, Grace, it's simply not on the surface like it used to be. Dig a bit deeper, and the man that buys heart-shaped cheese is still there."

Grace enjoyed the magic of the moment.

"He also mentioned that we should amalgamate our lives with the moon's cycle. Grace, I fell madly in love with your father when he revealed these ways of the world to me. Back then he was engrossed in the arts and sciences and open to everyone and everything. He explained that it wasn't enough to be aware of the moon's expansion and contraction, but that we had to meaningfully connect and feel its sequences inside ourselves. Gosh! And I thought these memories were lost in the recesses of my mind."

Grace hugged her mother tight. Drawing a line down the ridge of Grace's nose with her finger, Carla explained what Dylan meant. "The new moon is the time to give birth to fresh ideas and commence new projects. You then build your strength to consolidate the energy in the second quarter and during the full moon work on any imbalances in your undertaking, mirroring the moon in juxtaposition to the sun."

Grace couldn't recall listening this intently to her mother before.

"In the fourth quarter you digest the learnings, close the cycle and gear up for another new beginning or the next phase of your current venture."

Grace wished she had pen and paper on hand but knew this conversation couldn't be mentally captured, only intuitively felt.

The Wind entered. "Did you know that women's natural body rhythms correspond to the moon's cycle? Before electricity, women's bodies were influenced by the amount of moonlight they were exposed to and these levels triggered their hormones. Grace, as the moon journeys through its phases, so too does a woman move through her menstrual cycle. Creation resides in her blood, which is why it's so beneficial for women to harmonise their interior lives with the moon's chapters to heighten the narrative of their divine feminine nature."

Better revere these rhythmic cycles of life, I guess.

"Lunar traditions show a deep trust that the light always returns within the great web of life. The moon is a symbol of totality, a unified whole. The phases just represent time in the context of the eternal."

Grace's attention turned to her mother.

"It's a shame that I don't apply any of this knowledge myself," Carla sighed, and squeezed Grace's waist. "That night as your father described how to merge our daily calendar with nature's sequential events, I knew I wanted this man to be the father of my children."

How on earth did the Wind hijack Mum's body?

29 | Time Management

By day's end, Grace's to-do list had barely been touched, and it gnawed at her. She glanced at today's list of twelve entries and instantly felt overwhelmed and teary.

"Lose this goal-orientated approach to living, Grace. It's the quality you bring to the doing that counts, not the quantity."

There was no formal greeting between the Wind and herself, and their exchanges quickly got to the heart of the matter.

"The personality seeks approval by doing things as it believes that with enough externally-oriented effort you'll finally be complete. But you already are loved and accepted by the divine, Grace. You're made of the same cloth. You are already whole; it's just that you're not experiencing and making choices from your wholeness. Don't concern yourself with what needs doing, but focus instead on expressing the truth of who you are."

Grace no longer hesitated with her answers. "Well, I'd like to welcome opportunities into my life instead of rejecting them."

"Then do your doing as if time doesn't exist. Be in vertical time, not horizontal time."

"And how is that going to help me? Remember, I'm in school five days a week and don't have oodles of spare time." Obviously the Wind never read any of the time management books on *The New York Times* best-seller list.

"You can't achieve everything on your to-do list at full pace, Grace. If there's an emergency, rush, but don't treat every day like a crisis. And ask who is it that wants you to relentlessly race through your list? The personality, that's who."

Grace lay on her bed and pulled her knees up to her chest to stretch her back.

"When you browse in a bookstore when you've nowhere else to be, there's a whole different, magical quality to the time. As soon as you need to be elsewhere, browsing turns into clock-watching, and the next appointment creeps into your carefree time. There's no space for life's natural continuity to occur. You keep stunting your growth by dictating when and how things should happen. Grace, let life flow through you and stop forcing time into fixed blocks and rigid lists. Make space to be."

She stretched her legs and tried to touch her toes. Impossible! Her hands could only reach just below her knees so she turned around and buried her head in the pillows.

"Think of yourself as a bike with different gears. Which gear's best to complete each of the twelve tasks in front of you today?"

"You've lost me."

"A bike needs to be in a middle gear when it's on flat ground, in a higher gear to climb a hill and a lower gear to breeze downhill. It'd be silly, and difficult, to attempt all three terrains stuck in the same gear, as the gears aren't being used to their—or your—advantage."

"Okay, let me get this straight. Going downhill you let gravity do the hard work and uphill you make the gears work for you."

"Exactly. Why make it any harder than it needs to be?"

"It's the only way I know how!" Blurting out the truth made her laugh.

"Not everything in life requires accomplishing at top speed, like you're competing in a race. Get out of this paradigm where only 'sprint' and 'rest' exist. There are millions of gears in between to choose from, and you don't need to complete everything at the same tempo. Pace yourself!"

This was true. Grace lived life in only two gears—stop or go. She either had too much to do, running around like a headless chicken, or was crashed out in front of the TV watching fantasy drama DVDs with barely a registered pulse. She either slept for thirteen hours straight or had insomnia.

"You can choose a different gear for each task."

"I don't understand."

The Wind changed tack. "Say you have all these books to read for English class before end of semester. Will you speed-read the books the week before the deadline? Read a chapter a week? Or only when the mood strikes you?"

"Um, knowing me," she said, "I'd say it'd be deadline reading."

"But I know how much you love to read, and there's nothing worse than leisurely wanting to enjoy a book, wanting to grow with the characters and not being able to do so because the book report is due in the morning."

"Welcome to my life!"

"Do you remember that lemon scone recipe you once attempted to make for afternoon tea for your mother's friends?"

"Yep."

"And how you didn't give yourself enough time and hadn't finished before the guests arrived so you burst into tears and left the half-mixed dough in the bowl and walked away."

"It was a disaster from beginning to end." Of that Grace was certain.

"No, it wasn't. You interpreted the situation as a debacle, but it led you to realise that cooking is an act of love, not merely a results-orientated exercise."

Could she be gracious in defeat? "I guess I learned not to needlessly put myself in stressful situations, and that experimenting is much more fun when there are no time constraints."

"With self-imposed pressure from the personality, like this fixation to finish all these things on your list tonight, the agitation is all self-inflicted."

She said to herself, "I've got to stop rushing around like this and only spend focused, quality time on the projects and people I actually adore. I promised a few, dear friends I'd be here to walk this earth with them. I mustn't neglect them."

30 | Attuning to Your Inner Peace

Grace walked outside and sat under the pergola to contemplate the steep learning curve she found herself in. Although the clouds threatened rain, the night queen perfume from the frangipani tree scented the air, permeating the entire property.

"Speaking of feeling pushed for time, when you rush out the door without having a good look in the mirror, you end up spending the majority of the day agonising over what you look like."

"It's a false economy," Grace said, hoping she used the term correctly. She heard her father mention it when her mother wanted to buy a second-hand washing machine and Grace thought the word worked appropriately here.

"Infuse meaning into your actions by doing things at their proper pace. This makes them infinitely more enjoyable. So let's consider this list of twelve things. Can you quickly prioritise them?"

"They all need to get done," she said.

"Grace, not everything is important. Get better at distinguishing between what's indispensable and what's surplus to requirement. When a ship is sinking a lifejacket is essential; all else is superfluous."

"Okay, okay, point taken. So I guess only four things need my attention tonight, the other eight can wait."

"But Grace, those eight will roll on top of another list of twelve things you manufacture for yourself to agonise over tomorrow. Let's only focus on what's essential."

This was true. To-do lists were snowballs that gathered more snow with each day that rolled passed.

"Which two tasks will have consequences if left undone? And I don't mean what you'll berate yourself over, I mean real consequences that genuinely impact you or another."

"My mathematics assignment is due in the morning, and I promised I'd call Kosmos tonight."

"Now Grace, in time you'll come to know that completing your homework isn't a matter of life and death. Go call Kosmos now, as people—at all times—come first."

"Then my assignment?"

"Yes, and in which gear will you tackle it?"

"Well, it doesn't contribute to my grade at the end of semester, but I do still have to hand it in."

"Why don't we complete it to a level where you've comprehended the concept, but that you're not so burned out by it that you can still have an early night? I don't want you diminishing your flame unnecessarily. I want the fire within you to burn steadily as you wake up to the dimension of grace within you."

Grace was only half listening. "I can see what you mean. Living at a constant sprint is unsustainable."

"Don't let the pressure of time assault you, Grace. Be with the individual pace of the process. Don't try to jump the gun. Live at the centre, not the periphery where these pointless tasks exist. Keep bringing yourself back to centre. If you feel you should be doing something else, do it; if not, make peace with where you are."

"But I have to do everything perfectly—all the time—at maximum intensity." She suddenly wanted to take flight into the clouds above and escape the Wind, but it was a futile thought.

"Please stop that ridiculous chatter, Grace," the Wind said. "Watch your words—they concern doing. I'm asking you to be—to bring more of your compassionate, awakened self into this life. Express as much love as you can in each individual moment and recalibrate as one point of time folds into the next. Sometimes it's tough, your mind is elsewhere, you're drained and weak; but get over it and get over yourself. You can only work with the awareness available to you, and this level fluctuates from moment to moment, day to day, year to year."

Grace was now listening intently.

"Life is a process; it's a series of events. It's up, it's down, things make sense, and then they don't. It's within the alternation where life exists, in the tide-like ebb and flow. Discover the divine's constancy in change. Study the undercurrents. Value the inner life."

Grace begrudgingly returned to her room, opened her window to let the ominous, stormy air in, sat at her desk and started on her homework. She forgot to call Kosmos, even though he was the lifejacket on a capsizing ferry and the algorithm only a suitcase to let sink to the bottom of the ocean.

31 | Changing Gears

The next morning, out of the blue, Abel offered to drive Grace to school.

"This is a random act of kindness if I've ever received one," she pronounced.

"Don't have such a low opinion of me, sis."

"Man, I can't wait to get my license," Grace said, climbing into the RX7. "It'll be like busting out of jail. Total and utter freedom!"

"Nah, not really." Abel never gave any obvious emotion away. His face was permanently fixed in a look of 'it's all cool'.

The convertible roared down the hill. The beachfront four kilometres away glistened in the sun beyond the rooftops, trees and roads of suburbia. Stuck at the traffic lights, her brother, in a rare admission of vulnerability, admitted how frustrated he was.

"I'm here, but wanna be there." He illustrated the distance on the dashboard. "I wanna be earning the big bucks, but can't face sloggin' my ass off at university for years to get there. I wanna drop out."

Grace thought Abel loved his freewheeling, happy-go-lucky, big-man-on-campus lifestyle, but the lure of dollars beckoned.

"The in-between is as important as where you've come from and where you're going to."

"Whatcha on about?"

"I mean, so think of it like a car. For instance, this car doesn't automatically go straight to fifth gear, right?"

"Right." Abel looked at her as if she were deluded but she continued nonetheless.

"Stay with me. There's a process to follow: first gear to second to third to fourth to fifth. It's completely unnatural for the car to go straight to fifth from first."

Abel nodded in agreement.

"So what makes you think you can jump completing the degree, let alone the job-hunting process, and walk straight into a cushy, high-paying job?"

"Coz I can."

"How can you be so arrogant to demand life should answer to you on your limited terms of engagement?" she barked back, and then stopped. She suddenly caught a glimpse of herself.

How true! You always hate in others what they reveal in your own temperament.

"Yo! Do you wanna walk to school?"

While Abel was incredibly clever academically, his communication skills were severely lacking.

"Everything that comes to you is a blessing, Abe, appreciate it. Now, what was I saying? That's right, I mean, look at you and Lana." She was his latest squeeze of the week. "You expect a relationship at fourth speed when you haven't even moved the car from first to second. You're forever rushing, Abes." She now sounded like the older sibling. "There's beauty in each speed, but you're forever chasing the end goal and never valuing the subtleties of each gear change. Life's not about getting the car into fifth gear as quickly as possible and cruising from there."

Abel kept his eyes on the road. She could tell that what she had said unnerved him.

"Okay, brain box. Tell me more."

The Wind fed Grace the words. "Well, how we manage our behaviour through transitions, I mean gear changes, is crucial."

"It's okay, sis, I get the analogy."

"How we transition from the end of one relationship to the beginning of another, or how we leave our old job and start a new one, it all matters. And it definitely matters how we deal with uncertainty when there's a personal trauma in our lives. Transitions are the gateway into the next moment, they guide us into our future, just as the rainy season pre-empts the summer." She paused for a moment before continuing. "Each moment in your life paves the way for the next one to expand, that's why it's essential to be present for each point in time, as the quality you bring to that moment determines the features and attributes of the next. All endings lead to new beginnings."

"Let me get this straight." Abel stared intensely at Grace. "Hating uni is part of the transition from school to a career, and I should enjoy it, otherwise my future will suck."

"Yeah, I guess, pretty much."

When they arrived at school Grace didn't want to get out of the car; she felt they really shared a moment. She was staring into Abel, not through him. Reluctantly, she undid her seatbelt and slid out of the car. She wanted to say a few more words, but the Wind said them quietly to her instead. "Bring your soul to the moments that confuse you. Transitions remind us life is seamless, and it's us making them more jagged and rough than they need to be. Shift effortlessly through the gear changes."

32 | Being of Service

It was Sunday afternoon and her grandparents were over for a late lunch. Grace tried to bring the whole of her being to how she ate. She felt the weight of the cutlery and how the sparkling water bubbled in the back of her throat.

Nurturing connections with others will only come when I have a healthy and whole relationship with myself.

Once her grandparents left, Grace sat outside under the pergola admiring the mixture of burgundy and yellow cymbidium orchids Veronika gave her mother last Easter. She called out to the Wind, "So how do I stop placing myself at the centre of the universe?"

The Wind jumped right in. "Service."

"Oh."

"Service isn't about sitting on charity committees for the purpose of self-aggrandisement, or because it's what you think you should be doing. You don't serve to enhance your career prospects, Grace; your altruistic endeavours come from a true desire to help heal humanity. Don't think of service as some grand statement; it can be as subtle as smiling at a stranger."

"But smiling at a stranger surely can't be enough?"

"But it is, Grace. Yet again you're trapped in your 'not enough' paradigm."

"But I don't know how to be of service."

"Well, a noble act of service you can bring to the world is to share what I've taught you."

She was perplexed. "How?"

"You can't force this wisdom on people, Grace. They must come to it of their own accord, but by living these insights you will teach them. Impose the higher rhythm of the soul on your thoughts, feelings and actions and you'll educate by who you are. You can only teach what you live, which is why life's trials and tribulations are your training ground."

"I think I've heard something like this once before: from the test comes the testimony."

"First though you need to develop virtues into the very fabric of your being. And Grace, it's okay to make mistakes as you learn. No one gets it right straight off the bat. And I want you to communicate with nature and your inner child before attempting to reach any higher."

"But how?"

"Easy, be more playful. Do you even remember what it's like to play, Grace?"

She nodded, noticing how the flowers gently swayed.

"Return to your innocence, to when tears disappeared as quickly as they appeared, when life was lived lightly."

Grace moved closer to the orchids and fingered their leaves, feeling their vibrancy.

The Wind continued. "Selfishness is removed from our minds when we serve, as we honour life's web of interconnectedness. When offering our lives in service, we remember we're part of something far bigger than our limited personalities; that we're tiny parts of a much bigger whole."

Grace perked up. "So if I set up a community outreach program at school, I could boost my resume at the same time?"

"That's not exactly the correct intention, Grace," the Wind said. "When we serve, we do so for the benefit of the greater good, not for individual glory. Get into the habit of surrendering to the nobility of your soul. Don't let the personality dictate how, when and on what terms you'll serve, as serving is its own reward."

Grace thought it pointless. "What's the use of service if people can't see it?"

"We don't serve to be seen. I know it'll take some time for you to welcome this reality, but humility will steer you one day, not prestige and a life lived in the limelight."

Grace searched her interior landscape and admitted she yearned for significance and recognition.

"If you need the applause and appreciation so much, give it to yourself, Grace, or give it to another. What you give, you receive."

Her soul accepted the truth of what was said, but not her personality, which still wanted to be adored and put on a pedestal. A sparrow landed in the birdbath at the back of the garden. Grace had no idea who in the house regularly filled it with water. She decided to go and find out who it was to thank them.

33 | Personal Responsibility

On weekends Grace usually wore a tracksuit or jeans and a top picked from one of the dirty piles of clothes on the floor. She didn't even splash her face with water in the morning to wake herself up, like Abel always did. There were no conscious markers in her day. Time was one big blur.

On this particular Sunday she headed out of the house and began climbing up Atkinson Drive. It was uncharacteristically warm for Autumn. Grace hadn't even passed the first bend in their road, when the Wind commenced speaking.

"Grace, many of us forget how profoundly connected we are to the ancient rhythm of the rising and setting sun. We take this cycle of light and dark for granted; we've forgotten how intensely it influences our health and emotions."

"Okay, sure, but I thought we'd be chatting about something different today."

"What in particular?"

"Er, why we're talking."

"Grace, it was you who created this moment."

She stopped in her tracks and saw a red, single-storey brick house with a green wooden fence. She knew that a girl in third grade at her school lived there with her aunt. She spotted the brown hills sparsely covered with trees in the distance; they looked starved and uncared for.

"You don't stop at your skin, Grace; your environment is also an extension of you. You exhale your thoughts out into the air, and the atmosphere has no choice but to respond to what you're breathing into it."

It was far too early in the morning for her brain to absorb this expansive information.

"When you get home, Grace, you'll see a mess in your bedroom. Clothes on the floor, stacks of dirty coffee mugs, broken face powders, eye shadows missing lids and broken digital devices. All that junk is an extension of your thought process."

"I'm sorry, but I don't understand the purpose of this walk if all you're going to do is lecture me and tell me I'm junk," she said.

"Peace in the world depends on individuals cultivating peace in their own hearts and minds. Grace, my strongest desire is for you to accept yourself. I'm here to show you how everything in your field of perception can be an opportunity for your progression."

Her attention turned to some wilted daisies.

"We'll discuss how energy flows where attention goes later, but for now, don't try to figure it out, feel it out. The grace of life is accepting where the divine has placed you. Often during life's challenges your soul wants to impart a lesson for your growth and evolution, or reclaim some splintered, disowned fragments of your energy. It's trying to bring you back to your original wholeness and holiness."

Grace gave her attention back to the Wind. "But what if it's an awesome moment?"

"Like when you're floating like a starfish in the ocean?"

Grace nodded.

"With your arms and legs stretched in all directions, your ears submerged under water so you connect to the vibrations of some other plane of existence?"

"Aha, and I just float as the water happily takes the weight of my body, releasing all the pressures on my mind."

She stopped walking and visualised herself floating in an aquamarine sea, her arms and legs stretched to the side in a star shape, her face and belly just breaching the surface of the water. She pictured the sun on her face and her body crystallising into shimmering light particles as she floated for a few moments. When her feet sank and eventually touched the seabed floor, an intense clarity penetrated her consciousness. She'd truly been elsewhere, as surely as she was now standing on Atkinson Drive.

They had almost reached the end of the street. As she was downloading all this new information from the Wind, Grace thought it best to stick with the familiar, so she turned on her heels and walked back down the hill the way she came.

"I want to return your attention to the environmental cycle that's of greatest importance to all organisms on earth, the alternation of light and dark."

Whoa! Back in class.

"The wake-sleep cycle is synchronised to the day-night cycle. You know a calendar day lasts for twenty-four hours with four alternating rhythms?"

Grace concentrated. "Day, night, dawn and dusk."

"And these lengths are seasonally variable. You comprehend that, right?"

Grace did. She really hated winter's long, dark nights that stretched ad infinitum.

"There are many things humans do on a daily basis that fit within this twenty-four-hour cycle, like sleeping, eating and bathing. And you also have your own individual patterns."

"Like how I'm more of a morning person?" Grace knew to get anything important done it had to happen within the first few hours of waking.

"Yes, and you ignore this fact by pushing against your natural flow of energy long into the evenings, drinking energy drinks and reading the same passage of a book twenty times over. You become listless and unfocused. The fact that laundries, convenience stores and the internet are open 24/7 only makes it easier for people to disregard their inborn light-dark cycle."

"I guess all that neon advertising in cities, and those fluorescent lights in offices mess up people's cycles too."

"One of the greatest pleasures in life, Grace, is enjoying the transition from night to day and day to night. Unfortunately most adults miss the first changeover as they're asleep and for the second they're stuck in an office. It's why so many adults ease into their evenings with an alcoholic drink as they haven't naturally experienced the time shift, so force a cyclical and mental change through alcohol."

"But there's artificial lighting everywhere and people travel the world with constant jet lag plus there's all the lights emitted from digital devices."

"You're right, Grace. We're constantly resisting our natural human circadian rhythm—this roughly twenty-four to twenty-five-hour cycle going on within our bodies—which plants and animals follow too. Nourishing this internal body clock is crucial for our wellbeing. We need to live the way nature intended, in sync with the rhythms of the rising and setting sun. Harmonise with the light-dark cycle, as it's the inherited blueprint your body's cells and organs follow. Align yourself with the signals of nature to expand your awareness and intuitive knowledge of mother earth."

Grace was fired up to discover more. Could it be because she was connecting with an undeniable truth larger than herself?

"So there's a natural period of alertness in the morning and a time of restlessness after sundown but not for you, Grace, as you work on your laptop until the very second before bed."

Grace wished the Wind didn't know all her dirty habits.

"Every thought you think is visible to me and soon they'll be perceptible enough even to you, which will force you to take responsibility for the reality that each thought vibration creates in your life."

The ramifications of this terrified her and she didn't want to be accountable for the ripple effect of consequences her uninvestigated thoughts and beliefs were inflicting.

34 | Embodying Your Circadian Rhythm

G race suspected that the Wind had tried to enter her life on numerous occasions in the past, but only when she had allowed it in after Amber-Jane's party could it actually begin its work.

What do they say? Angels only help when you ask them.

About to start her third climb up the street, Grace walked past her house and glimpsed her father standing in the sitting room observing her.

The Wind resumed their dialogue on the circadian rhythm. "Start calibrating with this light-dark cycle, Grace. We all know the sun sets and rises, but how many of us truly fathom its principal meaning?"

"Which is?"

"That life is cyclical. There is day and there is night. There can't only be the day. There must be the going and the return. All living things are born, grow, die, and then are reborn. A twenty-four-hour day goes through the exact same iteration."

"True. A day is born, dies at night and then a new day begins."

"Rhythm is the context that gives meaning to your own experiences. Now there's certain preoccupations for individuals during daylight hours, while other activities take prominence as the night comes dancing in."

"Put simply?"

"Sundown means tools down. Switch off."

Grace paused to admire the colourful plumage of a pair of rainbow lorikeets in one of the magnolia trees. "On school camp last year the teacher explained how farmers worked the land as the sun rose and finished before sunset, but for us in big cities, life is 24/7. We really don't build any time into our lives to enjoy the setting phase."

"Too right," the Wind agreed. "The rising and setting of the natural world helps us release our trivial worries. The artificial falls by the wayside when we observe the swinging pendulum of nature and our sense of unity with the divine returns."

Grace felt as if she were conversing with a friend, not a teacher. "So how do I maximise the benefits?"

"When you can, rise with the sun to greet the world before the bustle of the day begins. Feel the divine perfection of natural order before the 'human' day grabs all your attention."

Grace felt ready to ask, "Wind, what's the divine?"

"What do you feel it is?"

She stuttered. "Well . . . um . . . I think it's something bigger than myself. I don't know? It's like something far more expansive than I can imagine, like a type of energy, a force. But I only feel it in glimpses, for no more than a second."

"Well, there's no one right answer, Grace. As you come to more intimately know yourself, you'll meet the divine on a recurrent basis. You'll even experience the divine's presence in acts you despise, like the vacuuming."

Grace laughed, knowing she'd never love this frustrating chore.

"For the moment simply know the celestial as your true self."

She looked to the sky.

"Now where were we? Bringing ourselves into line with the light-dark cycle reminds us of life's fleetingness. Ground yourself in the constancy of the rising and setting sun, as it's the divine at work. Find peace in its recurrence and flawlessness."

"Like family holidays when Mum forces us to watch the sunset every single day we're away?"

"Yes, you watch sunsets on vacation, but never at home. If you did, you'd honour in your heart something far more impressive than your own personality operating, something far grander than the petty problems that gnaw away at you. Unfortunately, much of the population take no notice of this daily, stirring ritual."

Grace wasn't aware of proper pauses in the Wind's thoughts.

"The sun never struggles to shine; it does so effortlessly and with great ease. It's a reminder for you to go about your day just as fluently, Grace. These twenty-four hours will never come again, and the sun's exultant path across the sky is a reminder of each day's uniqueness."

She paused, feeling there was something more the Wind was about to add. "Anything else, Wind?"

"By not witnessing the sun's movements on a regular basis, we miss the miracle of how each day comes to be and how quickly it vanishes like an apparition into the night sky. It becomes easier for us to complain and trudge our way through the daylight hours. Acknowledging each day as it opens and closes reminds us to be thankful for all the vast, indescribable beauty that exists in between."

The Wind brought their walk to a close. "That's enough for now. Let this conversation seep into your very being."

She entered the house. Her father was sitting at the dining room table and wanted to know why she kept charging up and down the street like that.

"That's what you do when you walk," she replied.

Though they had a challenging relationship, Grace knew in her heart that her father adored her; he just couldn't express his devotion in a way that resonated with her. As a property lawyer, Dylan was a 'rules man' and, to his chagrin, the custodian of a child who abhorred and disobeyed rules from a very young age.

Grace spent the rest of the day in front of the TV. She only moved from the sofa to help her mother prepare lunch. Watching Carla make a pastry base, Grace—for the first time—truly understood the amount of manual labour involved in food preparation.

Perhaps that's why she's always multi-tasking while cooking?

"We don't often acknowledge the amount of work—and love— that goes into a home-cooked meal, given how easy it is to buy all manner of pre-prepared and packaged food nowadays," Carla lamented.

Along with her dream of having children, Grace dreamt one future day of being a domestic goddess. She'd drift into a fantasy where, all grown up, she'd be in her fabulous, open-planned, stainless steel kitchen and could easily rustle up lavish spreads when friends popped by unannounced. Grace didn't as yet want to put in any of the required effort to start making the domestic goddess dream a reality though.

Evening approached, as did the time to start her homework. It was the last thing she wanted to do. Her mother could read her mind.

"Grace, you've been sitting in front of the TV for most of the afternoon," Carla sung out from behind the fridge door.

Grace dragged her feet up the stairs and collapsed onto her bed.

"Why not go to bed now and get up early to finish your homework?" the Wind said. "There's no rule that says homework is exclusively an evening activity; it merely needs to get done. Use the knowledge of your own inner body clock to your advantage, Grace. Stop trying to fit into a system that doesn't work for you."

Grace was exhausted, wanting the pillows to transport her to a cloud of feathers in the sky.

"Try to wake, eat, exercise and go to bed at the same time every day. Keeping a regular schedule, even on weekends, will help you enormously. I also want you to develop a ritual to help you shut down at night and another to greet the dawn."

Grace only heard that weekend sleep-ins were no longer allowed.

The Wind conceded. "Okay, once a month, but please, Grace, just try instilling some regular rituals into your daily routine. We wouldn't be having this conversation if things were going swimmingly well for you; what you've done in the past is obviously not working. Now in the beginning, there may be no pleasure in sticking to a routine, but when operating in unison with the to and fro streams of energy, the results will soon convert you."

"Ugh, there's always more to learn, more to do. When does it ever end? Does an end even exist?" she moaned.

The Wind ignored her grievances. "Tonight, as your father does, sleep with the blinds open, let the natural light wake you and turn off all the electronic gadgets and devices in your room emitting bright colours."

Grace leapt up, popped her head out the door and yelled downstairs that she was off to bed.

"What about your homework?" her father barked from his study.

"I'll do it in the morning."

"Grace, come down here!"

She trudged downstairs to feel the full force of her father's disapproval. He was wearing a sweatshirt from his college days, which her mother repeatedly encouraged him to throw out.

"Excuse me, young lady, what did you say?"

Grace decided instead of going up against him, that she should go around him. "It's an experiment, Papa. You know how drowsy I get in the evenings, so I'm planning to get up early—when I feel my best—and do my homework then. Hopefully I'll get it done in half the time because I'll be working at my peak."

He remained silent as Grace continued delivering her terms.

"If I don't have my homework done by the time I leave for school in the morning you can yell at me, but until then, please suspend judgment on my methods." It felt good to act so mature.

"As you wish," Dylan replied, smiling with surprise.

She kissed her father on the top of his bald head, then found her mother in the sitting room and pecked her good night on the cheek. She went back upstairs, brushed her teeth and even washed her face for a change. She knocked on Abel's door in a particular way: four quick knocks, one long one, followed by two short ones. It was their private code for good night, which they had developed as children.

Grace had never noticed before to what extent the laptop's screen illuminated the room at night with the main light turned off, nor how the space resembled a Christmas lights display: the red buttons in the extension cord, the blue glow of her mobile charging, the fluorescent orange hues of the alarm clock.

She unplugged the light show and crawled into bed.

35 | Inner Space

The next weekend arrived, and Grace had completed her homework on time every day that week. Her father was astounded. So was she. The new routine took a little getting used to: the alarm went off considerably earlier than usual as the sun was too subtle, and she too dense, to wake naturally. The Wind said the lighter she became in spirit, the more easily the sun would call her from slumber, but to use the alarm as a backup until then.

Only the other morning, the Wind whispered, "Feel yourself in the bed—the length of your back on the mattress coils, the thread count of the sheets covering your body, your head sinking into the soft pillow. Thank the universe you woke this morning and don't get out of bed until you've grasped how sacred each breath is." Today the Wind added, "Respect this life force within you, and vow not to waste it."

She silently repeated, "I honour my heart space and guard its value."

Grace climbed out of bed and instinctively knew it was the weekend, as five days' worth of mess had accumulated on the floor. She could barely make out the carpet. Books were everywhere (some marked with bookmarks, others with pages folded), teacups and mugs lined up on the desk interspersed with chocolate wrappers and hair bands. Her father called her room a pigsty.

Every Saturday began the same way, cleaning up the wreckage of the week before. Her mother was continuously on her back to do a little bit of tidying each night. It wasn't only her school uniform Grace picked up off the floor each morning but also the clothes she wore by choice. There was no discrimination in her lack of respect for her belongings.

Though she wanted a tidy bedroom floor and spotless mind, Grace wasn't yet willing to do the required work to get herself there. She was spent by day's end and cleaning up a little bit each night felt like being forced to partake in a gruelling army commando assault course.

Both Carla and Veronika kept telling Grace that clutter equalled a cluttered mind. She defended herself, saying, "Ask me to find something, and I'll tell you exactly where it is." To Grace, her clutter was a sign of creativity, though she secretly felt burdened by her mess.

"The clutter of your room drains you as much as your negative small talk. All this excess, ignored junk decreases your space, both physically and mentally."

Grace looked around her room and had no idea where and how to start. The mess paralysed her, and she just wanted to sit outside and soak in the few beams of sun poking through the clouds. And then the self-judgmental thoughts overtook her without warning.

Why did I scoff all that chocolate after dinner last night? I wasn't even hungry. No wonder I don't have a boyfriend.

"You don't have a boyfriend because of the way you treat yourself," the Wind replied.

Her throat closed up and the tears started.

"Grace, don't get so down on yourself. When you—or anyone—start contemplating changes big or small, the thoughts that don't serve you come out and attack with a vengeance. They want to keep you in a weakened state."

Grace pondered the intervention of the Wind in her life. The more she thought about it, the more it confused her.

"Just as we need inner space in our minds . . ."

"Inner what?" Grace interrupted.

"That inner space in our mind where we watch a thought come in, choose whether to follow it or not, and remain a witness to the process."

"Say again?"

111

"Grace, stuff pops into your head all the time, and you don't question any of it. There are too many unexamined thoughts going on in there, and they're usually the same destructive ones on repeat. You keep contaminating your mind with judgments that serve no purpose. Rather than embarking on a vicious assault of your personality defects, reconnect with the intrinsic wealth of your soul. There's still a core belief controlling you. You don't know it, but all your thoughts and behaviours line up to support this belief."

She drew in a concentrated breath.

"Grace, you believe you're not worthy, so you're always seeking worthiness, trying to prove your significance. You're just lost—not broken—and I'm helping you peel back the layers so you can connect to your true self."

Another immense gulp of air.

"When do you plan to start showing up for your life?" The Wind's tone was solemn. "How your body moves, your mind thinks and your heart feels—all are expressions of your divinity. You don't need to chase worth, Grace. Just make conscious choices that demon-strate your inherent worthiness."

Grace suddenly wanted a brown paper bag to hyperventilate into.

"Defer to your name for inspiration. Let grace move you and guide you. Believe that you are grace. I want this to be your dominant belief in life from now on. Refuse to fall from this altitude."

Grace experienced these intense moments with the Wind as one, huge download. It literally felt like a computer chip was implanted in her with new levels of understanding (but she didn't know where all the data was being stored).

"Don't just think of yourself as grace, but know yourself as grace. Your sense of separation is an illusion born of ignorance of the truth of reality and you find your way back to the source through ancient wisdom, not materialism. Grace, give up what's not working for you; jettison the baggage. Rewire yourself and illuminate your consciousness. Give your undivided attention to joy. Focus on the meaningful, not the meaningless."

Grace felt as though the old books filled with lies in the library of her mind were being systematically thrown out. A new, advanced system with increased functionality, awareness and compassion was being installed.

36 | Releasing Clutter

G race started tidying the rubbish tip in her room.
"We live in a synthetic and artificial environment and need the natural world around us. Grace, you'll struggle if you don't get in touch with your innate divine state and nature first."

"Fine. I'll decorate my room with some pot plants."

"This is not about peripheral decoration, Grace. You have to see yourself as part of nature and begin sensing the atmosphere of spaces and their connecting ecosystems. What is your space saying to you?"

Without skipping a beat, Grace replied, "Anxiety and stress."

"Okay, and what would you prefer it to say?"

"Cool, calm and collected."

"So create a space that nurtures serenity."

"Hello, I'm not an interior designer!"

"You don't need to be a professional designer, Grace. We can make this room flow better by placing your school stuff close to your desk, makeup by the vanity mirror and clothes in the wardrobe. Group things in their related activities. We also want to rearrange your room so that it's not centred on technology, which keeps you distracted."

"You've lost me." Grace only wished she could speak this honestly at school, instead of pretending to understand everything, which meant she understood nothing.

"Don't allow technology to use you. Use it instead of being used by it. So many living rooms in the West are focused around the TV, or even kitchens around the wireless connection. The technology dictates how the room is used and shaped, rather than us creating a comforting ambiance through the nourishing relationship we have with our body, mind and spirit."

"I don't think Mum and Papa will give us a massive financial budget to redesign my room."

"Like all things in life, Grace, we work with what we've got. Now let's first get rid of some of this clutter."

"But it's me." As soon as she blurted out the words, Grace realised how ridiculous she sounded.

"This stuff is not you. Don't confuse who you are with what you possess. You exist in a material world—enjoy its treasures—but don't be controlled by matter. Practice divine detachment."

Grace dislodged a spare phone charger stuck between her desk and the wall. "I may need this extra one someday."

"Holding onto the excess and unnecessary means you have no faith that the future will provide for you. You have the arrogance to believe you can foresee every future thing you'll need, and that's just plain laughable. Let go of the old so that the new can enter."

"But there's no space for anything new to come in. My room's jam-packed as it is."

"I don't mean just new stuff, Grace. Get out of this stuff-orientated way of thinking. I'm talking about new attitudes and ways of being, which come to you when you realise that the internal and external always reflect each other."

She sensed logic here. "I guess the less stuff I have, the less I'll have to look after and worry about."

"Aha, so let's go around the room and choose what's essential for living and toss the surplus."

Grace was amazed at how little of the products strewn across the surface of her dresser she actually used. Holding a raspberry-shade lipstick she'd only worn once, Grace said, "I never really liked this lipstick's texture anyway. And this moss green eyeliner runs every time I wear it." She picked up a coral-coloured powder blush and noted, "Juliet really likes this colour, and it looks far better on her than it does on me."

"Good, Grace. Be aware of how things influence you on an energetic level."

"I guess I don't have to keep these old maps from places I've travelled to either."

Her hands fingered the weathered London Underground map from her family's overseas trip to the United Kingdom when she was ten. Images of Buckingham Palace, Stonehenge, Tower Bridge, and Edinburgh Castle floated across her mind.

The Wind interjected. "It's why we become attached to mementos and take too many unnecessary photos when travelling. We're not really in the moment when the event is happening. When capturing amazing scenery through a lens, our mind is often elsewhere thinking of the following tourist sight to see or where to eat next."

This was true. No matter what Grace did, her thoughts always turned to the next thing. She'd be in the middle of reading one book and her mind would drift to starting another; while devouring breakfast she'd be devising what to eat for lunch; when watching a movie she'd mentally list things to do once the credits rolled.

"Grace, learn to create memories with all your senses; then you won't need to enter memory lane solely through your eyes."

Grace grabbed four matchboxes in each hand from various parts of Scotland and threw them in the bin.

"If something isn't working for you, Grace, toss it. If it's broken, bin it. Why wear something that doesn't suit you simply because you paid for it? Life is too short to feel awful and wear stuff that doesn't flatter you."

She looked at her tangled array of necklaces.

"You must take care of this costume jewellery, otherwise no one will ever entrust you with real gems, Grace. They won't believe you know how to look after them."

"I will, and anyway, I'll be much more sophisticated by then and I'll take better care of my possessions."

"So enlighten me, Grace, how will you go about acquiring this refined sophistication?" asked the Wind.

Grace didn't care for the truth at such close range. She wanted instantaneous change without having to work for it.

"I know you don't feel great after throwing your clothes on the floor, so when choosing the coat hanger or laundry basket over the ground, feel good. Assume a position of victory when hanging up your clothes, knowing you defeated slothfulness and its cousin, laziness."

Grace collapsed on the brown leather beanbag, a gift from her grandparents.

"Grace, get into the rhythm of feeling good. You don't make empowering choices for yourself, as you're under the misguided belief they'll cost you money or time, but the energy you expend in guilt and shame is a far higher outlay. Focus on what's to gain energetically, not what a decision will cost you materially."

Grace chose to take advantage of the moment, got off the beanbag and started picking the crumpled clothes up off the floor. It was a matter of making choices that demonstrated her inherent worth.

37 | Regular Maintenance

The next weekend Grace and Abel were at Kosmos and Veronika's house. Veronika was her usual serene self in the rose garden, and they found Kosmos in the bedroom standing next to the antique armoire, throwing shirts with his good arm onto the bed. Grace admired him, thinking how he lit the torch for living a principled life in his role as the backbone of this family.

"What are you doing?" Grace asked him, as she pecked his cheek.

"Spring cleaning, though it's not even spring." He hugged her close, then Abel too.

"Really?"

"A good clean out is exactly what nature does—she gets rid of the excess, so the necessary can shine. We're not separate from nature."

His voice had a permanent hoarseness to it, although Kosmos was never a smoker.

Why is it anyone I care for now sounds exactly like the Wind?

"Nature blooms, flourishes, withers, dies, re-blooms, and we also go through these same processes."

It's as if I'm talking to the Wind.

Abel looked at Grace and discreetly rolled his eyes. Though Kosmos clearly adored Abel and Abel his grandfather, they had a different connection, one based on 'manly values'.

"Regular maintenance is vital—of ourselves, the homes we live in, our circle of friends, and especially our attitudes as we question what's working for us and what's keeping us stuck. Maintenance can be boring, but it's what keeps the wheels ticking over."

"So I should ditch a few friends?" Abel asked.

"No, just check you don't have any decaying ones around you," Kosmos joked.

"Yeah, so many of your friends are real dropkicks, Abe."

"Whatever, ya geek. I'm gonna go see what Veronika's up to."

Abel left the room, leaving Grace to enjoy her grandfather's advice in peace. She sat down on the side of the bed and begged him to continue his spring cleaning metaphors.

"Make sure any new shoots in your life have adequate nutrients, water and sunlight, and also remember that when a new shoot is springing forth it will encounter resistance as it forces its way through the earth to the sun."

"So if I feel stuck, using your plant metaphor, I should make sure that I'm adequately fed and hydrated, and if that's not enough, find extra nourishment elsewhere?"

"Yes. Maybe uproot and plant yourself in another place, literally or figuratively."

Kosmos mostly wore dark brown leather loafers, tan trousers and classic blue dress shirts—often with a tie—which Veronika secured in a Windsor knot. He combed his thinning hair to the left, and a fine, grey stubble covered his face.

"Maintenance shouldn't be a yearly or seasonal activity, but a daily one."

"A stitch in time saves nine."

"Absolutely! Go over your studies a little bit each night to avoid the eleventh-hour panic before an exam, or look at how your father sorts his receipts each evening so there's no desperate commotion come tax time, or how your mother neatly closes each day by making sure there are no dirty dishes in the sink. Daily maintenance prevents massive overhauls." Kosmos noticed his granddaughter staring at him in a peculiar way. "Grace, are you okay?"

She was caught out. "You sound incredibly similar to a new teacher I've got, that's all. The words you're using and the tone and . . . but keep going."

"Regular maintenance creates optimal physical and mental health. We make minor alterations as needed rather than delaying them until a catastrophe demands massive changes from us. When we're responsive to what's happening around us, we transform for the better."

"So it's a process of constant tweaking?"

"Yes. Make the necessary adjustments as and when needed, Grace; don't let them fester. Check-in on your life often," said the man with seventy-five years of living behind him.

38 | Concentration

Another Sunday and the Wind was dispensing its wisdom while Grace was applying her makeup. Grace checked the mirror to make sure the black kohl eyeliner hadn't smudged.

"All things originate and manifest in their own good time. All people, plans and places have their own character and therefore their own timing. Events unfold when all the pieces are in their correct divine order. Let things bloom and wither, as they will, Grace. There's a higher timing than yours going on."

There wasn't enough light in her yet to internalise the Wind's words as truth.

"Although I'm trying to implement your wisdom, why is it I'm still feeling rushed and never seem to have enough time?"

"As I told you before, Grace, people can't see me, but I can make my force known, say by blowing up a gale, and it's the same with you. Your attitude—which is your invisible force—is what changes the physical environment. Every person either contributes to, or destroys, peace here on earth through the emotional vibrations they emit."

Grace let the Wind's words wash over her like a light summer drizzle, cool and refreshing.

"So no time is ever wasted if what you're doing is in alignment with your soul and in the attitude of love. Never, ever. And Grace, remember that being alive is an experience," the Wind said. "No gain in consciousness is ever lost. Learn this lesson well."

Lately Grace had been trying hard to focus her attention on whatever she was doing at any given time.

"When you're eating, do nothing else but eat—no watching TV, no absent-minded magazine reading, no checking emails. Just eat. Bring your soul to every bite."

This would mean distinguishing between physical hunger and symbolic hunger and Grace didn't know if she could do this.

"Keep working on focus and concentration. I want you to persist with the single-mindedness. If you're hanging out with a friend, enjoy your time together with all your heart; if you're doing the grocery shopping with your mother, concentrate on the positive aspects, not the drudgery. As I said earlier, if your doing isn't done from your soul, then the action is empty. Be love in action."

She was about to start analysing a past event from her personality's limited viewpoint but the Wind caught her just in time. "Accept that yesterday is gone. Not that it's wasted but that it's gone; it has passed and no longer exists. Feel light now, Grace—today—in this moment. You are the light, so act accordingly."

"So why do I keep forgetting who I am?" It was a constant identity crisis she faced.

"Because you allow yourself to plummet from grace. Yesterday brought you to today, which will carry you to tomorrow. Grace, your future is born in the now."

39 | Your Inner Tempo

Grace believed that her sphere of influence was miniscule and she mostly couldn't see past Gateshead. She wanted a broader playing field.

"Have you heard the line, 'There are no small parts, only small actors,' Grace?" the Wind asked.

"Yeah, my drama teacher said that to me once when I complained about only having three lines in the end-of-year play."

"And did you understand the meaning of the phrase?"

"Stop complaining?"

"No, Grace. It means you fully inhabit the role by making those few sentences your own and delivering them like they're the three most important lines in the play. Their length doesn't define you—you transcend them. In the same vein, your soul can't be contained to the limitations of the physical world, it goes beyond them."

"Oh." She double knotted the laces of her trainers.

"Yes, oh. So instead of wanting influence over greater lands, know the only territory you have dominion over is yourself. Don't try to control others; only over yourself will you ever have authority."

Grace craved a fresh start to her life, wanting a new city to bring about the desired changes. Sadly, reality dawned. Only when she changed could—and would—everything and everyone else.

"And you know why people don't take personal responsibility, Grace?"

"As it's easier to blame others than to look inside?"

"Exactly."

Later that day, Grace met Juliet and Ruby at the local mall and their first stop was the nut stand for hot honey-roasted cashews and smoked almonds. It was sales season and the shop windows flaunted their discounts with red balloons and signs with 50% OFF.

Grace sensed the Wind wanted to tell her something. She was beginning to get a feel for the topics and asked if it would elaborate more on the subject of flow and how rhythm is connected to it.

The Wind responded, "Flow is about dancing between the states of allowing and resisting, and mastering the expression of masculine and feminine forces. It's also about pace. Observe at what pace you're speaking with the girls right now."

"At the pace my mouth is moving," she joked.

"Just as you eat too fast and don't taste your food properly, you speak too quickly and don't hear your own words. Your voice is an instrument of expression; don't let it betray you. Most of the time you're not even conscious of what comes out of your mouth. Please endeavour to speak as kindly as possible, both to others and yourself."

"No swearing then?" she replied in jest.

"Definitely not. And while we're at it, lose the slang too. In general, don't use cheap things, whether it's materials, produce or language. I want you to avoid anything inferior and of poor quality—thoughts especially."

"You sound like Kosmos."

"And don't talk too much. Let other people get a word in. Give a feeling of peace to others by listening to their words with the whole of your being."

Grace noticed how quickly the three girls were walking, and they weren't even in a hurry. She then observed how rapidly they were speaking to each other. There was no silence, nor gaps, just a rat-a-tat-tat back and forth; quick-witted gossip followed by ironic banter, bitchy putdowns and clever word play. She wasn't consciously listening to what Juliet or Ruby were saying. It was merely noise, and she was struggling to hear the stillness underneath the repartee.

"That's right, Grace, too often we let our surroundings outpace us. Always ask yourself if it's you, other people or circumstances that are dictating your tempo."

Grace slowed her stride a little, and the girls dropped back in line with her. As her pace slackened, she remembered to breathe from her belly, not her chest. She said to them, "Let's go and browse in the bookshop."

⁂

Later in the afternoon, Grace called on the Wind. "Why are some cities fast-paced and others slow-paced?"

The Wind replied, "Big, fast-paced cities often have a frenetic energy at their core composed of lots of 'doing' whilst places that respect a slower pace of life usually have 'being' as their modus operandi though . . ."

"I disagree. People living in these slower towns could simply just be lazy," she interrupted.

"Grace, you didn't let me finish. In these smaller places sometimes the 'doing' isn't as rushed. But all fast and slow-paced cities, towns, situations, and spaces have their polarities."

"So I should know what inner and external pace suits me for my current life stage and then find geographical places to complement the tempo?"

"Exactly. It's about monitoring, then responding appropriately."

"?" Grace was getting better at sending symbols to the Wind.

"Monitor means conscious awareness. Be the observer of the momentum with which you live your life and have the feedback loop running, so you can respond to what is and isn't working. Remember, Grace, all change initially happens on the inside, so check what's going on in there first."

Grace examined her inner thoughts and feelings.

"Are your thoughts racing too fast about silly things? Are you dwelling on stuff that doesn't matter?"

"Okay, I'll try to be more mindful of the stories I'm telling myself that take me out of experiencing the present moment," she replied.

40 | Claim Your Assets

"You will come in time to know the power of words, and not make yourself a victim of circumstance by the language you use with all your 'could've, would've, should've' talk."

Grace already sat through English class this morning and wasn't in the mood for another lecture on language. "But maybe there are times I should've done something?"

"Well, express your choices using phrases like 'I choose to' or 'I choose not to' instead of passive words that victimise you."

"Such as?"

"You'd usually say, 'I wish I could spend the weekend swimming at the beach, but I've got too much homework to do.' Change it instead to, 'If I choose to spend the weekend swimming, I'll need to finish my homework on Friday night.' Active tense, Grace. Spend your time finding reasons why you can do something, rather than mulling over the reasons why you can't."

"I'll try. I mean, I will."

"And your tone of voice and posture can't be in conflict. Be congruent—your thoughts, emotions and actions must function as one."

"Alright, I admit I've chosen to be in this situation. I know there's something here for me to learn."

"And the best way to learn, Grace, is by being childlike."

"Say what?"

"Play, Grace, play. See life as a ball, not a prison. Choreograph your own dance. You are only just now beginning to embrace the visionary archetype in you, but in the future you'll guide others to live a more connected and nourishing life by example. You're an original, Grace. Claim and own your assets."

"But how do I play to my strengths?"

"Well, you're great with big picture thinking and not so great with details."

"Ahem, excuse me, I'm here. I can hear everything you're saying."

"Grace, you have a wonderful deftness in how you approach certain things, but while you're terrific at overall creative concepts, you quickly tire of the details. You know this about yourself. And while you're incredibly empathetic and intuitive—when you choose to be— follow-through and implementation just don't come naturally to you. Now don't take all criticism as personal attack. See it as a pathway leading to a higher turn of the spiral where you can view the same situation with a more rounded sense of vision."

She nodded her head and ran her hands through her hair.

"And Grace, when speaking with others, aim to keep the personal references to a minimum."

"Like how?"

"Imagine that a friend returns from holiday and you start chatting about how you've also been to the same place . . ."

Grace interrupted. "I thought that showed empathy."

"Yes, if you're speaking as an observer—modestly and with the voice of the soul—but so often you're engaging from your personality. You're engrossed in your own story and aren't even listening to theirs. Trust me on this Grace; leave the personal references to a minimum. And . . ."

She sighed. With the Wind there was always another 'and'.

"Try not to butt in. Give them your grace by letting them finish their train of thought. Maintain eye contact, greet the speaker in your heart and don't converse too quickly, loudly or talk over them. Learn to let silence in and this will create an irresistible energy field around you. Soon others will come from near and far to experience your serene presence."

41| Dissolving Habits

Grace and Ruby were hanging out at Juliet's house deciding what to do later that night. Gateshead wasn't a small town, but it was no Paris, New York or Berlin. Grace often fantasised about these sophisticated destinations. To her, life in the world's international cities appeared infinitely more alluring. No glamour existed in Gateshead; it was a world of tacky underage nightclubs, average pizzerias and greasy fish and chip shops by the beach.

Carla occasionally took her to the ballet, but although she tried, Grace couldn't grasp the finer points of cultural living. Folks in Gateshead went to work, raised their families and in their limited free time enjoyed sports and the great outdoors. Being cultured was not a priority. Her definition of beauty came from teen magazines, not from Renaissance sculptures or Italian arias.

"Man, my hair is a disaster. I look a mess."

Grace fell easily back into her old ways. While she knew her ingrained habits—pessimistic thinking, talking while eating, frequent procrastination—were unconstructive, it was hard to elevate her consciousness to another level.

"Not all habits are bad; they're merely learned ways of behaving. Grace, you need to establish repetitive behaviours that serve you, not destroy you, and learn to make choices that connect you to your heart instead of disconnect you from it."

"Why don't people change if they know how destructive their behaviours are?"

"Very few people want to look at their shadow and into their reactive, compulsive, shame-based behaviours. It's easier not to, but

Grace, that's where the treasure that will set you free lies," the Wind went on.

"But I do want to change," Grace insisted.

"Are you willing to accept all parts of yourself without judgement? Can you be inclusive instead of trying to rid yourself of all the things you don't like about yourself?"

There was a lot she detested about her character.

"The current habits that keep you from feeling your emotions and being in present time have their own energetic imprint. They currently serve you by providing a sense of relief. Grace, you can't overcome what you perceive as 'negative' within you as this puts you at war with yourself. Resisting these aspects leads to self-hate and you can't run from your shadow—it follows you everywhere you go. Accepting and approving of the things you don't like about yourself, and then transforming them into their highest aspects, is how you turn lead into gold on an inner level. Stop fighting yourself and instead fall in love with the elevated form of these character traits and put them to good use. Be the alchemist."

Grace found her thoughts wandering to avoid dealing with the Wind's advice, as she sought relief in her mind rather than feeling the uncomfortable emotions in her body.

"Earth to Grace. Come in."

"I don't want to."

"You need to embrace who you really are. To express more of your empowerment you need to be here in present time."

"Okay, I'm bringing my attention back to my body," and she felt deep into her rage, which expressed itself like an uncontrollable fire burning through her skin.

"You can't force yourself to break a habit, instead you energetically drop from your head to your heart and release your resistance to it. You allow it to be there. You feel into the initial motivation behind why you developed the habit and this understanding and acceptance is what reconstructs your perception. You don't fight the habit; instead you surrender it to the light of your awareness and it will transform of its own accord."

Over the next week Grace observed many of her habits and caught herself reading gossip magazines at the checkout counter at the local supermarket. She loved looking at pictures of movie stars without their makeup, as well as examining close-ups of their cellulite and disintegrating marriages. It was her stress release.

On cue, in came the Wind. "Grace, thinking constructively means raising your vibration. Speech is thought energised and gossip sits at a lower frequency. Don't read or discuss these trashy celebrity magazines; they bring your soul down. They don't display the values you were born with, only make you compare yourself to others and tempt you to desire what is unnecessary. Gossip is small-minded thinking, and therefore non-essential. I want you to focus and connect with what's essential."

Grace couldn't see the harm of flicking through a couple of these magazines while waiting in the supermarket queue with her mother.

"It's a chain reaction. You look at these images of celebrities for a few seconds, but feel bad about yourself for hours. Conserve your creative energy."

"I guess it's true. These magazine images do stay with me and they're the standard I'm constantly holding myself up to."

"So let the intensity of the soul's light melt the pointless and artificial out of your inner landscape so that the authentic can shine. And please Grace, surrender the notion that you have to be any more than who you already are."

42 | Befriending the Mirror

Another Saturday night had rolled around and the girls were back at Juliet's place. The sweet aroma of the coconut and mango-scented candle permeated the room. Wearing floral-embossed white jeans, Juliet sat on her bed painting her toenails brick red.

Grace glared at her reflection in the mirror. "Ugh. What am I supposed to do? Walk out of here with a matted mess on the top of my head?"

"Relax, Grace, it doesn't look that bad," Juliet comforted.

"Stop comparing your hair with what you think it should look like. Don't critique as you create."

Is it the Wind or Juliet speaking?

"Jules, why do you always wear the same red on your toes?"

"Because when I look down at my toes the colour makes me happy. It looks grown up, and you know red lipstick doesn't suit me."

Juliet cultivated a classic fashion style. Though only fifteen, she had already accumulated the basic staples that formed the backbone of a mature woman's wardrobe—the white shirt, little black dress, pencil skirt and cashmere cardigan. She was fifteen going on thirty.

The Moors were playing in the background as Ruby began reading questions out loud from a magazine questionnaire. One question asked to list five things you loved. For Grace this was easy: swimming, dancing, afternoon tea, reading, and travel. Pity she rarely carved out any time to fully engage in these activities.

"Do you want to try that new light-defusing primer my mother bought me?" Juliet asked.

"What's a primer?" asked Ruby, whose makeup routine only involved clear lip gloss and a single coat of brown mascara.

"It evens out your skin tone and helps the foundation to stay on longer."

How did Juliet even know all this stuff?

Grace wished her mother imparted tips like this instead of teaching her to put lemon juice on an avocado to prevent it discolouring.

Carla never wore much makeup. No foundation, only shimmery lilac eye shadow and a pink pearl finish lipstick, and it struck Grace how girly and childish the colours were. Grace revered the idea of beauty wisdom being passed down through the ages from mother to daughter; secrets of sensuality that journeyed through generations like precious jewellery.

The Wind blew behind her as she tried out Juliet's new eyelash curler. "Grace, relish being a teenager. You don't need to slather your face with all this makeup; just let your youth shine through. Stop desiring a grown up's life."

"But I'm sick of being fifteen. I'm over it."

"You're a teenager living at home with your parents and brother, with pimples and problems fitting in at school. This is your reality. Embrace the age you are now." The Wind had the timbre of a positive affirmation CD. "Love being fifteen, as this is the only time that counts. Yes, you have spotty skin but it's a phase you'll grow out of. If you're not accepting of your pimples now, how will you comfort your own children when they experience the same issue? How will you empathise with the social alienation they feel if you're not present to your own experience now?"

Grace went to the window to let in some fresh air. The scent of mango and toasted coconut was sickly and annoying.

"So who else is going tonight?" Juliet asked as she finished her toes and began to paint clear varnish on her fingernails.

"Emmy and Jo said they're going, and I think Sebastian said he'd pop by."

Grace zipped up her jeans wishing she'd brought her burgundy suede skirt to wear instead. "Man, look at my thighs. They look huge. I can't wear these jeans out."

"Do you want to pass your negative body image on to your daughter, Grace? The weight you are today is unconditionally perfect for you. It may be less tomorrow—or more—but your body weighs exactly what it needs to weigh today. Cherish your body as it is and be grateful for all the functions it performs to keep you alive."

"What are you talking about? You look fine," Ruby reassured.

"Yeah, you do," Juliet said without taking her eyes off her nails.

"That's because you're super slim, Jules, and anything looks good on you. I have to strategise and hide."

Grace hated how Juliet's body came from discipline and her own from the lack of it.

"You're crazy, Grace, and it's so dark in the club that no one can see anything anyway."

The lies that keep friendships intact.

"Ugh, I'm starving," she said.

"Here, I've got some potato chips in my bag," Ruby offered.

Grace started devouring them two and three at a time. Only later would she make the connection between complaining about her weight and her hand in the chip packet. For now, they were two unrelated facts.

"To feel healthy, Grace, listen to the messages your body gives you. If you don't feel so great after that second brownie, why are you watching your hand go out and grab a third? When your inner voice tells you to choose the fruit salad over the chocolate cake, why ignore it? Grace, you're always receiving guidance. It is unfailing. Use it, and your mental anguish will end as this voice directs you to what your body and soul most need."

"Why am I even eating these? I don't even like salt and vinegar chips." Grace threw the almost empty packet onto the coffee table.

"You're also drowning out your body's message to rest. If you listened to your body you wouldn't have to pile all that concealer—which fools no one—around your eyes."

Grace flopped ungraciously onto the sofa.

"Guys, I don't feel like going out tonight."

"What? Is this about the jeans?" Juliet looked up from her nails. "Everyone's going to be there tonight."

"No, I mean, you guys go without me. I just want to go home and crash."

"Don't be so stupid, Grace. You're coming with us, and that's that."

And Grace did end up going to the club. It's what you did to maintain the delicate art of female friendship.

After their night out, Grace still thought herself unattractive.

The Wind said, "That's just a thought, Grace, and it's impinging on your reality. Stop placing so much emphasis on how you look; it's only the teeniest, tiniest part of you. Connect to the cosmic beauty in the world—not physical appearances—and certainly not to the false myths of 'looking good' that are sold to you in fashion magazines. Turn your gaze to the exquisite beauty that lives in nature instead."

43 | Rebalancing

Grace woke to her mother next to her bed shouting that she'd miss the bus if she didn't get moving immediately. Startled, she jumped out of bed and tripped over her tennis shoes as she hurried to the bathroom. Grace was out of the shower in two minutes flat and mindlessly brushed her teeth. There was no time to eat anything as she grabbed her school bag and ran out the door with only the briefest whisper of a kiss to her mother, who was heading out to her own appointment on the opposite side of town.

Grace power-walked to the bus stop but she felt flat and groggy and knew a headache wasn't too far away. She felt incredibly out of sorts and ran the last stretch to catch the bus. When she got to the main road, the bus was already pulling away. Grace burst into tears.

What am I going to do?

The only money Grace had was for lunch, not enough for a taxi, so she'd have to go home and wait for her mother to return and drive her to school, but she didn't know what time she'd be back. She decided to walk to school, figuring it'd take well over an hour, but in this moment she didn't really care. She just wanted to fall into a heap and sob hysterically.

"Grace, what's wrong?"

"Why did I miss the stupid bus? Now my day's all messed up. Why didn't I get up when I was supposed to? If Mum had woken me earlier, none of this would've happened. And she should've driven me to school. She should've known I wouldn't make the bus in time."

"Stop blaming your mother, Grace. It was you that slept in."

"But I'm going to be in massive trouble at school for being late and Mum will be furious."

"Grace, can I tell you something?"

"Do I have any choice?" She was still standing at the bus stop staring wistfully down the hill.

"We have a deluded idea of balance. We believe it's static, and it causes us tremendous agony because nothing in life stands still; absolutely nothing stays the same. Do you know what being out of equilibrium feels like in your body?"

"Of course! I'm in it now! I've missed the bus, and now my whole day is ruined."

"You need . . ."

"Oh joy! Just what I want! Another 'you need to' lecture that helps nobody. I know what I need to do, what I require help with is actually doing it!"

". . . to listen to your body. Your body is part of the body of nature, listen to her inner intelligence."

"And what does this have to do with the price of eggs?"

"Nature, like balance, is dynamic. You shape-shift to the rhythm of the moment as it moves with and through you. That's how."

Grace recalled a beginners' yoga class she attended, where the teacher told her not to beat herself up if one week she couldn't stretch as far as the week before. This was this week and that was last week, each separate moments with their own uniqueness, just as no two nights at the opera are ever the same.

"Each second of time is its own incomparable and individual moment. Enjoy the irreplaceable sequence of time within the larger composition."

Grace panicked now, as she'd only travelled to school by bus or car and never paid any real attention to the route.

"So here you are again, wishing the present moment to be other than it is. All your domineering mind does is halt the flow of life. You must respect the divine design of your life. Are you even listening to me, Grace?"

"Yes, you gain balance by controlling the situation," she replied. The Wind blew up a gust of leaves. "That's the last thing you do. You can't control, Grace. Ever. You're not in charge of the forces of creation. You can only accept and adapt, lessen your resistance and allow. Lose your rigid ideas about how things should be and work with how they actually are instead. Make the container of your mind vast and spacious."

"But I should get up on time to catch the bus every morning."

"Yes, maybe you should, but today you didn't, so we have what we have. Rebalancing is a moment-to-moment activity as we adapt ourselves to what the current situation requires from us. We're constantly in motion. Right now, the light will never fall this way again to cast these particular shadows. Can you become one with this wonder, Grace?"

Oh man, now here comes the oneness speech.

"I'm only attempting to point the way, Grace. Belief, love and trust are the pillars of balance—believe you're exactly where you're meant to be, love where you are and trust the process."

"What? I'm supposed to find pleasure in walking down this hill with the cars hurtling beside me, starving, with my tights twisted where they shouldn't be?" Grace felt the chills. "Just leave me alone!"

She couldn't hear the Wind anymore and began walking and replaying the morning's events in her mind. If only she went to bed earlier and got up the minute the alarm went off, then she'd definitely have made the bus and none of this mess would be happening now. But it did happen. Analysing and replaying the morning wasn't helping her get to school any quicker, only wasting precious energy.

"Wind," Grace wailed. "Please come back. Please, please help me stop these 'if only' thoughts. They're killing me, I seem powerless to stop them."

The Wind was back in an instant. "Simple, Grace. Believe this is where you need to be, love the situation as it is and trust in a higher wisdom."

"Break it down in a way I can understand."

"Grace, can you place your life in the context of the wider cycles that govern the planet? The world is larger than you missing the bus, can you tap into that?"

Grace didn't want to but knew with enough perspective she could.

"Trust that the universe is giving you a gift and stop fighting the situation. Accept this moment as pure perfection."

"Alright, explain to me how this situation is perfect."

"Because there's no other way for it to be other than how it is."

Grace couldn't comprehend the Wind's response. She immersed herself in her breathing in an attempt to maintain what little composure she had left.

"How does this help me when I'm off kilter?"

"Think of balance as balance with the now—not maintaining equilibrium as a permanent state—but constantly rebalancing yourself to each new step like a tightrope walker."

"So I'll feel better if I accept the situation as it is and orientate myself to what the present moment requires from me?" Grace felt suddenly lighter, as if a massive weight had been removed.

"And what does this slice of time want from you?"

"It wants me to place my bag on both shoulders to evenly distribute the weight of my books, to stop at a restroom to rearrange my tights so they don't chafe and to give thanks that it's not raining."

"Right, so rebalance yourself in the rhythm of now, go back to your breathing and be one with the action of walking, feeling the weight of each foot gliding along the earth. Be the witness and view yourself from a great height. Feel your inner aliveness as you stroll to school and bring a sense of beauty and finesse to how you hold your body, keeping a watchful eye on both your form and mind."

"Wind, I'm sorry I snapped at you."

"Don't worry about it, Grace. Just remember, trying to force balance will unbalance you every single time."

44 | Relationships

Grace and Kosmos were always welcomed with open arms when they entered their favourite restaurant in Market Park. When Lorenzo (who had owned the Italian restaurant since Abel was a baby) smiled, the knock-on effect was instantaneous; all the diners beamed from the wattage of his grin.

Grace was absorbed in thinking how nothing ever happens in isolation and the Wind added its two cents' worth. "Life is a continuous thread of relationships and no thread is ever broken. The mesh of life means all things are interdependent and interrelated; these threads, like a spider's web, envelop us here on earth. These connecting filaments remind us of our role in the collective energetic experience."

"Where are you, Grace?" Her grandfather was smiling at her. He treasured spending quality time with his granddaughter.

"Oh, I was just reflecting on the group art installation project our teacher gave us and how crazy the deadline was."

"Did you meet it?" His voice was raspier than usual today.

"Yeah, even though we had absolutely no time to prepare."

"Bread fresh from the oven for signorina," Lorenzo said.

Kosmos knew that any kind of handmade bread, still warm to the touch, helped Grace locate a path to inner harmony. The comforting, warm dough filled her mouth and silenced her mind.

"Oh, heaven," she uttered.

"If you're ever out of sync, Grace, and can't find the stillness you crave, then make this restaurant your church."

"It has and always will be, for both of us," she said and touched his hand.

Their booth was backlit by a stained glass window of yellow tulips (the décor wasn't particularly Italian). Kosmos mentioned that he especially liked the restaurant's use of light dimmers; he couldn't stand lighting that was one-dimensional.

In between hunks of bread with butter, she confided to her grandfather, "I can't wait to have my own place. I feel I've got no control at home, especially with how the place looks. Mum and Papa chose the house's location, bought all the furniture and arranged it all how they wanted. Abel and I just have to live with it."

Kosmos, after some time, replied, "True, but can't you choose how to act in the space?"

She loved how her grandfather deliberated over her words as if they were the most important creations in the world. "I mean, I guess."

"Look at your parents. Your mother enjoys sleeping in, and your father rises with the larks."

"Oh yeah, Mum's such a late sleeper."

Lorenzo brought some wild asparagus and handmade tagliatelle to the table. There was no need for a menu, which is why Kosmos kept his horn-rimmed glasses firmly in his shirt pocket.

"She always has been. They respect their individual rhythms but know that they must work together to create a morning routine that suits them both."

"That's why Papa leaves his suit out the night before in the bathroom so he can get dressed in there and not disturb her too much before leaving for work."

"They've found a way to make their mornings flow. Now, there'll continuously be ups and downs," said Kosmos, who had a way of directly looking into Grace as though he was seeing her very life force, "and days when they're out of sync, but as in any situation it's about responding, not reacting. I'm sure with your art project you responded to the pressures of the deadline as a team, not as individuals, just as your mother and father as a couple make their mornings work for them."

Grace didn't want to chat about rhythms and routines with her grandfather; she had enough of this mentoring from the Wind. Their voices were becoming increasingly interchangeable, and right now, Grace couldn't deal with the implications of this. She just wanted to focus on the pasta and its rich, creamy gorgonzola and mushroom sauce.

In the taxi on the way home after the meal, the Wind chirped in, "Just as nature goes through cycles, so will your relationships."

Grace was muddled.

"It's important to know where you are in the cycles of your relationships. Some are just beginning, others are stagnant, a few are changing into another form entirely, and several need ending."

She ran through the last few days in her mind.

What was bringing this topic up now?

She closed her eyes. "Okay, got it. Yesterday I was thinking that when I first met Madison in eighth grade, she presumed she was my best friend after meeting me for all of five seconds and started to tell me her deepest secrets. I mean, I just met her."

"As I said, it's important to know where you are on the continuum of the cycle. This way you'll appreciate the infinite merit each particular point of time brings."

"They're big words, Wind."

"Grace, when you first met Madison you probably liked not knowing anything about her, the distance and awkwardness were to be relished. As the relationship progressed, this phase melted into the next layer of familiarity, then another level of camaraderie, each time building a different type of closeness. Stay alert to the subtle—and obvious—changes a relationship goes through during its lifecycle."

"Okay, I get it."

"And some friendships will dry up as you've become a drain on each other, and that's fine too. Not all things are to be kept. Let what doesn't serve you drift by the wayside."

Carla once in a reminiscent mood told Grace how much she liked

Dylan after their first date, but that it took him a couple of days to call her again. She was worried that she'd said something to offend him and that he didn't feel the same way about her. She wished she had acted more aloof. He finally called three days later.

"Grace," Carla said, "I wish I had enjoyed that uncertainty of 'will he/won't he' call more."

Now that Carla knew her husband would always call when he said he would, she chided herself for not taking more delight in those few moments of doubting. As the Wind phrased it, Carla's anxiousness had a necessary place within the relationship's development.

45 | Raising Your Vibration

As Grace climbed into bed, the Wind began explaining how every thought is a vibration. "Every object has an energy field."

"Hold up a second. I'm lost. Go back to the beginning."

"Every thought you think has its own energetic pattern and can be read by the friends you're with, strangers in the room, the universe . . . everyone."

"Hold up. So when I was chatting with Jenny and thought she was dead boring the universe heard that thought?" Grace hoped it wasn't true.

"Yes, as the thought had an emotional charge and intent behind it that both Jenny and the universe picked up on. They didn't hear the thought literally, but on one level the message was received. You are an open book, Grace. The universe is always responding to the feeling vibrations—these unseen ripples—which are attached to your thoughts."

Grace felt a little inkling of panic begin to stir in her stomach. She didn't want others to know her distorted thinking patterns and she especially didn't want the universe to show them back to her as the sum total of her life experience. Most of her vibrations weren't harmonious in the slightest.

"A loving thought carries a completely different charge to a fearful one, and the frequency you exude from your heart determines the quality of what you bring into your life, as well as what you block out. Everything in the universe retains a frequency. For example, that chair you hate in your bedroom holds an energetic imprint that doesn't sit well with you. It's not the salmon polka-dot pattern that you detest, but the feeling it emits. It feels too formal, especially in your bedroom, and this unnerves you."

Grace hated the chair. She didn't even want the damn thing in her room, but her mother insisted that there was nowhere else in the house for it to go.

"As much as possible, check your thoughts to monitor what vibration you're sending out to the universe. Think of yourself as a vibrational being affecting everyone and everything by the thoughts and feelings you're emitting and the actions you take. Imagine every thought you think as radiating outward and coming back to you. A negative, hateful thought only poisons you, so regularly check the intentions behind your thoughts. Are they driven by not wanting to be humiliated or are they filled with kindness and understanding? Either way, the emotion driving the thought will be reflected back to you in the circumstances of your life. Be aware of what you're placing out into the world, Grace."

Only a few weeks ago she announced to the Wind that what she most wanted was a still mind and to live from her soul.

The Wind continued, "Remember, you're not your thoughts, you're the awareness of them, and that there's a higher power operating than your thoughts."

"But I feel powerless to stop this obsessive thinking."

"Don't oppose your thoughts and judge them, Grace. Observe them. Don't let them own you; refuse to identify with them. And don't hate yourself for having them, as that only energises another destructive vibration. Just be aware that when thoughts arise in your mind that aren't in your noblest interest, you don't have to think them through. Let them vaporise into thin air."

Could it be that easy?

"Your thoughts are just sitting there on the side of the road trying to hitch a ride, and it's in your power to drive on by, but each time you stop to collect one of these travellers, you let them share the seat up front with you and switch the radio to a station of their own choosing. No more picking up self-sabotaging thoughts like roadside hitchhikers, Grace. Let them stay by the side of the road. Show some discrimination in who you allow to ride up front with you."

Is this why people speak of the journey being the purpose of life?

If so, Grace thought she better start bringing a degree of quality to the journey quick smart. What did her grandfather once say? "Choose quality, and quality will choose you."

"Your mind is only a small part of you. Yes, it builds reality, but it takes its orders from your soul, from your heart's intelligence. Remember, the universe is constantly speaking to you, and you to it through your thoughts, feelings, beliefs and actions."

Grace was wishing that she didn't know about this direct line of communication between herself and the wider world. Personal responsibility would never look the same again.

"Draw your energy from the internal instead of the external."

Grace couldn't even manage a "huh" or "what" so stayed silent.

"Use the times when you're feeling flat, Grace, to not gulp down an energy drink to perk you up, but instead use your thoughts and feelings to lift you up. If you're feeling frustrated, and you don't accept and honour the emotion, it taints your surroundings, and the universe can only respond to what you've unconsciously given it— even more frustration. Get curious about your feelings and make space for them."

"I've had enough. I'm going to sleep."

"If you half-heartedly give a gift, that half-heartedness resides with the gift—and in you—always."

"I'm drowning you out," Grace said, placing the pillow over her head.

"You are co-creating your experience with every thought you think, every emotion you express and every action you take both consciously and unconsciously."

"I can't hear you." But Grace knew the pillow was useless in silencing the Wind's voice because it came from inside her.

46 | Surrender

It was Friday afternoon and Grace was in the lockers getting changed for sports class. It was freezing outside and she drew the rugby shirt's collar through the crew neck of her jumper for an extra layer of warmth. "Man, I hate these track pants. They look like they're from the 70s they flare so much," she muttered.

"Grace, too much of your life is spent fighting that which you can't change. Let the complaints about the sports uniform go."

"Wind, I have this voice inside my head which keeps telling me I should be accomplishing more than I am."

"Get curious, Grace. Who is this voice?"

"I guess through us spending time together I'm aware enough to know it's my inner critic." She made finger quotes around the word "aware."

"Very good, Grace, but it's no good throwing words around unless you understand their meaning and purpose."

I guess this eagle isn't quite ready to soar.

Today's sports lesson was hockey. The sports teacher blew her whistle and selected Madison and Gisele as the two captains and then asked them to select their teams.

"Grace, if this voice which controls your life is anonymous, how can you ever confront it?"

"What do you mean?"

"You champion many causes, Grace, so why don't you ever demand better treatment from your inner critic?"

Grace pondered that thought. It was true; she easily stood up for the rights of others but rarely for herself.

146

"Saying it's your inner critic is the equivalent of boxing shadows; you're speaking unconvincingly and not actually saying what you mean."

What! Gisele chose me for her team before Madison did. There's a first!

"You master your enemies, Grace, by knowing the combat methods they use. Now this voice in your head, is it male or female?"

"Male," Grace replied.

"Is it someone you know?"

Grace replayed the voice. "You said you'd call Ruby last night and you didn't, and here you are daydreaming again. And you haven't done any exercise all week and you're useless at hockey and . . ."

"Okay enough, Grace, whose voice is it?"

"I thought it could be Papa, but it's not. It's kind of like an aristocratic male voice, full of disapproval, relentlessly reminding me what an abject failure I am."

Out on the field, Grace started dribbling with the ball.

"He speaks like he's a military drill sergeant, with a British accent, and acts all grandiose like he's from some titled background and expects all my thoughts and actions to be executed with the precision of a military drill, with no room for mistakes. He also keeps saying I should know the right thing to do at all times."

"Now that you know who is criticising you, Grace, why is this voice so interested in telling you that you're no good?"

"Because I'm not following orders."

"And do you agree with his orders?"

Grace was remarkably clear in her response. "No, he's out of control. He picks on every small thing. His standard of perfection is impossible to meet and maintain. Nobody could live with this pressure; what he expects from people is completely unrealistic."

"So why do you allow him to demand these expectations of you?"

"Because I don't stand up to him." Grace stumbled. "I mean . . . I can't. I don't even have a backbone when he's around."

"Grace, run!" shouted Gisele, and passed the ball.

Grace sprinted with the breeze behind her, got her stick to the ball before it went out of play and fired it directly back to Gisele.

She didn't want to spend any more time with the ball than necessary. There was nothing worse than being the most physically inept (and therefore hated) person on a sports team, and hopefully Grace just saved herself and her honour.

"Grace, have you ever thought to treat this voice as an ally, not an enemy? That maybe the voice is here to help you?"

It took Grace a few seconds to catch her breath from the intense burst of speed. Boy, was she unfit. "But he goes way overboard."

"Then say that to him. Tell him to let it go, that it's not worth getting worked up about."

Smiling, she replied, "So I should tell him he's insane and to go take a chill pill?"

"Quite right. Grace, the power of decision is yours, so take your control back."

"But I should be able to accomplish all my tasks."

"Grace, if only you knew how little you have to do and how much you need to be."

The words washed over Grace as she stared at the sheds behind the oval.

"Let the grand harmony of life flow through you instead of funnelling life via your trivial tasks. Why not take your orders from a higher source?"

It was half-time, and the teacher brought out a tray of cut oranges from the cooler. Grace didn't particularly care for oranges, but enjoyed sucking on the fruit's flesh in the middle of a game, liking how the skin resembled a mouth guard.

"But how am I meant to trust anything other than myself?"

"That's an incredibly sceptical point of view, Grace."

Why can't I let go and trust the force powering the universe?

"So you're telling me you can't depend on the source of all life? The source that gives your lungs each breath, pumps the blood around your body and brings the sun up each morning—you can't count on this? Then who or what can you rely on, Grace? Do you believe that you're bigger than the divine cosmos?"

"No, I didn't mean that," she said.

"Then what do you mean, Grace? Where do you place your devotion?" the Wind asked.

Caught off guard, Grace thought about it for a moment.

Do I have more faith in my thoughts—the very thing that's gotten me into most of my messes—than in the supreme source of energy? Do I trust my muddied, harmful thinking more than that which pulls the moon into the night sky?

"I know there's something higher than me that makes this world exist and breathes my body," she said, "it's just that I find it hard to surrender my life over to it."

"It shouldn't be so difficult. You've already surrendered your bodily functions. You don't stress each day about how you're going to get your kidneys to filter the waste out of your blood, so why not trust this same source to also guide your life?"

The whistle sounded, and it was time to throw the orange mouth guard in the bin.

"Keep awake out there!" Gisele yelled at Grace as they jogged back out onto the oval.

Grace took up her position on the northern outer edges of the grassy field. Then she answered the Wind's question. "Because it means giving up control."

"You're fooling yourself if you think you're the one controlling time, when it's a higher power that decides if you even first get to take a breath. Breath comes before your doing, Grace, not the other way around," the Wind replied.

I don't trust that which gave birth to me and sustains me. How warped is that?

She whispered a silent prayer for the ball not to come anywhere near her during the final half.

"Unfortunately it's how most people think, Grace. Never let that which matters least rule your life. Remember your priorities, not the ones written down on your to-do list. Commit to memory that you're a soul first and foremost, and that this is the lens from which you perceive and interact with the world."

Most of the play was occurring on the other side of the field now. Grace was part of the game, but not actively engaged.

"Navigate the multiple responsibilities in your life with this single-mindedness and you'll learn to view life impersonally. Living small and through the personality brings you great anguish, yet if you only looked up to the heavens more you'd begin setting your course by the stars."

"I have a feeling I know what you're going to say next. You want me to find time to meditate each day, but I'm telling you, I can't."

"Because silence doesn't yet mean more to you than all the other things in your day. When you experience this stillness—and surrender to the peace it brings—only then will you commit to a regular meditation practice."

Grace saw Madison fling out her stick to stop the ball going out of play, but it went flying from her hands and she fell with a loud thud.

"Higher power isn't pushy, Grace, but the non-essential constantly makes its presence felt by its overbearing manner."

Counting down the minutes until the whistle blew, and not caring if her side won or lost, Grace digested the Wind's words. So true. Her soul's blueprint never forced itself on her, but the guilt of all the inconsequential things she didn't get around to doing each day screamed and jostled for her attention. There were enough hours in the day; she just chose to spend most of them in a noisy, limiting mindset.

Maybe it's time to really experience stillness?

47 | Travel Detours

It was Grace's turn to cook breakfast for the family this Sunday. The Roses were discussing where to go for their annual family holiday, and with no influence from the Wind whatsoever, Dylan said, "Places have their own rhythm and become more agreeable once you align with their pace. Do we want to vacation at the speed of a New York minute or at the tempo of a Spanish siesta? Then I can start planning."

"Dylan, you can't plan every step of our trip the way you micromanage your department's chargeable hours. Our vacation is not an Excel spreadsheet!" Carla declared.

"Er, Mum, Papa likes to think it is." Grace didn't know what had come over her parents.

Carla continued, "Travel is a series of scenes, not a one-act play. The destination isn't as important as the steps you take to get there."

"Well, your mother also holds false beliefs, like all the peace in the world awaits her the minute her toes touch the sand at a beach resort, and—poof!—her worries will instantly evaporate." Dylan clapped his hands for effect.

"Peace doesn't lie in the next moment, only this one." Nobody around the table understood the depth of Grace's words.

"You can't plan every second of our holiday, Dylan. Travel needs to change you, and the best experiences happen through unplanned detours," Carla said. "Things not going to plan are an essential aspect of the journey. It's why people like you go crazy when their travel plans go awry, because they expect the planes to leave on time and the weather to be exactly as forecast."

Everybody laughed. They knew their father too well.

"My dear husband, you want the travel gods to march to the itinerary you downloaded onto your Blackberry, but resisting the unscheduled events is what sours the trip. Yield to the detours. The unplanned is the very stuff that makes the journey worthwhile. Interruptions don't disrupt the schedule—they are the schedule."

"Yeah, Papa, have faith that the unplanned, random events along the way are placed there for your benefit," Grace added.

"Thank you for the love and support my family has shown me from the floor," Dylan said in jest.

After breakfast, Grace went outside into the cold air to feel the Wind even closer to her.

"Your father's right about travelling in the cultural time of the destination you're in, whether that's Cairo, Buenos Aires or Moscow. And it's important to learn from the rituals and routines of the locals knowing that each encounter on your travels is uniquely designed for you."

"What do you mean?"

"Remember last year when Madison's family travelled to Hawaii for summer break, and she told you all the things they got up to, and you wished you'd done those things too instead of the activities your family did?"

"Well, they did go swimming with dolphins and paragliding," Grace replied.

"But Grace, you devalue your own family's adventure by wanting the carbon copy of another's. Both scheduled and random happenings are purpose-built for you. If the universe wanted you to experience what Madison did, then you would've. You must learn to cherish your own path, Grace."

"So explain to me why I constantly feel that I should be eating a different meal to the one I ordered, or be eating at another restaurant than the one I'm in?" Grace questioned, unable to think of better metaphors.

"Focus your consciousness on the restaurant you're in, enjoy the dish you've ordered and know it's for your highest good. The moment was tailor-made for you."

Grace couldn't say, "I know" anymore, so tactfully nodded.

"Have you ever considered that other people might be admiring what's on your plate?"

"Now that's a step too far of an exaggeration, Wind."

Grace still didn't get it.

48 | Stillness Whispers

While she was listening to her iPod, the Wind came through the stereo headphones and softly whispered, "The spaces between sounds are as important as the musical notes themselves."

Grace wanted to tune the Wind out as much as its monotonous tone of voice drowned out the song.

"It's the same with your thoughts, Grace."

She sang *Summer Sun* by The Wolves out loud instead. It was number one on the music charts this week. Her singing didn't disrupt the Wind though; it broadcast from a more powerful station.

"When your thoughts are racing you're incapable of extracting yourself, like the whirlpool of bath water flushing down the drain. Allow gaps to exist between your thoughts, as this is where true creativity lies. In that stillness the very essence of life exists."

There was no stillness in Grace. She was humming along to the instrumental and visualising the video clip to the song. She had a major crush on Ferrier, the lead singer and guitarist with his elfish grin and lanky body, whose voice cracked with passion and pain, as if he was serenading only her.

"When we're thinking at a million miles a minute our thoughts become one long drone, like the annoying hiss when you can't pick up a radio signal. It tells you that you're not in tune with the receiver, and the receiver is the universe." Before she could reply, the Wind went on, "The holes give Swiss cheese its texture and appeal, just as the zero in the binary code system is what allows the one to function. Equally, it's the still gap between our thoughts where true originality and creativity exists."

Grace was getting annoyed. "So you're saying that silence is where creation exists? Isn't that an oxymoron?"

"It's the truth," the Wind stated. "When your thoughts are racing around with no gaps, you must return your attention to your breath, which connects both your conscious and subconscious mind. Disconnect from your over-analytical brain and place your attention elsewhere in your body."

It felt almost physically impossible to move her awareness out of her head and into her feet.

"It's not about shutting off your thoughts, but rather letting the space shine through. Allow the transitions between thoughts and sounds to act as mini-breaks for your soul. Luxuriate in these creative pauses—lap them up."

"But sound is how we speak and hear the music we listen to. It means everything on planet earth."

"All I'm suggesting, Grace, is changing what to value. Give the same worth to silence as noise."

"What are you saying? I can't listen to my iPod anymore?"

"Not to the complete exclusion of silence, Grace. Your soul will tell you when to lose yourself in a rousing chorus, embrace the stillness between beats or when it's time to completely unplug, disengage and withdraw into solitude. But you must listen to that voice, my sweet. Many of us get the urge to disconnect—but don't know how—so we keep pushing and trucking on."

She nodded her head in sympathy.

"Sound has driven our lives this last century. It's now time to let silence lead."

Grace added, "It's like that metaphor about the silence at the bottom of the ocean, right? Even though movements occur on the water's surface, they don't disrupt the intrinsic stillness underneath."

49 | Celebrating the Seasons

Grace was over at her grandparents' place. In the kitchen, Veronika's natural finesse and relaxed grace radiated outwards. She operated in 'the zone', crushing basil, mincing garlic and grating Parmigiano-Reggiano for the pesto, unified with the intention of nourishing her beloved family. With every mouthful of food, Grace was drawn closer to her grandmother's quintessence.

In contrast, Carla distractedly prepared the family's meals; there was no single-mindedness of attention. Grace wondered how her mother actually got a completed meal to the table, because she wasn't 'there' most of the time, whereas Veronika expressed her devotion through her attentiveness.

Frequenting the Central Markets with her was also an adventure of delight and wisdom. On their previous visit, Veronika had mentioned regional typicality and how to choose food that tastes of where it comes from.

"As you verbalise your thoughts, your pronunciation tells people where you're from." Veronika held Grace's chin. "Pumpkin, please don't lose your accent, no matter how widely you may travel in the future. Never forget your roots. The same goes with food; buy that which speaks of where it comes from. The French call it terroir, how the geography and climate of a location influences certain foods and drinks, embedding them with special characteristics."

Veronika took great pleasure in interacting with the grocery stall owners. She had a magnetism that led all sorts of people to seek her out. She charmed everybody—the barista, baker, florist—all admired her delightful openness. She took great care in bringing people together, introducing one special soul to another.

Grace watched as she selected produce as if it were fine jewellery. Grace wanted some strawberries, but Veronika categorically said, "No, they're not in season."

"But they're here in the market," Grace protested.

"Yes, that's true, but they've been flown here from halfway around the world. They don't come from our city, let alone our country. We need to eat what the local crops provide for us at this time of year; they know what's best for us."

Grace picked up a punnet of strawberries. They didn't even smell of anything.

"Strawberries aren't in season; you'll have to wait until later in the year."

"But I want them now."

"My darling, knowing you can't have them every day, makes you appreciate them even more when they are in season."

"But we should be able to eat strawberries every day."

"Why? Too many of life's treasures are devalued as they're too easily accessible and we take them for granted. We lose all sense of their value, and I'm talking about people here as well." Veronika gently pressed some avocados to find one that was both firm and soft. "Fruits and vegetables in season are at their peak, so they contain the greatest number of nutrients. Eating foods that are in season brings a reassuring rhythm to our lives with great dietary benefits."

"So what you're saying is, if I can only have local strawberries for three to four weeks each year, I'd enjoy eating them more?"

Veronika was wearing a fawn, mohair cardigan that she'd knitted herself. Leaning over to touch and smell some persimmons, the cardigan's fuchsia pink lining peeked through.

"Yes, knowing you won't have them again until next season heightens your appreciation and reminds you to pay attention to their shape, smell, texture, taste, and consistency."

Veronika always spoke in a poetic, lyrical manner, but since Grace met the Wind, she could more readily absorb her grandmother's phrasing. Veronika's words usually washed over her—they were more melodic than meaningful—but today she listened attentively to her grandmother's soothing tone.

"Eating seasonally we notice everything else special about that time of year; which insects are buzzing about, what flowers are blooming, the changes in the air. It's a particular point in time on the calendar that can't be frozen; it must pass."

"We should be one with the seasons as they fleetingly make their way through us," Grace said.

Veronika didn't miss a beat. "Deeply enjoy your transitory strawberry pleasures. They're to be intensely savoured when in bloom. Don't try to capture what's ephemeral, because you'll only diminish its beauty and imprison its legacy."

"Now I'm kicking myself that I didn't enjoy the local strawberry season more."

"It's okay, Grace. We incorrectly assume everything should be accessible according to our own selfish whims and fancies, but it's best for us to live in parallel with nature's cycles, to tune into the seasons and enjoy the brief windows of time they present."

Grace stared lovingly at her grandmother.

50 | It's All About Attitude

"Plan your life by the seasons and not by the school semester, Grace." It was the Wind speaking to her again. "Don't think in terms of what you want to achieve in the third term, but what your hopes are for the spring. Allow the seasons and their idiosyncratic rhythms to rule your day, not a daily planner. Look at the Mongolian farmers and their nomadic lifestyles; they let nature guide them and their animals, and it's this fluidity that's missing from your life. Grace, unite with the land."

She glanced at her iPhone for the time.

"And stop valuing clock time over the natural movements of the sun and moon. Connect to time through sensation and lose the logic of your digital timepiece."

At the southeastern end of the market, Grace spied the merry-go-round. As a child, the black horse was her favourite. Another child once sat on 'her' horse and Veronika calmly told her then eight-year-old granddaughter, "The horse isn't yours, my darling. When it's free, it's yours to ride, but if someone else is in the saddle first, give them the freedom to enjoy the horse, just as you hope they'll do the same for you."

She turned to face her grandmother, who knew exactly which memory just played through her mind. Veronika opened her purse and said, "Go, here's some money. Ride that horse and contemplate how far you've come."

Grace paid the elderly female attendant and mounted the black horse. Holding onto the gold pole of the Victorian carousel, she only caught sight of her current world, and then with a jolt the horses began their diminutive dips up and down as they set off on their circular path. She often considered her life to be permanently stuck on pause, but moving around and around with the organ music playing, Grace was aware of life curving at a higher turn of the spiral.

If I must go over the same ground, at least I can approach it from a higher perspective.

All these years she believed she wasn't moving forward, and in a way it was true. Instead of progressing horizontally along a one-way path, Grace was, bit by bit, vertically winding her way in a helix back to the source of life.

When the ride came to a halt with a slight shudder, Grace didn't want to get off. It—life—made sense as she twirled around and around. Covering old ground with every spin, there were vast swathes of wisdom to be gained from each previous rotation. The carousel reminded Grace of how progress occurs through cycles.

Grace rejoined her grandmother out the front of Amber's Ice Creamery & Dessert Bar. She chose three flavours: white chocolate and strawberry cheesecake, honey peanut butter pretzel and bubble gum in a large chocolate-sprinkled waffle cone.

Veronika ordered one scoop of vanilla in a cup with a single maraschino cherry on top and laughed at Grace's choice of flavours. "My darling, you make life so chaotic and complicated. When you're older, you'll come to appreciate the elegance of simplicity."

After their ice cream break they visited another fruit and vegetable stall. Veronika touched the beautiful, ruby red tomatoes and said, "When you're eating foods at their peak, they encourage you to also live life at the apex and fully express your magnificence."

The stall owner, wearing a blue- and white-pinstriped apron, said, "This wise lady here speaks the truth. Back in Italy we eat purely out of love, for food connects us back to ourselves."

"When eating with the seasons we witness life's passing and remind ourselves that we won't last forever either," Veronika replied.

Grace didn't want to think of this morbid fact. "I just love being here with you." She squeezed her hand. "It's so much fun. I want to have this much fun every day." To Grace, her grandmother was the living embodiment of refined, sensuous enjoyment.

"And you can, dear, by discovering there's a rhythm to all things—including washing the dishes. We shouldn't only take pleasure in the food we eat, but in all the steps involved in food preparation and presentation. As we did now; we made a shopping list, travelled to the market to buy the food . . ."

"And some items not on the list!"

"Always," Veronika agreed. "And then we'll get home, and Kosmos will tell us off for not buying him enough treats, and then we'll lay the table . . ."

"But it's so boring when I do it at home by myself. I can't stand it."

"Because you've turned it into a chore, pumpkin."

They were now outside the market waiting for the bus, each holding an overflowing, canvas tote bag.

"It's because of the attitude in which you approach it. Everything in life is neutral; it's our attitude that brings the meaning. At home when your mother asks you to set the table, you consider it a burden. Do you ever lay the dining room table out of love?"

"At Christmas I do."

"But what about a Monday evening in October?"

"Why should I? It's just the four of us."

"And you four aren't worth it?"

"We are; but not every day."

"Then which day? Grace, you're not honouring the never-to-be-repeated uniqueness of the moment. The meal could provide much needed comfort and support to your father after a hard day at the office, or your mother may have exciting news to share, or Abel might unexpectedly bring home a new girlfriend. It's one of life's privileges to share a meal with people you love, so bring joy to what is seen as routine."

The bus pulled up and Veronika greeted the bus driver, smiled at a few of the other passengers and let Grace take the window seat.

51 | Living Wisdom

As the bus trundled past the local Member of Parliament's office and the council hall, Veronika turned to Grace and said, "Witness the artistry in each minor event. This is not just a bus ride to get us from point A to point B, but it offers us an alternative view of our surroundings. We're being presented with a different outlook on life."

Grace became aware of the many stories occurring both inside and outside the bus. She transposed it to the whole world.

Seven billion stories and counting.

"See each event as its own finale," Veronika said, smoothing the matted hair behind her granddaughter's left ear.

Some time passed and Grace still had not spoken.

"I can see by that puzzled expression that you don't understand what I mean."

Actually, Grace did. The puzzled look came from thinking she was conversing with the Wind, not to her grandmother.

"Don't make what you're doing a means to an end. It is both the means and the end. You do it for its own sake, not because of where it will get you or what will result from it. Say you're at home laying the table, smooth the bumps out of the tablecloth with the palms of your hands, feel the stretch in your arms as you place each piece of cutlery down on the surface, line up the plates and glasses with a symmetrical eye and be in the movement of your body; completely forget the end result and feel the process."

Grace knew when she slowed her actions down she more easily connected to the stillness within her.

"And pumpkin," Veronika continued, "when sitting at the table;

feel the inner fullness that comes from sharing a meal with your nearest and dearest. How you eat is just as important as what you eat."

Veronika always concerned herself with the 'how' of living. To her, how you did the small things demonstrated how you'd tackle the big things. You'd never catch her eating tuna out of a can while standing in front of the fridge. The very idea was sacrilege.

"Meal times are a way to share intimate moments with your family and friends, as well as with yourself. They're opportunities to feel the abundance of the earth, its nourishment and wholesomeness."

Grace made a mental note to book in for a haircut this week.

"And even when clearing the table and washing the dishes, tap into the pulsating rhythm of life running underneath the moment."

Grace asked, "But how do you know all of this?"

"By living, dumpling."

"But I'm alive too, so why don't I have access to the same information as you?"

"You possess the exact same knowledge as I, Grace Rose. It's in your bones just as it's in my bones. The difference is that you don't act on it, and knowledge without action is useless."

"So you're saying I know exactly what you know, but by not accessing and living this same knowledge it lays dormant?"

"Precisely." Veronika gave Grace the look self-confident women do when they know they're right—one eyebrow arched and a lengthy stare down the nose.

"You're a great student, Grace, always wanting to learn more, but you're not implementing the knowledge you acquire. Living wisdom means applying your insights to manoeuvre your way through life. Your knowledge is only as deep as your actions."

This was the Wind talking, its words stark in their honesty.

"We shouldn't view our time at the market today as a chore," Veronika explained. "The planning and shopping weren't tasks to get through so that we could get to the main event—dinner this evening—but individual steps to take great pleasure in and relish."

Grace rested her head on Veronika's shoulder and breathed in the scent from the trumpet lilies peeking out of the tote bag.

"Yes, we have to get dinner on the table this evening, but each aspect—planning the menu, buying the produce, chatting with the stall owners, riding the carousel, pausing for ice cream, catching the bus home—each of these is a main event in and of itself."

Grace realised at that moment what her grandparents gave her—the space to be herself. She didn't have to try to be anything other than who she is. Grace looked up and kissed Veronika on her neck.

"Pumpkin, one day you'll come to recognise anticipation and preparation as end states in themselves—not precursors—for they are the main event." Veronika stressed the word 'are'. "They're not mere steps, but destinations in themselves."

52 | The Journey
of Co-Creation

Grace awoke, and her first thought wandered to when someone would recognise her brilliance and sweep her away from the drudgery of her life.

"That person is you, Grace."

"Good morning, Wind." She hadn't slept well.

"Grace, the person you are seeking is you. You are the only person who can transport yourself to another world. You create your experience in this world by the attitude in which you meet the chosen milestones on your life's journey."

Grace rolled over and hugged her knees close to her chest. "You just don't get it, Wind, you really don't get it!"

"Grace, what are your frustrations? What am I not getting?"

"I'm failing science class, Amber-Jane and the 'cool' gang still hate me, Gabriel's started dating Vivian, none of my clothes look good on me, I'm permanently stressed, chronically tired and never have enough energy."

"Anything else?"

"I'll never find a boyfriend, a decent job, learn to cut loose and get rid of my super-critical mind that . . ."

"I was joking, Grace," the Wind said.

"Oh."

"Grace, let me remind you that you are only fifteen-years-old."

"And?"

"Imagine looking back at the end of your life and realising that, instead of living your destiny, you chose to make your journey one

165

long, constant frustration. Can you picture the sorrow you'll feel knowing that you had the right life all along, but that you spent all your energy believing the timing and circumstances of it wrong?"

It sounded awful, like hell on earth, to know that she could possibly throw the brilliance of her life away on one false assumption.

"You presume the universe made a mistake, that you were destined for another life, but by some bad luck of the draw you were given this one?"

"Kind of," she said.

"There are no errors in this world," said the Wind. "Ever. You're exactly where you need to be with this precise name and body, facing these specific trials and tribulations. Definitively accept this."

"Oh man! Not acceptance again," she groaned.

"Yes, acceptance. Honour your personal journey. Stop assuming that the world is against you. Claim the peace and equanimity that lives within you. It's your divine birthright."

She let out a huge sigh.

"Remember, Grace, that you're precious beyond measure and imagination."

Grace complained all week how tired she was, but this Saturday morning she cursed herself for not waking earlier. She practically begged all week for a day to sleep in and now that she finally had it, didn't want it.

"You spurn your life, and your inability to go with the flow is what breaks you. Allow situations and other people to just 'be' and you'll grant this same peace to yourself. If you judge another, it's you who becomes the victim."

I know I can't reverse my longstanding habits overnight, but how long will this transformation process take?

"You place a ceiling on your own awareness when you judge. And here's another home truth for you, Grace. Life isn't what you wish it to be, it is what it is."

"Okay, okay, you win, you're right."

In time she would perceive what a privilege it was to get out of bed with no physical aches and pains, but not today, not from a teenager's perspective.

"You fit into life, Grace. You more than fit in—you belong—so take your proper place in the order of things."

Then an understated, yet palpable shift occurred. She almost missed it, like she had missed the bus, because of sleepiness. It wasn't a dramatic moment, but an equally valid shift in perspective.

"So, if everything is for me, the least I can do is be appreciative, I guess?"

"You're finally beginning to awaken to the wisdom that's been lying inside you for eternity. You're beginning to see that everything's happening through you."

She sat up. "Wait up! I thought you said everything was happening for me."

"It's a higher turn of the spiral, Grace. Not for you, or to you, but through you. You open all the doorways for the universe to step through. Your soul has brought in these experiences for your expansion, so gratefully receive what you've called in."

Something in that line resonated with Grace, and she rephrased it in her own words: "Be with what I've brought into my life."

"Yes, be with the situations without wanting to change them and cherish those who are in the moment with you, yourself included."

"Let me get this straight. I know we've been through this before, but just so I'm perfectly clear, I'm co-creating my life with the divine by the beliefs I hold, choices I make, emotions I feel, and actions I pursue as I meet circumstances in my life that I sometimes have no control over."

"Absolutely!"

"So why do I spend so much time feeling dreadful?"

"I know; how crazy to think it's you who keeps viewing your days as one long-suffering drama series, permanently stuck on repeat?"

Although the Wind quietened, Grace had the notion that it wanted to impress on her something else, something important; how each re-occurrence of trauma, whether emotional, mental or physical, was a chance to heal her psyche by allowing her soul to respond, instead of the personality reacting. She had the feeling the Wind wanted to teach her how the unexplored parts of herself were governing her life, but could only mentor her at the level she was at now. But the Wind remained silent, and all Grace had to hold on to were vague insights and unspoken truths.

She returned to their conversation. "Part of me agrees with what you said, but I'm not totally convinced yet. Why am I addicted to feeling bad?"

"Grace, you are a work in progress, not a finished masterpiece."

"Well, that brings me little comfort," she replied.

The Wind changed tack. "So why do you feel you struggle making congruent choices?"

She blurted, "Because I can't see their knock-on effects."

"And are you now beginning to grasp the associated ramifications and consequences?"

"Kind of."

"And how they separate you from the divine?"

She bowed her head.

"The disconnectedness you feel is the signal to return to love."

"Cause and effect?"

"That's right. If what you selected isn't working for you, Grace, why stick with it?"

"Because change is so impossibly hard," she moaned.

"Change is one of life's only constants, Grace."

"But it means taking responsibility for my life, which scares me no end. It means being accountable and not getting trapped in thoughts that take me out of the present moment and into past regrets and future worries."

"Which is why I want you to regularly ask yourself if your thoughts are serving you and your fellow kindred on earth?"

"But that means resisting less and being more awake. It means operating from a more dignified height."

"The problem being?"

"The air up there is too pure. I just . . . I just don't know if my lungs could breathe in air so virtuous."

"This is not about what the personality wants, but what the soul needs, Grace. You're worthy for the mere fact that you're breathing. You don't need to prove your worth."

Grace started crying and while she'd usually use the corner of the quilt to wipe her eyes, this time she reached for a tissue.

"Grace, you're forgetting all the amazing things in your world."

"Remind me?" she gasped.

"Me."

53 | The Responsive Universe

Gabriel walked by Grace with a nonchalant look on his face. The Wind quickly tried to pull her out of any detrimental thought processes. "No tears, Grace. You are worthy of a life filled with royal abundance."

"No I'm not."

"Negativity will only taint all future good times coming your way. It paralyses you and stops you dancing with life. Step into your gifts, Grace."

She listened to the Wind.

"Learn to float above life. Detach yourself from your thoughts and feel your heartbeat. When you're so self-involved, you can't see beyond yourself. Work with—not against—life."

"But everything is wrong," she stuttered.

"Of course it is, because that's how you're interpreting it."

On the weekend Grace had felt like a mature adult venturing into a world of creative thought, but today she felt like a toddler.

"A fall from grace, it's the chronicle of your life up to this point."

"Oh, the play on my name again, great! Just what I need!"

"When your thoughts next hold you hostage I want you to tell yourself, 'I won't allow myself to nose-dive from grace.'"

She let out a long groan.

"Why must others validate your significance? Don't you believe you're a good friend?"

"I'm a great friend," she shot back.

"Then why chase relationships? If you're such amazing company, wouldn't people naturally flock to your side?"

She couldn't even bring herself to nod her head.

"Grace, you're incomparable. Don't you believe this?"

She sighed. "Kind of."

"Then why chase approval from Gabriel and everybody else? Why must others acknowledge your uniqueness? This striving for acceptance clothes you in a lesser vibration. Convey poise and vivaciousness. This is what attracts people."

Maybe her failings weren't due to lack of willpower or discipline, but an inability to embody her true nature?

"Your internal state of grace is what you radiate outward, not something you chase."

Grace could see the error of her ways, and it hurt.

"You're looking for someone to confirm your unique specialness, aren't you?"

She didn't respond.

"You want Gabriel to vouch for your right to exist?"

Silence.

"Stop hoping that someone outside of you will fix you, Grace. No one will confirm your worth until you first believe it yourself. Start acting like the prized, rare gem you are. Love already exists in you, so let it pour out, and then that which you seek will be attracted to you like a magnet."

She sat in one of the arches in the cloister and chewed the ends of her hair.

"Grace, if you're constantly disappointed, you'll only ever attract more things to be disappointed about into your experience of life. You can't attract love by attacking yourself. If you hate the world today, the world must respond to your spiteful energy tomorrow. The universe is always responding to you."

"Alright! I get it."

"The universe is always responding to you."

"I said I get it."

"The universe is always responding to you."

"Are you deaf? I heard you the first time you three-peated yourself!" she shouted.

"The universe is always responding to you."

"I know, alright! Quit it, would you!"

"Though I admire this feistiness in you, Grace, 'getting it' is not enough, nor is understanding it. You have to live it, just as reading a book on meditation can't be substituted for the personal experience of meditating. Direct experience is the truth your soul lives by."

"Oh."

"Trust in your bones that the universe matches you thought for thought, feeling for feeling, action for action. It'll replicate your fears as equally as it'll reflect your joys and reproduce your dissatisfaction as much as your elation. So what do you wish the universe to mirror back to you?"

Grace searched her heart for a considered answer. Finally, she replied, "Peace. And I don't mean that in response to a question in a Miss Universe beauty contest, I mean peace of mind."

"You're not alone. The universe only wants to help you with your desires, but first you must help yourself. What does peace of mind look and feel like to you? You need to know this because it all starts internally; the universe can only match the emotional state you're vibrating. You're the starting point, Grace. It can't come from anyone else."

In the past, Grace thought others were responsible for delivering the solutions to her problems directly to her front door. She saw the errors behind her beliefs. From now on, it had to begin within.

54 | Living Tradition

"I don't want to go to the stupid fair."

"You have to. It's part of our family tradition."

"But, Mum, I didn't choose my part in it."

"Fine, stay at home, but the rest of us are going."

"Don't be such a tool, Sis."

Grace bit her tongue. If Abel succumbed, so could she. But she refused to submit gracefully, so she purposely slammed the car door as she climbed into the back seat.

"It's true, Grace." The Wind was with her again. "We rarely question our traditions and follow many of them without rhyme or reason. Some are meant to stay, a few evolve and others die off. Blindly sticking with traditions when we have no special affinity with them—well, that's ridiculous."

"Exactly! What meaning does this fair bring to my life? It serves no purpose whatsoever."

"Yes, some traditions are forced on you, but Grace, perhaps there's a better way of approaching the issue? Why not find out what meaning this tradition holds for your parents?"

Grace refused, unable to put her own needs on the backburner.

"Adapting tradition to the present is what keeps it relevant."

Grace was transfixed on the scene outside the window. It appeared as if the car and sun were travelling at the exact same speed. She begrudgingly opened up. "I thought traditions weren't meant to change, that's why they're traditions?"

"They need to evolve, Grace, otherwise they'll become irrelevant. Long-standing ancient traditions ground us at our very core because they centre on love, joy and peace, but they need to be celebrated in the context of how people live today."

She nodded in understanding.

"Without relevance there's no meaning, and without meaning there's no reason for them to exist," the Wind said in a no-nonsense manner.

Her mother began speaking. "Grace, we have traditions in our school, working, family, and community lives to remind us that we're greater than what we do. They remind us of who we are."

Grace folded her hands in her lap.

Carla continued. "As much as we respect tradition, we must also value transition."

"I agree. We're constantly in a state of unfolding as we're always in the process of expansion."

"And who are you quoting there, Grace?" her father asked.

She knew he didn't believe she could create such elegant phrasing of her own accord. "Me, myself and I."

Abel snickered.

Grace said, "I wish to start a tradition where family and friends come to our house for a pancake breakfast on each of our birthdays."

"And how would this remind us that we're greater than what we do?" her father asked.

"We'd go around the kitchen table and each say what we'd learned about ourselves over the past year and what we hoped to experience in the coming year. As everyone leaves to begin their day, whoever's birthday it is would tell every person there why they're especially grateful that they're in their lives."

Her father softened. "Why, Grace, that's beautiful."

The Rose family arrived at the country fair in the hills in a relaxed mood after listening to Mahler's Symphony No. 8 in the car. Her mother invariably went to the cake stalls first, Abel headed for the amusement rides, Dylan staked out the artisanal beer tents, and Grace just ambled around the bric-à-brac stalls.

"Keep looking at traditions of the past through the lens of the present and reinvigorate them when necessary."

Grace wasn't listening. All the handcrafted products on display enamoured her: jewellery, candles, doorknobs, mosaic tiles, and wheat bags in the shape of eye masks.

The Wind interrupted her browsing and changed the topic. "Good design means that products flow; they ease into your life. Using the right product at the right time helps accentuate pace."

Grace instinctively thought of the champagne-coloured cashmere throw she snuggled under in the sitting room when rereading chapters from her favourite fantasy novels.

"Rhythm is as much about sensuality as it is about function. Contemplate which products you want close to you in life, both mentally and physically."

Grace moved to get a better look at the dressing gowns on the rack.

"Products close to your skin should heighten your sensuality. How does the dressing gown feel?"

"Indulgent," she said as she brought the linen to touch her cheek. She read somewhere that people's hands are often desensitised, so it's best to feel a material's quality on the cheek.

"Grace, try to buy clothes made of materials which feel as if they're softly stroking your skin as you wear them. Choose items which help move you into a flowing rhythm and ditch the rest."

She knew exactly what the Wind was on about. The fountain pen she owned that leaked, the skirt that unattractively bunched up at her hips, the inconvenient power socket behind the desk in her room that she struggled to reach each day. Grace amazingly put up with lots of things in her life that weren't right, didn't suit her or were broken.

"Let them go, Grace. Choose products that put you in a good mood. The moisturiser that emerges smoothly out of the tube and doesn't splatter all over your clothes, the soy milk carton with the easy screw-top lid, the office chair that moulds to your back, so that doing your homework is a dream for your body, diffusing essential oils that help focus your awareness. Find these enablers in life, as these little things make the big things happen."

Grace never thought of products in this way before.

"These enablers help you tap into the relevant rhythm you require, so view them as energy facilitators. Be responsible for the forces you create around you."

"Oh, all that vibrational stuff again."

The Wind spoke with patience. "Grace, you're a vibrational being, remember?"

She replied, "Got it. I mean living it," while trying on a malachite necklace.

"And . . ."

Grace could sense the Wind wanted to say something else.

"Create markers of ordinary, as well as extraordinary, time."

"Not only for big, annual, noteworthy events?"

"Correct, Grace. Have annual markers, but also focus on the daily and weekly rhythms you share as a family. Is it saying grace before the evening meal? A walk in the park on Sunday mornings after breakfast? A regular movie night?"

"I guess it's about finding individual customs, as well as ones to share with others."

"Right again. But how will you embrace and encourage these individual practices? Will a busy personal schedule prevent you from committing to family and community rites? Don't devalue the ritualistic elements of the human experience."

Grace decided that her family's annual trip to the country fair was a tradition worth keeping.

55 | Connect to Your Passion

"Where's your focus, Grace? Not much brilliance can shine through you when your fear-based thoughts are running the show."

Why Grace was remembering the Wind's advice from a few weeks back she couldn't recall.

"Treating the present moment as an obstacle means that you've separated yourself from your vital life force and aren't one with the living streams of life. It's in this moment that we plant the seeds of our future, so watch what you're busy planting, Grace. Don't sow a future of dissatisfaction, sorrow and emotional disturbances. Just imagine what others will lose if you succumb to fear and its children."

"Children?"

"Insecurity, doubt, rage, depression."

Grace walked into the kitchen, dumped her school bag by the pantry and opened the fridge. She saw her mother on the phone, sitting by the teakwood sideboard, which her parents had shipped over from Thailand. Carla's tone of voice implied it wasn't a close friend on the line.

The Wind said, "You can't beat your mind, Grace, only learn to live with it. You can't automatically halt the thoughts that crucify you; they don't go away by force. It's only when you consciously choose thoughts of a higher vibration that the attacking and debilitating ones begin to release their grip."

After Carla hung up the phone, Grace volunteered, between bites of an apple, "In class today, our teacher said that if you follow your passion you'd never have to work a day in your life, but I don't believe her."

"Well, Grace, what are you passionate about?" Carla put her diary down and focused her attention on her daughter's words. "Who is your divine muse?"

Not a word came out. She hated being put on the spot like this.

"You don't allow passion to enter your life and move through you, Grace, as you're too absorbed in the past or unnecessarily preoccupied with the future," the Wind said.

Her mother wasn't so direct, and said, "Passion can be things you do without thinking they're anything special, like jotting down interesting quotes, taking photographs, hiking, or knitting. Or it's what you read when you think no one's watching, like your father placing his golfing magazines inside business ones, thinking we're none the wiser."

"I know! Why does he do that?"

They both laughed.

"Passion sits close to the surface of a person's identity, so some individuals want to keep it private. It could be the only thing that makes them feel alive, so they don't want it visible, lest others take it from them or judge them because of it."

Grace called on the Wind to clarify its point of view.

"Passion is an energy which is never forced, it spontaneously flows through you. Rather than waiting for enthusiasm to catch up, instead let your passion for life touch everything." As Grace tried to take it all in, the Wind continued, "Have a zest for living. Don't make this passion private, find a way to share it with others."

Grace turned to her mother, who was making a pot of Lapsang Souchong. "But what if you don't know what you're passionate about, Mum?"

"Grace, some people on their death beds don't even know what their real enthusiasms are. Some creep up on you, like my gardening for example. What is it that inspires you?"

Grace was silent and turned to the Wind for its opinion.

"Keep living in the moment until a particular fervour arises. Be still and you'll be called to it. Don't dismiss anything. Watch the emotional shifts that come up in you and you'll soon know what you're committed to from a soul perspective."

Carla spoke. "You love reading, Grace, and you'd make a wonderful researcher or writer, but rather than a career, maybe it's a calling you're seeking?"

Grace caught her mother's eyes welling up. Carla composed herself and said, "Not all passions need to be fulfilled within the context of some sort of commercial work."

Grace twigged. This had something to do with her mother's failed attempt at running a gallery after completing her fine arts degree. She was dating another man, the one before her father, who nobody speaks of. This was her mother's Pandora's box, and there was no way on earth on Carla's watch that it'd ever be opened.

Carla pushed her bobbed hair behind her ears, poured them both the strong and smoky tea and, with a touch of synchronicity, said, "You've been given, identical to Pandora in Greek mythology, the gift of curiosity, Grace. But your inquisitiveness doesn't need to have a career as the end goal. Don't force yourself to make it the destination, instead make curiosity your path."

If Grace were to be summed up in one word, 'curious' would be it. She wanted to know how the world worked and what the best way was to travel through it. Though she considered herself open-minded, Grace was also threatened by new and different approaches. She inherited her father's 'my way or the highway' thinking. Change scared them both. But what frightened Grace more was being okay with the unknown.

"Look at your grandmother, Grace, she's passionate about everything involved in the cooking process, and undertakes each laborious task in a light-hearted manner. Or consider your father's ardent approach to his work. He communicates with his staff about the humdrum details of property contracts with the same excitement as when making a flamboyant submission before a judge and jury in court."

Grace sipped her tea as her mother continued.

"It's not that you become passionate about something, but rather that passion is its own state of grace. When you find what you love, it's as though you can't not do it, and you can't not be curious, my darling daughter. Tap into that inquisitive energy, which is your gift. Don't despise it; feel its force and respect it."

56 | Divine Timing

"Change does and doesn't happen overnight; some flowers bloom in the blink of an eye, while others unfurl more gradually. You can't hurry natural phenomena. Growth doesn't always happen at a rational speed."

As she ate her cereal, Grace enjoyed the peace and quiet in the house. Both parents were working this weekend, and the only time Abel got out of bed before midday was when he had lectures.

"Today I want to speak to you about divine timing and how to train yourself to look inward. Ask yourself what really needs doing in each moment, Grace. Which decisions best serve your inner life as well as the people in your outer life? And the only way you'll know this is by checking in with your soul."

"Okay, I'll listen to my soul instead of letting my personality dictate its preferences," she said while shovelling a spoonful of muesli into her mouth.

"It's not that the personality is inherently bad, Grace; it's a form of expression for your soul and is necessary for life here on earth, but we want it infused with the soul's will, so that it conveys only the highest aspects of the celestial."

Grace sprinkled three and a half heaped teaspoons of raw sugar over the organic muesli to make it more palatable.

"As Sting sang, 'Let your soul be your pilot.'"

Grace laughed at the Wind's reference to pop culture.

"Also, remember that time is only a concept in your mind. It can go quickly or painfully slow, all depending on how you think about it."

"I think you've mentioned this to me before."

"You control your attitude towards time. If you believe you have all the time in the world, you will, and if you feel there's never enough of it, that's true also."

These intense downloads Grace received from the Wind made her feel as if her circuits were overloading.

"Unfortunately 'lack' is the lens through which you're currently interacting with time. Let life unfold to its own schedule. Universal rhythms of time aren't something to believe in with your mind, they're cycles to feel and live. Rhythm unites all aspects of life."

Grace let out a loud, forceful sigh, causing her recently trimmed fringe to puff away from her forehead like she was blow drying it, then settle back again.

"From your limited vision you can't comprehend exactly how the past, present and future interlink. You're not appreciating the fullness of the scenic landscape because you're not viewing life from a high enough altitude."

"You're saying that I can't perceive the greater meaning and purpose behind situations if I live through the personality?"

"You got it."

"I get worked up about my problems, but really each challenge is expanding my soul in some way."

"Yes, you're finally recognising that each moment is always for the highest good of all involved, even though in the personality's eyes it may appear otherwise."

Grace got up to rinse the bowl. She prompted the Wind, "So, back to time."

"What's meant to be will be—so don't sweat it out in the meantime. The soul has its own timeline, which often runs counter to the personality's agenda . . ."

Grace interjected. "You mean me and my to-do list and my expectation of how things should happen."

"Right, but you must get by now, Grace, that the soul is working to a divine schedule. It's not always for you to know the order of events. All you can do is consult your internal compass and trust that your life is unfolding perfectly. So while you may think you're busy studying tenth grade at school this semester, your soul is working on an entirely different schedule of learning."

So my life is not out of order or off course. I've been on my path all along.

57 | Connecting the Dots

Grace locked the front door with one key and the security door with another. Walking down the driveway, she noticed that the grass looked greener after the recent rain and that it contrasted nicely with the bark of the bare trees. She waved to the next door neighbour as he collected the newspaper from his front lawn.

"Regard periods of complete immobilisation as enforced destinations for your required growth. From the personality's viewpoint it might appear as if you're going nowhere fast, but to the soul you're right on target." The Wind paused. "This involves faith, because the personality only sees a holding pattern."

She was ten minutes early for the bus, a rarity.

"Grace, do you recall that time at the airport when you and your family were on your way to the United Kingdom and your plane was delayed? To you the delay was off schedule—it wasn't fitting in with your personality's plans—but the holdup was perfectly calculated to your soul's timetable."

"I guess I can see that now," Grace conceded. "I know I initially resisted it," she recounted, "but then I tried to, I guess in your language, surrender to the delay."

"And didn't a certain sense of peace wash over you?"

"You'd say I gave up wanting to control the situation and accepted the change in plans, but deep down I knew there was nothing I could personally do about the delay."

The Wind said, "You can't always predict certain setbacks, so all you can do in these situations is roll with the punches and enjoy the benefits the delay brings. It could create the space for a new idea to come through, or prevent you from being in an accident, or cause you to sit next to the most perfect person on the following flight. Never forget, there's great beauty in all moments."

The bus eventually arrived and she sat at the front behind the driver and continued her conversation with the Wind. "Once I calmed down I noticed all the other travellers in the same boat as us," she said. "The delay wasn't personal to me. That's when I came up with the idea to take Kosmos to the recital given by that visiting Russian string quartet."

"That concert was a treasured evening out with your grandfather, wasn't it?"

"I know. I'm usually not so fond of the viola, but the solo really moved me that night, and then I don't know how, but when the second movement of Bach's Orchestral Suite No.3 played, I knew that I wanted to compile a book of poetry for my final English project."

"It brings me great joy when you trust life's interconnectedness, Grace. There are no isolated events in life; everything is a 'connect the dots' game. When you perceive events from a deeper perspective you realise nothing's an isolated experience, only interrelated dots connecting to reveal more and more of the divine on earth."

Grace leaned her head on the bus window.

"Every point is a sequence. Each one leads you to think or behave differently and leads to another point. Seemingly random, disjointed dots are actually stepping stones leading you to your true nature."

"At the airport when we finally boarded our plane I felt really soft, like I could melt into the chair I sat in."

"It's always a matter of allowing, Grace. When you stopped resisting the delay and treating it as an enemy, you became friends with the present moment and whole new possibilities revealed themselves."

The bus slowed down as the traffic lights turned amber.

"Hindsight only exists in retrospect, so all you can do is align yourself with the now. That's why it's so important to be in the present—it's where everything happens."

She stared at the red light, surrendering to the moment, neither wishing it to change nor stay static.

"You forgot another crucial lesson the airport delay taught you."

Grace searched her mind. "Oh, that's right," she replied. "At the salad bar when I brought my plate back to the table I wrongly guessed the orange thing in there was mango. I was cross with myself because I didn't want any fruit in my salad, but when I actually tasted it, it was pumpkin."

"And until you actually tasted it you were severely rebuking yourself over a misperception."

"Please don't remind me how much energy I squander on irrelevant details each day."

"But these small things form the quality of your life. Don't undervalue them, but equally don't make them any bigger than they or you are. There are great paradoxes at play in this world, Grace."

"Meaning?"

"Contradictions exist, and the trick is understanding the ebb and flow between these opposites."

58 | Wise Counsel

The bus caught every single red light to school.

"The small things matter, yet they don't. Can you feel the undeniable truth of this statement?"

Grace was brooding.

"Not in your mind, Grace, in your heart."

Grace repeated what she'd heard: "The small things matter, yet they don't."

"Don't try to understand it, Grace, but feel if this has happened in your own life. Can you know it as a truth instead of a statement of fact made by me?"

"Um, it's important to spell-check my emails, but it also doesn't matter in the wider scheme of things?"

"Aha."

"But Wind, back to what you said about knowing something as a truth rather than reading or hearing it. Is that why most self-help books don't seem to work?"

"That's right. They work for the author who lived the advice she or he is dishing out, but until you as a reader can internalise their counsel and apply it in your own life, their words are just rhetoric. They're lost to you until you can experience them yourself," the Wind clarified.

Grace's mobile rang with the *Walking on Sunshine* ringtone and Ruby's name flashed up on the screen.

"Hey, Rubes, what's up?"

"Ah, not much, I'm just stressing about my workload this week. Best to share the misery, so thought I'd call. Where are you?"

Grace thought it completely out of character for Ruby to feel overwhelmed. She was one of those lucky people who seemed to just breeze through life without a care or worry in the world.

"On the bus." Grace didn't bother speaking in a hushed tone, as whoever else sat at the front of the bus wasn't a threat to her social standing at school.

"Rubes, out of the three of us, you're the one that makes life the most simple and straightforward. It's usually you telling me to take the path of least resistance."

"I know!" Ruby laughed.

Grace decided to apply some of the Wind's teachings. "Believe you have enough time to do everything. Rubes, don't even contemplate the next task at hand, just be fully present with whatever it is you're feeling and doing in the moment."

"Say what, girlfriend? What are you reading from?"

Grace knew it was much too soon to explain to Ruby that 'being' comes before 'doing', and that bringing focused attention to the completion of a single action was better than doing many things in an unconscious state. She couldn't bring herself to tell her best friend about the Wind's entry into her life yet, so she said, "Oh, I read it on some blog post on procrastination. Anyway, stop freaking out, it's all cool, just get yourself to school."

Ruby only lived ten minutes walking distance from her school in the eastern suburbs. There was no torturous bus ride for her today or any other day.

"I don't know what came over me."

Grace guessed it must've been an isolated shockwave of fear that rocked her foundations and caused her momentary wobble of self-doubt.

"Before I forget, the Cold Hearts music festival is on in a few weeks, and we should really get our tickets organised this weekend. I'll call you tonight to arrange."

The festival was called Cold Hearts because it was held in the depths of winter at the Gateshead Convention Centre, not like the summer events in the parklands or at the beach.

Grace simply replied, "Okay, cool. Chat then," and hung up.

As the bus was held up at yet another red light, Grace murmured a prayer to Ruby and also herself. "Don't apply your restricted view of time on life. Focus instead on the timeless dimension within you."

59 | Looking for the Quick Fix

The following day Grace headed to the local shops. On her way out the front door, she observed a final, fragrant, creamy white flower hanging off the crooked branch of the frangipani tree in their garden.

At the newsstand she picked up some gardening magazines for her mother and then stopped at the fish and chips shop. The chalkboard menu listed far more than just fish and chips: hamburgers, dim sum, pizza, falafels, salads, hot dogs.

It should change its shop window to 'All food served here.'

She ordered a toasted sandwich with bacon and extra cheese and a chocolate milkshake. As Grace handed over the money to the cashier, she felt pained.

What happened to trying to eat for my soul's nourishment? Why is it so hard for me to do the right thing by my body?

Usually she'd proclaim there was nothing healthy on the menu, but there was—even in this fish and chips shop!—yet she still couldn't bring herself to choose foods that nourished, not depleted, her.

"Grace, don't beat yourself up. Your junk food habit is currently far stronger than your desire to be healthy, as you still believe a bag of chips gives you something a salad can't," the Wind explained. "It's not possible to eliminate all your bad habits overnight; it's more a little here, a little there. You seem to have swallowed the myth of instant reinvention hook, line and sinker."

"I guess no one wants to know that it can be a long and taxing process."

"Too right, Grace. People want freedom from their addictions in one easy step. They forget that they acquired these patterns of behaviour over the length of one or multiple lifetimes. Before tackling a large mountain, you must first scale a smaller one. The Western culture, though, is in love with the quick fix."

"Yeah, like all those plastic surgery and total makeover programs on TV." Grace's worn and shabby jacket fell off the back of the chair as she tucked her hair into her woollen beanie.

"That's right, Grace, but look at nature. Change can happen instantaneously—a flower can bloom overnight—but mostly it's a gradual process where the growth is in proportion to the bud's capabilities. It's the same for you; you can't outpace that which hasn't opened yet."

Grace felt stagnant and stupid but reminded herself not to chase wisdom, and instead let it rise from within her.

The Wind added, "You can only let in what you're ready for."

She tightened her grey cable-knit scarf underneath her neck.

"Keep starving the self-defeating habits while feeding the beneficial ones."

⚮

In the food court at Woodcroft mall after school on Monday—where a dense air pocket smelling of deep-fried batter floated above the shoppers—Grace virtuously chose a Caesar salad. As the fresh donut smell entered her nostrils, she craved them solely to inhale their sugar content.

Halfway through her 'healthy' meal—which wasn't filling her up in the slightest—she noticed how much grated and processed cheese was in the salad.

Here I am thinking I'm doing a good thing and I slip up again.

She berated herself until the Wind intervened.

"It's not so bad, Grace," the Wind said, "it's the intentions behind our decisions that are crucial. You chose the healthier option. Your intention was pure, it's okay, relax. Why we do something is as significant as what we actually do. For example, it may appear that someone has performed a noble act, but if driven by the desire for public recognition, the nobility doesn't hold true."

She nodded and kept eating.

"You're not losing anything by giving up what's toxic from your life. Stop obsessing over what you're missing out on and focus instead on what you're gaining; more health, energy, radiance, and a greater sense of wellbeing. Grace, if you eat junk, you think junk. Eating a diet of natural, whole foods is one of the best ways to cleanse your thoughts."

Grace felt full of shame and remorse.

"Only the personality lets guilt control it, Grace."

She called on her soul to lead.

"Of course we all want the quick fix solution; to be a flawed person in the evening and a faultless angel by the next morning, but Grace, it doesn't happen that way. Just as you want to be more refined and agile in your mannerisms, it doesn't happen overnight. It's nigh on impossible to instantaneously change the ways you've done things the majority of your life. If you can even be fully conscious with just one action—and complete it with finesse—that's a huge victory. Striving to achieve these huge energetic shifts overnight only leads to disappointment and more resistance."

Grace felt defeated but no sound came from her mouth.

"To effect change you have to start at a psychic level. Change happens first in the inner realm before it's reflected externally."

The pull was too strong. Grace walked up to the counter and ordered a bag of six cinnamon donuts. She returned to her seat, and boy did the first bite taste good. The crunchy crust and light interior melted in her mouth, so she took an even larger second bite of the soft, fluffy, air-filled dough. The mix of nutmeg, cinnamon and sugar clung to her lips. Before she knew it, Grace was staring at an empty bag of batter crumbs.

"You must hold your intention tight whenever you enter a difficult situation."

The tears started, and the napkin was already covered in grease. "Rely on me for added strength and resolve, Grace, don't attempt to walk this life single-handedly. Call on the guardians of the light that exist all around you as no one succeeds on their own. If you believe you can get by in this world without the influence of the gods, you'll only have a lifetime of pointless struggle ahead of you."

60 | Honouring Your Body

Grace was absentmindedly going through the motions of shopping with her mother in Bells department store. Carla was trying on a white, funnel-neck jacket that she said she'd wear to Dylan's annual summer work event later in the year. "Just so your dad doesn't think it was an impulse buy," she said.

Grace sat on the uncomfortable stool outside the changing room. "Mum, when you're trying something new on, don't think how good it looks in the mirror, feel how good it looks. Interact with your image from an emotive—not visual—perspective."

Carla sharply pulled the curtain back and saw Grace swinging her legs back and forth under the stool. "Sorry? What did you say?"

"Are you going deaf, Mum?"

"No, not deaf, sweetheart, I'm just disbelieving my own ears."

"Meaning?"

Carla quickly reframed her answer. "I agree, meaning yes, you're right, darling. I don't like the way this jacket makes me feel, so let's keep looking until I find one that feels like a dream."

"There's a first, Mum. The only reason your wardrobe is so massive, yet you still complain you have nothing to wear, is because you buy what you think looks right on you, rather than what feels right."

Carla couldn't muster a response to her daughter's insight. She pulled the curtain shut and leaned back against the changing room wall to compose herself.

At home and getting ready to play in a basketball match later that afternoon, Grace brushed her hair and remembered to sense the brush's bristles on her scalp. She was looking forward to the Swedish massage her mother had booked for her at a new spa set up by one of her father's clients.

The Wind didn't need to tell her, she told herself. "When you lie on the massage table, attune yourself to the rhythm of the masseur's hands. Feel each stroke and its subsequent vibration, and lose yourself in the sensations as your body and the masseur's hands become one." She even added a caveat, as the Wind so often did. "When you hop off the massage table, don't rush and get dressed too quickly. Slow down and prolong the experience."

"Grace, why don't you learn to massage yourself?"

"Why would I do that? It sounds like too much hard work."

"But that's part of the issue, Grace. People think they don't have time to walk their pets or wash their cars, but they do. We have the means to take care of ourselves, but out of sheer laziness or a sense of entitlement we expect others to do many of these things for us. Adults especially outsource so many aspects of their lives and this is one of the reasons their existence becomes barely recognisable to them."

"How would getting a monthly massage from a trained masseur make me dependent?"

"That deep relaxation—the feeling you desperately long for—I want you to learn how to give it to yourself. Right now you're relying on an external source to give you what you crave, and that characterises dependence to me."

Grace frowned.

"It's easy to learn to massage yourself."

Grace rolled her eyes.

"You rub your sense organs: ears, eyes and nose," the Wind began. "Squeeze your neck gently and massage your body with languid hand movements from your shoulders all the way down to your feet. Lightly tap your head and face with your fingertips, then place your hands over your face and breathe in visualised images of divine grace. Do this in the shower every morning to help increase your blood flow and carry oxygen to your soft tissues and organs."

She closed her eyes to find her centre.

"It'll also improve your sensory awareness. Knowing you're the one giving yourself these sensations—they're born from your hands—means relaxation is always at your own fingertips. Grace, I'm trying to teach you ways to feel good in all you do. Honour your body, as it contains your soul in the world of form."

Grace understood what the Wind was saying, but she still wanted someone other than herself to care for her.

"Massage yourself to work with your moods. When you feel out of sorts, rub your temples. When you feel tired, press the centre point of the palms of your hands. When you feel overwhelmed, rub the insides of your feet. Touch should be felt at both the inner and outer levels. I want you tonight, Grace, to feel your father's lips when they press against your cheek as he kisses you good night and to experience the comfort his kiss brings you."

Her heart constricted. All the kisses doled out by her father during her lifetime and she couldn't actually remember feeling a single one.

"Another thing," the Wind said. "I'd like you to contemplate how it is you're touching moments and other people? What are the experiences you're creating and leaving as an imprint for others? This world wasn't made for us to suffer through—though you unfortunately believe it is—and this has become your default viewfinder of the world."

Grace searched for the rainbow inside herself, the one that led to the pot of gold, her soul.

"Let the universe flow through you, Grace," the Wind said, "as you channel a tender, loving vibration through your thoughts, feelings and actions. Don't ever deny yourself an opportunity to touch another's soul with your radiant grace."

Her team lost the basketball match by only one point but this was of no consequence to Grace. That night her exhilaration came from feeling the softness of her father's lips on her cheek as he wished her good night.

61 | Just Be

"When you wake, first be grateful for your breath. Can you possibly imagine how many thousands of people around the world will breathe their last breath today? And how they would do anything for just a few more gasps of air?"

Earth school has started early this morning.

"Don't literally think of your breath, Grace," said the Wind, "physically feel the air moving through your airways and into your lungs. Savour its nourishment and cyclical nature as you unite with its recurring rhythm."

Grace dutifully repeated, "I respect my life force and refuse to waste it. Everything happens for my soul's highest good. Always."

"And?" the Wind prodded.

"I will no longer dwell in the world of 'shoulds'—only in the land of acceptance."

"Now here's another paradox for you to wrap your head around, Grace: there's meaning in everything, but not everything needs deciphering. Have faith that your worldly experiences are leading you in the right direction."

Does the Wind mean the rhythm of life dances this way for a bit, then that way, and doesn't require my constant scrutinising and measuring?

"When you constantly replay the past in your mind, you block the stream of life. Your soul lives in the now and can't express itself fully when your mind keeps travelling back in time. The only time that matters is now, so fully inhabit it."

Grace knew that she leaked energy by not fully occupying present time and sabotaged her aliveness by dwelling in the past and living for the future.

It's just that the thoughts that drag me away seem so much more seductive than the current moment in front of me.

"I want you to reconnect regularly with the natural world, to the web of life, Grace, and this will help you lose your addiction to doing. You actually do by not doing."

To Grace, this conversation was like having multiple advanced lessons of physics and philosophy delivered simultaneously.

"Don't condemn your thoughts when they wander, merely bring yourself back and once again take up residence as the witness. Grace, I'm trying to point you back to yourself. I'm bringing you back home."

Grace knew the Wind was only trying to help her understand why she made certain choices, and point her to the divine within, but some days it was difficult just to get out of bed, let alone reconnect to her inner wisdom.

Returning to the topic of effortless doing, it said, "You expect doing more will make you be more, but all that's necessary for you to do in this lifetime, Grace, is to be. Just be. That's it."

In her heart, Grace knew the Wind's words to be accurate. She only wished it wasn't so hard to both remember and live this truth.

"Learn to take an unselfish, long-term view of life. The more this universal wisdom infuses your narrative and nature, the less you'll condemn yourself and others." The Wind took a long pause. "Grace, be realistic. A basketballer doesn't spin a ball on the tip of her finger the first time she tries and not drop it. Practice, practice, practice."

62 | Embracing the
Present Moment

Grace and Juliet were waiting at the bus stop by Jade's Café. While Grace was content with her novels and gossip magazines, Juliet read anything to do with tips and hints for the 'real' world: advice on how to walk in high heels, fashionable holiday how-to's, making face masks from leftover food items in the fridge. This was Juliet's world. She was also full of wanderlust and had an odd obsession with France.

"If I come back in another life I'd be a Parisian female living on the Left Bank."

Grace looked at Juliet perplexed, wondering where this was leading.

"It's said in Paris that women approach men for assistance, and men approach women. If there's a choice, a woman wouldn't go to another woman to ask for some minor form of help, and a man never another man."

"Jules, who cares?"

"Grace, you go ask the opposite sex, as it's less about executing the practical nature of your request and more a practice of sensuality. A French woman seduces everyone she meets. And yes, before you say it, I know that's a vast generalisation."

Grace thought Juliet had a way of speaking that went well beyond her teenage years.

Maybe it's all those how-to books she reads?

She was about to comment, when Juliet said, "I don't mean that way, Grace, but the way a French woman moves, whether it's picking up a croissant from the pâtisserie, to sipping a double espresso in a café or walking her dog. Every movement is sensual." Juliet held an imaginary dog leash in her hand as she wiggled her hips.

The Wind blew in and said, "Perceiving the truth of a situation is harder than actually seeing it. Perceiving means going behind your five physical senses to get to the heart of the matter."

Grace couldn't find the link between the Wind's comment and the current conversation, but then made the connection. "So why aren't you happy with where you are, Jules?"

"Sorry?"

Juliet wore a black velvet jacket with skin-tight jeans. Even with heels on, she was still shorter than Grace.

"You're constantly dreaming of a fantasy life far away from Gateshead. What is it that you so dislike about your life here?"

"I don't know what you're talking about."

"It's as though there's another life you feel you should be living, and it's by some bad luck of the draw that you're stuck with this one in Gateshead."

The bus arrived and they sat at the front, Juliet by the window, Grace the aisle.

"You try to make the best of it, Jules, but it feels as if you're just lying in wait for your real life to begin."

"Well, you know when we finish school I'm travelling around Europe."

"But I always assumed you'd come back."

"I mean I am. I promised James I would."

"I thought you'd travel together. Why doesn't he want to join you?"

"He wants to start university. He enjoys the system, Grace. He does well in it; he's not like you. If you're in it—and it works for you—it can be the most wonderful thing."

Grace bit her tongue. The only reason James 'worked' in the social system was because he made himself visible when needed and blended into the background at all other times.

He's just like the colour beige.

She suppressed a cynical comment before asking, "He's okay with you going away for a year on your own?"

"He doesn't really have a choice, does he? It's what I want to do."

"And what, you'll stay together while you're away?"

Grace did though secretly admire the way Juliet approached her studies and pursued her goals. She thought in cause and effect, choice and consequence, while she herself was still resisting these universal laws.

"Of course. I mean, we're not going to break up; we're just going to enjoy different things with our time. The affection isn't going to change."

Grace thought the whole rationale mad, and Juliet delusional.

"Shouldn't you be doing something that's so important to you with the person you love? How can you isolate what will be such a distinct, defining experience for you from the rest of your relationship?"

"Why not? It may put some strain on the relationship but it wouldn't necessarily break it."

Grace remembered her mother telling her father once, when he was moaning about his job at the previous firm, to stop complaining and just quit. Her father had defended his predicament, saying, "It's only the office politics I despise. I love everything else in my life. I can stick it out."

"Dylan, you can't be happy with your health, home life and golf handicap, then be miserable at work from nine to five and think that's okay," Carla said. "You can't fence off one part of your life and expect it not to influence the other aspects. Grievances about the job will seep in and slowly start to impact upon your health, golf swing and life at home with me and the kids."

"Carla, I love you, but occasionally you can take it too far with all this integrated living, holistic mumbo jumbo stuff. I'm fine. I can push through."

The week after their conversation, Dylan quit the job. Carla was incredibly persuasive when she wanted to be.

Grace, in all sincerity, said to Juliet, "I think you should break up with James before you leave and fully commit yourself to your time overseas. You want to involve yourself in everything over there— all the new, exciting opportunities—and you can't do that if you're worrying about what James is doing here."

"We'll see." Juliet kept her eyes fixed outside the bus.

Grace knew this topic was no longer a point of discussion. Juliet wouldn't deviate from her plans. She had it all worked out in her head and nothing would alter this, so she quickly changed the subject. "Well, if you adore all things French, why don't you start living aspects of your dream Parisian lifestyle today?"

"What? Wear a red beret, buy a baguette, some cheese and ride around town on a moped?" Juliet joked.

"No, I don't mean that way, Jules. What I'm trying to say is that it's not like you'll arrive in Paris and fit right in. This idealised French lifestyle exists only in your head, so why not embrace some Gallic attitudes now to make the culture shock less severe?"

Now it was Juliet's turn to think Grace delusional, and she told her as much.

"I know you complain that Gateshead has no real history or culture, but it's not like you'll travel to Europe and suddenly find yourself in paradise. You're the one, Jules, who brings the excitement and meaning to life. You'll still have to take the bus over there. Why would it be any different to the bus we're riding in now?"

Juliet looked out the bus window. They were approaching the Gateshead Racecourse. "Because of what's outside the window, you fool. Like hello, we'd be staring at the Eiffel Tower!"

"So you're telling me you can only be happy when the view outside the window is agreeable to you?"

Juliet shifted her body to look Grace dead in the eye. "Yeah, pretty much."

Grace desperately wanted to counsel Juliet not to depend on the scene outside the window for her happiness and to stop seeking satisfaction in things outside herself. Instead, she said, "You can't only be happy when the sun's shining."

She also wanted to tell Juliet that expecting the world to appear a certain way guaranteed a painful existence if she couldn't accept all views from all bus windows exactly as they appeared in the moment. Only loving acceptance of the current view—the racecourse and its historic grandstand—would allow Juliet to appreciate the sight of the Eiffel Tower one day.

Grace knew her words would fall on deaf ears, so stayed silent.

63 | Finding the Extra in the Ordinary

Grace finished helping her mother prepare lunch in the kitchen and then went outside. She sat on the plastic chair under the pergola and gazed onto the flower garden. She spied a tightly curled bud on the yellow rose bush. Her mother had told her the variety's name, but she'd forgotten it.

"How easy it is to take flowers for granted," Grace said without a sense of awe or amazement in her voice, simply a disinterested observation of fact. She found gardening extremely tedious and couldn't comprehend how her mother found so much gratification in this pastime.

"Grace, nature will soon teach you the same philosophy I've been teaching you but without words," the Wind said. "Unfortunately, it's a misguided expectation that life should perennially be in bloom. If you spent more time in nature you would know that this was biologically impossible."

Carla opened the back screen door and shouted to Dylan and Abel still inside, "Seeing the sun's out and it's not too cold, we'll eat out here. There's no need to be cooped up indoors."

On Carla's orders, Abel and Dylan ended up moving the outdoor table three times during the course of the meal in order to remain in the warmth of the sun. Grace, though, was preoccupied with the changing shadow patterns. She had never bothered in the past to notice the subtleties of light falling across the garden like this before.

"Witness the variations nature brings to spaces as you deeply connect with various cycles of energy," the Wind reminded.

After a dessert of poached pears with chocolate ganache and custard, the table was cleared. Grace stayed in her seat.

"Train yourself to view the ordinary with fresh eyes, Grace, otherwise you'll forever be chasing extraordinary future moments, which whisk you away from the now. Witness the rare in the everyday, not only on holidays and special occasions."

"Tell me then, what's so special about this here and now?"

"Well, Grace, you've mistakenly entered this scene with a false sense of entitlement. Believing that you deserve to witness something exceptional, and demanding the universe put on a little song and dance for you, is what destroys the beauty that lies untouched in this moment. Be content with life as it is, then all of life's brilliance will touch you."

"Okay, I think I get it," said Grace, "but how do I distinguish between the extra and the ordinary?"

"Breathe in and out and feel the waves of your breath as you tap into the rhythm of your being that lies beneath whatever it is you're doing. Herein rests the extra in the ordinary."

"But I'm not doing anything at the moment."

"Yes, you are, Grace, you're being. So as you're sitting here, sense your legs touching the ground, tailbone sinking into the cushion and spine resting on the back of the chair."

"Alright."

"Now pick up the glass tumbler in front of you and feel your fingers wrap around the circumference of the glass."

"Aha," she replied.

"And then really taste the water as it trickles its way down the back of your throat and notice the weight of the glass as you place it back on the table."

Scores of sensations and minor gestures she'd never paid much attention to erupted to the surface, like how quickly she dragged the glass away from her lips after taking a sip.

"Mindfulness, Grace. Where are you focusing your attention? Your past decisions and actions led you here, and today's choices will determine the quality of your tomorrows."

Where is my attention?

"You were aware of this last mouthful of water, but where were you for all the other sips you took at lunch?"

Grace couldn't answer. Most of the practicalities that constituted everyday living—food, shelter and a certain sanitary level—she took for granted. She barely acknowledged the continuous stream of fresh, clean water in the house—in her glass, the shower, the dishwasher— let alone the availability of electricity and the basic infrastructure that made Gateshead function as a city.

Carla called out, "Okay, young miss, enough with the daydreaming, let's go do the food shopping."

Grace instantly forgot her lack of gratitude for the water that cleansed and revived her, and followed her mother to the car.

64 | Ebb and Flow

G race was frustrated and impatient waiting for the traffic lights
to change to allow Carla to turn right onto the main road.

The Wind told her to sense the ebb and flow of the traffic. "Feel
as if you're captured by the red light, then liberated as it turns green
and the traffic is free-flowing again."

It was a succession of ebb and flow all the way to the Central
Markets, which bothered her poor mother, who kept cursing the
traffic while kicking herself for not taking a different route.

"Rhythm and flow arise from alternation—ebb and flow—as one
state smoothly blends into another. We are permanently in a state
of change, Grace, because life is not static, it's transitional. You're
continually adjusting and fluctuating," the Wind reminded her.

"So how can I help Mum enjoy, or at least accept, this undulating
journey?"

"Grace, I don't think she's willing to tune into the serenity of the
stop-start traffic just yet, so simply tell her that you love her and feel
the affection emanating so strongly from your heart that the love
you have for her can't be contained within this car, that it expands
far beyond the shell of the vehicle."

Months ago, she would've resisted the Wind's instructions, but it
was a sign of how far she'd come that she now knew it best to act
on them. Grace thought, felt and told her mother how much she
loved her, and automatically Carla's hunched shoulders dropped and
a tranquil smile returned to her face.

"Can I add one more thing?" the Wind asked. "When you pick

up that underlying current—the uninhibited expression of each moment that transcends the mind—the flow on the surface may appear rough or choppy, but know that underneath it is seamless. Getting frustrated by traffic jams and red lights is the equivalent of swimming upstream. By becoming one with the pulse that runs beneath the traffic, you turn into the witness. By observing the direction of the stream, you're far better able to surrender to its flow and let it effortlessly carry you to your next destination."

Grace looked down at her hands crossed neatly in her lap. The sheer exhaustion that usually cloaked her body released itself as she consciously forfeited the many battles raging in her mind.

"One more word, if I may? Just as you relaxed into the traffic's ebb and flow, use this experience to mine the stillness that exists between each rising and falling movement in your life."

⁂

Later that evening at the dinner table, Grace hastily polished off her meal, barely putting her knife and fork down between bites.

"With food, Grace, taste it, don't think about it," the Wind said. "Enjoy your food with your eyes and nose as well as with your taste buds. Slow down and merge with the food's texture, whether it's the crunchiness of coarse ground peanut butter or the fleshy suppleness of a fig."

"I know, I know. I eat too quickly."

She was aware how frequently she snacked on food and sipped herbal teas while wandering from room to room around the house. She ate apples while typing on the laptop, tahini from the jar with a teaspoon and Nutella with her fingers. Being around bowls of nuts or chips was also something of a challenge for Grace; she could never have just the one.

"I know you can't resist a bowl of nuts, especially honey-roasted cashews, but I've watched you, Grace. You reach across the table and surreptitiously grab a massive handful as you eat each cashew individually, but it's still a greedy, grasping gesture."

She was embarrassed; there was no escaping the Wind. Grace desperately reached for things across tables all the time, hardly ever asking the person next to her to pass the salt and pepper or butter, or whatever it was she wanted.

"Grace, from now on take only one nut from the bowl at a time," the Wind said. "Witness the rhythm of your eating style. At what pace are you lifting the fork into your mouth? How quickly are you guzzling your drink? I want you to get into the routine of waiting ten seconds between each mouthful of food."

The first time Grace tried to wait ten seconds between bites was torture. She was so used to quickly shovelling food into her mouth to reach that instant high.

"The same approach applies when you're responding to your emails. Are you firing replies off without any contemplation of their content whatsoever?" Grace didn't have a chance to respond before the Wind added, "Agonising and stressing over them doesn't count as contemplation."

"Excuse me, but when did it become 'Let's pick on Grace day?'"

"Grace, when you have enough self-respect to step into the life you're destined to live—the life of your soul—you will quit letting your grace spill into the drains of life."

"But how? How do I this?" she implored.

"By being loving and appreciative of all people and all circumstances."

"Well, I obviously just can't go around hugging trees and people and that." Her sarcasm had come to the fore. "That's just plain ridiculous."

"Grace, subtle is the language of the soul; forceful is the personality's voice. Love isn't just about the obvious acts, but also the unseen realm. When you can sense minuscule changes—within yourself, others and the atmosphere—you're moving closer to your imperial command centre," the Wind said. "The universe will first send subtle hints, and if you don't listen, then you'll really be sent messages that grab your attention."

"Like what?"

"Diminishing health, a disastrous accident or the meltdown of a relationship. Through these challenges we are forced to start paying attention to the signals we're receiving that we consistently ignore, from the understated to the glaringly obvious."

65 | Sensing the Subtle

In the car on the way home from school, Carla brought Grace up-to-date with her best friend's circumstances.

"I love Caroline, but at times I want to strangle her," she said.

Grace had often heard from Carla how Caroline hated her job as a pharmaceutical sales representative and dreamed of opening a corner deli in one of the more affluent parts of town.

In Caroline's words, "It'd serve antipasti; marinated olives, char-grilled artichoke hearts and caramelised figs stuffed with goat cheese. Just a beautiful little deli you could pop into after work and pick up some indulgences for supper."

Carla's response was the same every time. "Stop talking about it, Carol, and just do it."

Caroline had enough money saved for the venture and knew enough about the produce she wished to stock. What she didn't know about running a retail operation she could easily learn. Her numerous responses differed, but the meaning stayed the same. The defeatist procrastination ranged from, "It's not the right time," to "I need to work a bit longer to save for my retirement," to "Health insurance is so expensive." On and on the litany of excuses went.

"I block my ears now, Grace," her mother said.

"I don't understand. If Caroline wants this gourmet deli so much, why doesn't she just get on and do it?" Grace asked.

Carla replied, "Darling, at your age I'd say the same thing, but as you get older your fears become more powerful than your desires. You don't believe security exists in newness, and so fears, not your passions, begin dictating your life."

The Wind explained to Grace that Caroline continuously received soft messages from the universe—her amount of hours at work were cut, there was a great retail space going with a cheap lease in the most swanky part of town, and she had met an interior designer who offered to do the project at cost so he could promote the retail fit-out in his portfolio. Although she felt energised and excited when speaking about this business idea, she was otherwise drained.

The Wind added, "Caroline's been guided all along to pursue her dream, but didn't follow the first dot that would've led to the next, so eventually a completed picture could materialise. When we can't sense the faint, it means we'll only listen to the obvious, and so something dramatic needs to happen to gain our attention for a course re-correction."

Grace nodded, recalling a previous conversation with the Wind about connecting the dots. How had the Wind put it?

There aren't isolated events in life; everything is a connect-the-dots game. Look at events from a deeper perspective; nothing's an isolated experience, only interrelated dots allowing new light to shine through so more of your soul can be revealed on earth.

"The subtle is the colossal," the Wind now said. "Don't for a minute believe it's small, for it's the way in and through the lessons of life. Learn to perceive these soft and subtle distinctions: changes in the air, the amount of light in the sky, a person's facial reactions and messages your body gives you, coupled with your inner guidance. They all prophesy the unfolding future. Partner with the faint and the hushed, Grace; act in partnership. The obvious will force you into a position of reaction, whereas the subtle offers power and discernment. Don't mistake it as weak and insignificant."

Yet another divine paradox.

66 | Peace Within

It was Wednesday after recess and Grace had a tummy ache. She went to visit the surgery nurse who told her rather dismissively that there was nothing seriously wrong with her, to take some paracetamol and return to class.

Grace was indignant. "What would you know? You're useless!" she screamed and slammed the surgery door behind her. She hugged her stomach while crossing the courtyard back to the history lesson. As soon as she sat back down in her chair, she castigated herself for not responding more calmly.

"How could you when you weren't even thinking calm thoughts before you walked into her office?"

"Man, I don't even know where my mind was."

Actually she did know. She was replaying a particular childhood memory. On her second birthday, Grace (with a pixie hair cut), wasn't allowed to lean too close to her birthday cake to blow out the candles. Her father held her back from the candle flames to protect her, but as a two-year-old she intuited this action as a denial of life's pleasures. From that moment on, happiness—at all times—felt at least an arm's distance away.

The Wind cut short her flashback. "Grace, really get to know the triggers that hook into you, so that you can unhook them before they start tearing you apart. Responding calmly isn't an option if that emotion isn't a dominant vibration in you. You can't draw on what you don't have, so I want you to develop an internal peace bank account."

A smile formed on her lips. "An internal peace bank account?"

"Yes," the Wind replied. "An account you can draw on for peace in situations such as these. You build this bank account up with regular deposits of peaceful thoughts, feelings and actions, which you can then call on at will when you're required to make a withdrawal. Remember, you can't draw on an account that's not in credit."

The Wind went on to remind Grace that her most consistent thoughts and beliefs determined the quality of her life. Angry thoughts running through her mind before an incident meant that she would more than likely react in anger, while loving thoughts allowed for a completely different response. A belief that all men in the world were no good meant she'd experience exactly that, to the detriment of every future relationship she'd have with the opposite sex.

While she understood the concept intellectually, Grace rarely responded in a composed manner as her mind was usually preoccupied in a futile attempt to alter and erase past memories.

"Don't take the nurse's judgment personally. Just see it as a missed opportunity to watch your reaction as an observer."

Grace knew she had messed up, but instead of forgiving herself and learning from the experience, her instinct was to lash out.

⁓

After class, Madison wanted to join Grace at the canteen for lunch.

"Don't feel like it," she said and blew her off.

Man, why do I have to deal with people? I can't wait for the day when robots rule the world.

"But life is all about relationships, Grace. And the quality of your relationships reflects your progress because they mirror the degree of peace—or angst—you're connecting to inside. Ask yourself how others are responding to you energetically."

"Sorry, I'm not open to hearing this right now."

"Everyone's just doing the best they can from the position they are in, Grace. If they knew better, they'd do better, and even when they know better, acting from this higher perspective takes an enormous amount of courage, energy, commitment, and awareness. Changing your beliefs and behaviours—when you've lived unconsciously most of your life—is not an easy proposition."

215

Grace marched to the canteen (hoping Madison wouldn't see her), grabbed a chocolate bar and pushed to the front of the queue with no "excuse me," "pardon" or "sorry." She knew what she was doing, but this habit of self-medicating through food was a life-long pattern. She wished she could be still and observe her emotions like a passer-by, watching a raging river from the safety of the riverbank, but dealing with her discomfort by devouring sweets and entering a state of numbness was routine behaviour.

She greedily demolished the chocolate in the girls' restrooms, the cubicle acting as a cone of both silence and shame. With barely a breath between each bite, Grace didn't even taste the chocolate. Brooding, she made a mental hit list of people to direct her anger at.

Jenny hadn't returned her email about visiting the national archives so they could work on their jointly-authored history paper together.

Right, a bitchy follow-up email to remind her.

Oliver still hadn't lent her the latest Missy Black novel like he promised weeks ago.

From now on I'm not talking to him. I'll permanently freeze him out of my life.

Making others feel bad made her feel better about herself.

Is this the only route I know to get high?

"Your personality got a little dusted up and wants revenge, so yes to the above."

"It is personal. That dumb nurse didn't take my stomach ache seriously."

"And you think she'll take you more seriously after you told her she's useless? Do you realise how you keep backsliding by repeating the same behaviour over and over, never once breaking the cycle? I know that change is a slow process, but you must commit to it."

Grace knew the Wind was right. It was time for some serious homework. She flipped the toilet lid down, found a pen at the bottom of her bag, opened the back of her graph book, sat, and began writing line upon line.

Bring awareness to my doing through consciously connected breathing.

When I'm holding on so tight it's impossible to detach and float effortlessly.

Witness the wider cycles at play and tap into the current flowing beneath them.

Listening to the beat inside will bring me back to myself.

I block the flow of life when I judge people and situations.

There is benefit in each and every unfolding life scene.

Though I move through transitory states, my soul—the truth—is constant.

Every problem holds the solution within it.

Thinking shouldn't replace experiencing.

All moments are impermanent, ever-changing and in divine order.

Acknowledging planetary rhythms stops me placing my worries at the centre of the universe.

Grace recalled as many of the Wind's teachings as possible. She had to take this moment into a field of light.

I'm so sick of breaking myself.

67 | Ingenuity

Later that afternoon in her bedroom, the Wind returned with a new topic for Grace to ponder. "Be ingenious instead of innovative because ingenuity comes from your intuition; it's not linear. From now on I want you accessing knowledge from different realms, not solely these books in front of you. Ordered thinking is fortified by creative thinking."

Grace felt a draft of cool air surround the stack of books on her desk. "But my intuition only provides me with fragments, never the complete picture."

"And think how boring it would be to have the whole story in one go!"

"Not really. It'd solve all my problems."

"We've been through this, Grace. That's not the point of life."

Grace wanted to argue back but refrained herself.

"Behind those fragments and flashes of intuition, a certain knowing exists. Follow that knowing; chase all its possible realities. There are more pearls of wisdom in the fragments than in the sum total of all these books in front of you."

She yawned, actually wishing for the mindless preoccupation of *Teen Vogue*.

"Occasionally epiphanies do strike," the Wind said, "and on other occasions understanding unfolds over time. Who's to know? Time can't be boxed in, which is why I want you to draw on the far-distant past and the far-flung future to solve your problems. Tap into alternate realities that exist—not just you in your bedroom bashing out words on a laptop. Travel to other realms and places."

What? Aren't I supposed to be on a constant upward trajectory?
She felt as lost as the first day the Wind entered her life.

"Grace, remember the process is two steps forward, one step back, on a higher turn of the spiral, eventually arriving full circle. Now, where were we? Intuitive flashes are both a fraction and an entirety."

"Oh, the land of contradictions again—unfinished and finished. Pray tell, how does one do that?"

"One would intrinsically recognise an idea's complete form and enjoy the process of making it visible."

"Doublespeak. Just great! Precisely what I want to hear."

"Allow the ingenuity to come from within."

She closed her eyes, swept clean the inner recesses of her mind and focused on her breath. A few seconds later, she gave up in total desperation.

"Don't force it, Grace. Intuition comes to you, it doesn't appear on demand. You feel your way into it."

She focused her awareness within herself and felt infinite love and gratitude for her and the Wind's original and inspired relationship. She recalled a recent history project at school where she was required to research the Great Chicago Fire and then later that same afternoon she spied a billboard for *Chicago*, the musical.

"Signs and synchronicities are forever being sent, Grace. It's up to you to respond to the serendipity," the Wind said. "Time to take a break. What do you feel?"

"Me? What do I feel?"

"Yes, you. You're responsible for what you're producing, and your thoughts are creating this feeling of imagined difficulty with your homework. Why do you suppose you're doing this?"

Grace was dumbfounded.

"I'll be with you for the rest of your life, Grace, but if there's one lesson I can press the importance of on you . . ."

How often had she heard this? The Wind said practically every tutorial in its syllabus was vital.

". . . you must take personal responsibility for your own life; nobody else will do it for you. This is not something you outsource,

Grace. Everything in your life—the good, bad and the very ugly—represents your belief patterns. If you have an off day, you own it, and if it's an awesome day, you claim it too."

Grace pondered the Wind's words, and the silence between them appeared to stretch for eternity.

"Be in touch with your emotions, but know they're not you. Be in union with the invisible source underneath them."

"Okay. I'll go for a quick walk around the block to clear my head and be open to a new way of approaching my homework."

"And muse on the fact that ingenuity comes from curiosity."

Another fundamental lesson in the curriculum.

68 | Patterns in Nature

Grace walked down the driveway thinking about her study routine. When sitting down at her desk, she usually mucked about on the internet for a good hour or two, and by the time she tackled her homework, she was spent. Her best energy went to reading gossip websites and social networking, not completing her assignments.

"Grace, again, it's not about what you're doing, but where your head and heart are at while you're doing it. Clearing your mind is fundamental to conserving your power; it assists you in holding on to one particular stream of energy for any length of time."

As she conversed with the Wind, it became clear that most things required both a planning and preparation stage. It wasn't as though she miraculously turned up to a friend's place with a birthday present in hand. She first needed to think of a thoughtful gift, go to the shops, buy the present and card, carry them home, wrap the gift, find some ribbon in her mother's stationery drawer to match the wrapping paper, compose a draft message of the birthday card, then actually write the card, and finally deliver the parcel to her friend. The present with the perfect bow didn't magically appear on the night of the party. A series of steps were needed to achieve the desired outcome, and the planning usually took far more time and thought than the actual doing.

Grace crossed the park to climb up the oak tree by the mini-roundabout. She wanted to sit in one of its lower branches. She placed her hands on one branch and both legs on the trunk to hoist herself up.

Maybe while walking home from the bus each day I can plan how to tackle my homework?

She knew what the Wind would say to this. "When you're walking home, focus on where your feet are treading, not the thoughts treading water in your mind."

She did sometimes think about her assignments during the day, but when sitting down to start them in the evening she mostly drew a blank. Perhaps if she carried a notebook around during the day to jot her itinerant thoughts down, she wouldn't be forced to start with the 'dreaded blank page' when she finally sat down to commence the work. Grace often felt she should've finished her homework before even starting it, given how much brain power and emotional energy she'd already devoted to the issue. Some assignments could've been completed thrice over given the amount of mental effort she'd already expended on them.

Already stressed about an essay due in three weeks' time, she coached herself as the Wind would. "Banish the unease from your system, otherwise it'll be a long three weeks carrying that dead weight around your neck."

The notebook idea was good. It would get the thoughts out of her head and onto the page and stop her dwelling on them. Starting with a blank canvas always made her anxious, and this way the first line would already be drawn. And she was a far better editor than writer anyway. She flashed back to the Wind's words on stillness and how this was the first step towards creativity and ingenuity the second.

Invite ingenuity in by being lost in stillness.

She found a way to balance herself in the tree so that her back fit snugly against the trunk and her legs ran out horizontally along the branch, then closed her eyes.

The Wind said, "Appreciate the complexity of the problem, move to stillness and let your intuition deliver the ingenious solution," before adding another caveat. "But first, appreciate your stuckness. Only by accepting where you are, can you change any and everything."

Grace awoke what appeared like hours later, but in reality only a few minutes had passed. Surprised she hadn't fallen out of the tree, she felt like she'd been transported elsewhere.

"Grace, appreciating your predicaments means knowing yourself. When, and for what, do you have the most energy? Which environments bring out your genius? Who or what revives you? When do you prefer to eat? These preferences are not your identity, but knowing how to be in sync with them will help your life flow with greater ease."

"To the last point, I'd rather have a bigger lunch than dinner," Grace replied. "I'm not as hungry in the evening, but that's when we eat as a family and when the majority of people go to restaurants. Anyway, most people are either too busy with work or studies for a big lunch during the weekday, so it's a sandwich on the go or at your desk. It sucks."

"Nothing is good or bad, Grace. I want you to really be with the moment that's happening before you. Know your body's internal biological clock and how to work with—not against—it. Your body goes through a cycle every twenty-four to twenty-five hours, so synchronise with your circadian rhythm."

"My what?"

"Summon it back in your mind, Grace; we already spoke about it—your roughly twenty-four hour personal cycle."

"Oh, yeah, gotcha."

"Cues from outside rhythms influence our internal biorhythms. Unfortunately for many adults though, artificial lighting, long working hours and jet lag from international travel leads corporate life to dictate their circadian rhythm more than nature."

"I am this," Grace said, patting the knobbly branch of the tree.

"Yes, you are. You're made of the very same matrix of energy. Everything in the universe is."

Grace sank further into the branch holding her aloft, imagining it and her melding as one.

"See how much presence you can bring to the cycles of waking, bathing, eating, and sleeping," the Wind said.

"So the gist of what you're saying is, knowing there's a daily cycle we each go through, I should figure out how to make mine best work for me, like Mum and Papa do with their morning routine?"

"Yes, Grace. Observe the light-dark patterns and the associated increase and decrease of activity within you. How can you take advantage of these changing conditions? You maximise or minimise the natural rhythm of your life by understanding the choices you make."

"And my life situation is the sum of my choices."

"Those you make consciously and subconsciously and those made today as well as at a time before here."

Grace in time discovered dusk was the most powerful time of day for her, each sunset electrifying her heart.

"The underlying cosmic patterns affect every aspect of daily life, as they influence when we wake, sleep, work, rest, eat, and procreate. Grace, how we spend our days is how we spend our lives."

Grace was confused. "But why do I need to know these patterns?"

"By reading patterns in nature—and in yourself—you'll come to recognise the changing and the changeless and how all events in life occur in the order they're meant to. You'll be one with the interactions between heaven and earth. You'll also become more radiant, fiery and compelling in your manner as you connect to the dark, rich, cosmic and mysterious divine order of all things."

To Grace, the Wind really was the fount of all knowledge. "Do all patterns show movement?"

"Many types of patterns exist and within them variation and contrast are crucial. While flow implies natural ease, it occasionally comes through mastering pull and push, as well as alternation and repetition. It's why I want you to learn how to move freely between the different modes of operating in this world."

"Hmmm. Wind, you don't really 'live' on this planet and we, us humans, often have to do stuff we don't really want to do. We're exhausted but have a deadline, so have to push on through; we're tired and want to sleep in but need to get up and go to school; we want a break in the middle of the day to relax but can't as we have classes. So while what you're saying sounds great in theory," Grace said, "it's pretty much impossible to synchronise our wake-sleep patterns with the sun's rising and setting in today's modern world." She didn't even mention doctors, nurses, police, paramedics, security staff, and many others who work nightshifts.

"You're right, Grace, this modern day life isn't geared to respecting nature's living wisdom, but that's no excuse to abdicate responsibility and not try," the Wind said. "When you know in your soul where in their cycles the sun and moon are, you connect to the force powering you and this earth. Feel the gift of life you're receiving every moment—without fail."

Grace noted with displeasure how she always seemed to see problems whereas the Wind saw solutions.

A glass half empty or half full?

"You inherently understand this, Grace, you see it with your own physical eyes. For nature to grow it needs water and sunlight. Plants are utterly dependent on this nourishment, and if you're also made from the same energy, consider how it is you're nurturing yourself," the Wind said.

"I guess it's one thing you've really impressed on me. When people aim for balance, they're trying to balance external things out 'there'," and she stretched her arms out wide, "but I need to achieve balance in 'here'," then quietly pointed both index fingers to her heart. "Then I can take this balance in 'here' to the world out 'there'," she said, elongating her arms again. "But Wind, why do so many people chase balance? Why is it seen as the Holy Grail?"

"The balance most people chase is an illusion, Grace. They forget that balance is ever-elusive due to its constantly changing form. They think they've conquered it and with the flap of a butterfly's wings, they've lost it again. It's a constantly moving target, which is why rhythm is fundamental to wellbeing."

Grace leapt from the branch, landing smoothly on the grass and began walking home. "But all the women's magazines tell us perfect balance exists, and it's our fault if we're not achieving it."

"Grace, the version of balance these magazines sell implies a fixed, one-off ending of 'happily ever after'. You bring balance to your internal mind as a frequently repeating process."

"But I want to be perfect and in balance," she wailed.

The Wind replied, "You must be your natural form of grace first. You can't chase perfection or balance outside of yourself. Grace, ponder this truth from Ralph Waldo Emerson: 'Beauty without grace is the hook without the bait.'"

This was not the response she wanted.

69 | Trust

The Wind began educating Grace on the stages involved in the unfolding process as she walked home from the bus stop the following Monday.

"When something—anything—begins making itself known within or outside of you, it may only be partly visible. You might notice an inkling of something there, but it's a prerequisite of the process that the hunch must be carried for a length of time before it's birthed into reality."

Grace nodded and felt herself to be lit from within. Such was the strength of the feeling she now understood why the Wind sought time and again to train her inner eye to pay attention to subtle sensations and discover beauty in the most miniscule of details.

"Can you catch the possibility of an idea not yet born to fruition? Would you even know how to shepherd it into the light of day? And can you be the space for the inspiration to blossom in its own time without you stamping your personal agenda all over it?"

When the Wind spoke in questions Grace felt as if it'd take her a week for a half-intelligent response to materialise.

"The universe needs a vacuum of space to work through."

Grace tried to open the front security door, but it was locked. Her mother must have popped out to run some errands.

"We've spoken about this before, but it's such an important point to readdress: Mother Nature unfolds in her own time, at her own pace, when the conditions are conducive for her to do so," the Wind said. "Life can only unfurl as quickly as it's able to. Grace, remember to be fifteen and not twenty-nine. Live your high school years to the full and learn to drop this angst about the future, about your life after graduation. Enjoy your adolescence within the total scheme of your life and find comfort in the mystery. Be okay with the vagueness of the unknown and through the unknowable you'll be born into a new glory."

Grace figured this lesson on cycles, rhythm and timing was worth repeating given how much she struggled to embody the principles.

As she went to sit by the lounge room window, the Wind said, "Grace, it'll take you the better half of your life to integrate this wisdom."

She didn't fight the Wind's words, instead imagined the magic of life revealing itself around her.

"You don't know when—or how—the flower will blossom, and therein lies life's splendour. The seed eventually flowers, then dies, and soon you'll be viewing this exquisite process from my perspective."

She knew better than to question the Wind on points such as these, so she tilted her head back and closed her eyes.

"We can't force time, Grace. There's an organic naturalness to how life reveals itself to us and fits the requirements of the moment. Life divinely opens up when we rise to meet it, and the universe responds to our rising."

Grace's body relaxed and her mind disengaged as her soul stirred. Whispering in her ears as she dozed off were the words, "When you wake, fall into the rhythm of surrender. On me you can trust."

70 | The Importance of Dreams

The next morning her dream was still playing itself out as her eyes slowly opened, heavy with sleep. Grace tried capturing the visions in her dreams, but there was no pen or paper nearby. A thought about her dreaded physics class now entered her mind and the dream vanished. Annoyed, she attempted to go back in but couldn't find the entry point.

Where did the dream go?

The next evening before bed, Grace placed a pen and notebook by her pillow. She drifted off to sleep and put in a request to the Wind. "Can you please come with me into the slumber world and bring my dream back for me in the morning? Pretty please?"

She stirred the next morning with bits and pieces of the dream coming to her—a shopping mall, eating junk food, a police officer—but beyond that she couldn't recall much else. The tighter she squeezed her eyes, the less there was to recall. There was no cohesive story, just a few random images.

The Wind gently said, "Allow yourself to remember. Don't force the dream to reappear; instead invite it to awaken within you. Fully inhabit the feeling you first woke with, then capture the specifics."

Grace yawned, still half-asleep.

"What's the predominant emotion? Did you wake up feeling scared, excited or nervous? The feeling the dream leaves us with when we open our eyes gives us a clue as to how the images relate to our waking life. Be with this feeling and question why you needed to awaken with this particular sensation, and we'll go from there."

"Does everybody dream, Wind?" Grace asked while yanking her pyjama sleeves down from her elbows.

"Everybody dreams, though only a few have opened themselves up to their inner life, of which dreams are merely one small part."

That night after a meal at her grandparents' house, she stirred some honey into a warm glass of milk and spritzed lavender aromatherapy spray on her pillows.

"These are just crutches, Grace. Dreams occur with or without the trinkets. But they're nice symbolic gestures, so carry on."

As she dozed off, she heard the Wind whispering in her ear, "Sweet dreams."

Grace woke before the alarm with a feeling of calm steadiness. She scribbled down what imagery she retained of the dream—stars, houses, telescopes, and a baseball game. Once she finished, class began.

"Okay, so you woke up feeling peaceful. Where in the last twenty-four hours have you experienced that emotion in your waking life?"

"In Veronika's kitchen last night when she described how cooking teaches you about quality, quantity and texture, as well as embellishment and reduction," Grace answered. "And that these are important life skills too."

"Tell me the essence of each scene of the dream."

"Firstly, I was looking at the stars through a telescope."

"So that could be distilled to . . ."

"What do you mean?"

"We're wanting to sum up what happened in each stage of the dream in order for the main theme to reveal itself. You wanted to magnify an issue? Or bring some distant thing closer?"

"The latter, I think."

They went through each of Grace's scribbled lines to summarise each scene.

"Next, look at the symbols in the dream. Houses have universal meanings, but certain types of houses have significance only to you.

Let's now go through the dream again and this time interpret what the symbols represent."

"But why do we dream, Wind?"

"Our dreams exist to guide and connect us to the eternal part of ourselves and to provide us with feedback on how we lived and expressed our truth over the past twenty-four hours. They also weave additional material into the memory system."

"Why do they speak to us in symbols?" she asked.

"You have studied ancient Egyptian history and learned that they communicated through hieroglyphics, right?"

"Aha."

"Well, words are just a mental interpretation of symbols. Universal symbols speak to the subconscious mind and they're independent of language. Unfortunately, most of us have lost—or never learned—the art of reading life symbolically."

"But why are symbols important? Doesn't language communicate everything anyway?"

"In symbols deeper meanings and associations exist, and while these associations are individual to us, they're also part of the greater collective," the Wind explained. "Dreams remind us to first know ourselves, as only then the wisdom of the world can reach us. It means opening ourselves up to the invisible, to the 99% of existence we can't see with our naked eye. You set your course in the darkness by the stars."

Grace wanted to go back to sleep, to further traverse the terrain of her dream state.

"I want you to perceive your dreams and life symbolically, Grace."

"But how?"

"Begin each day by decoding your dream's communication to you —the feeling you woke with, the distilled interpretations of each scene, the symbols and their associations; the messages contained therein."

"Dreams aren't literal then?"

"More often than not, dreams read deeper than their initial appearance."

"I sense that this dream's trying to tell me to let go of what others think of me, but I already know that," Grace said.

"Dreams might not always provide new insights, but instead confirm what we already know, remind us that we're on the right track, or nudge us to integrate the message more fully into our day-to-day lives. Be grateful for their guidance and open yourself to receiving further communication."

Grace wriggled her head free from the crevice of pillows.

"So what do you think your dream's bringing to your attention?"

"Well, after I looked at the stars, I was on a field and part of this famous baseball team, though I wasn't chosen to play that day. I don't know which team it was—you know I don't even like baseball—but I definitely had a seat on the bench. While I'm sitting there it hits me how much pressure the players are under—especially from the fans—and for some reason during the seventh-inning stretch I turn my back on the team and go sit in the bleachers as a spectator. I don't want to play with such intense pressure bearing down on me."

Grace was enjoying analysing her dream with the Wind and didn't want to get up and go to school.

"Wonderful, Grace! You're learning to view life from a different angle. We forget how limited we sometimes are in our day-to-day problem-solving abilities, and dreams help show us another way, if we let them."

"Can I trust them?"

"Absolutely, you can. Dreams come from us; this means their guidance is created specifically for us," the Wind said. "Let me ask you something. Whose advice would you trust more, a friend's or your dream's?"

"I'm not sure." She didn't consider that there was only one right answer.

"Always trust your dreams over an external source, because your dreams are an inner two-way dialogue with your soul."

"Oh, okay."

"Ask your soul for guidance while you're sleeping. Ask for doors that appear closed in your waking life to be open in your dreams. Focus on that intention throughout the day and right before bed reaffirm it, but most importantly . . ."

"Yes?"

"Believe that an answer will come to you."

She trusted the Wind's words.

"Train your eyes to see as well in the darkness as they do in the light. A vibrant dream life reminds us we're in constant communication with the divine, and it with us."

Grace finally rose.

71 | Breath of Life

"Take a breath, a deep inhale of fresh life force into your belly that pushes your ribs out to the side, and exhale the stale energy and let your tummy go flat. Don't think about what happened this morning; just know each breath in is an infusion of life. Believe this truth."

Grace admired the yoga teacher's calm serenity. With her platinum blonde hair scraped back into a tight bun she resembled a ballet dancer. With health and wellness becoming a greater social priority in society, her school had started offering weekly, Friday lunchtime yoga sessions to promote its holistic personal development program.

"Know every inhale is life being breathed into you and every exhale an opportunity to release all that drains you. Let this centre you as you use your breath to bring yourself back to the present moment. Your mind protests, but life waits to flow through you now, the only moment that ever exists."

Why do yoga teachers go on and on about the breath?

During savasana (corpse pose), Grace's shoulders melted into the rubber mat on top of the cold, hardwood gymnasium floor. She opened her eyes to see the yoga teacher tiptoe amongst the students lying on the ground. She sensed Grace's gaze and gave a smile that conveyed the knowing of her soul.

"Honour this moment, for it won't come again. Don't let your mind replay that argument with your parents this morning. The past no longer exists, and the future is only a fanciful idea. Deepen the length of your breath. No shallow breathing. Don't limit your greatness by not taking the breath you deserve. Use its rhythmic presence to bring you back to present moment awareness," the teacher said.

Some of the eleventh grade girls next to Grace were snickering.

Why bother being here then?

It wasn't as if the lesson was held during class time. Students (mainly girls) were here of their own volition, so Grace thought the least they could do was commit to the class instead of giggling their way through it.

"The most vital relationship you'll ever have in this world is with your breath. It's your essential life source. Inhale, exhale and pause. Again: inhale, exhale and pause." She waited a moment until she could see her students breathing in time. "Now this time inhale, pause, and exhale, pause. Breathe in and feel the world's possibilities, breathe out and let go of any stress and tension trapped in the body. Inhale, pause. Exhale, pause. The breath helps cultivate our sensing abilities, so build breath awareness into as many moments as possible during your school day. Grace. Love. Light."

Was she called by name, or was her name's resonance drawn on? Either way, Grace felt her next inhale bringing in a greater capacity for love and light to shine through her life.

72 | Mastering Waves

As the warmer weather made its first palpable appearance, the smell of new life began to burst through the spring air. To Grace's delight, her parents had arranged for her to have surfing lessons as part of her birthday present. She wanted to be a fully-fledged surfer chick by summer's start.

The local surf lifesaving club ran the lessons on alternate Saturday mornings at Headland's Bay, and she'd already had two lessons. The instructor said it took twenty years to learn to surf, and only at this point did the real fun commence. Grace instinctively felt she could learn a lot about life from the ocean.

Last time everyone in the class was able to stand upright on the board by lesson's end. Everyone, that was, bar Grace. By the time her brain told her legs to move and get into place, it was too late. She couldn't for the life of her catch a wave, or even the resulting foam. She looked at the others in the class, all girls mostly her own age, and surmised that they must've been surfing for years and now just wanted to refine their technique.

Grace vowed today's class would be a fresh start, like spring, and a reversal of fortune. But she still had no luck standing up. She had been given a different foam board from the other week, this one yellow, a little longer and a touch wider.

A general negativity crept into her, a dissatisfaction that swelled like one of the waves she couldn't catch. Floating in the water next to the instructor, Grace tried to keep the emotion out of her voice, but couldn't. "It's this board. I want the board I had last time; that's why I can't stand up. I don't know where to place my feet on this one. I can't concentrate properly."

This week's instructor, whose sand-washed, shoulder-length hair had taken on a natural, tousled windswept look, bellowed back across the white-capped waves, "Okay, I think there's some others in the van. What did it look like?"

"I can't remember exactly, but it was blue."

"Okay. Stay in the water, and I'll see if I can go find it."

The instructor eventually paddled back out and they swapped boards where the water was shallower. Grace strapped on her leg rope and headed back out into the ocean, psyching herself up.

Okay, I'm going to stand up. This is it, I can do it.

Grace saw the wave come and start to peak. She tried to get her feet in place before it broke but again was dumped. Her eyes welled with tears. She couldn't help it.

Why can't I do this?

She let out a scream in her mind and submerged herself underwater.

"Wind, where are you?"

"Grace, I am always here. Now, let me help. You're trying too hard; instead feel the water and join the expanse of the ocean."

Grace burst back up through the water's surface.

The Wind then said, "You believe that being able to stand on the board will mean that you've succeeded. But that's not success. Success lies in experiencing the present moment, irrespective of whether you're up standing on the board or not. The fact that you haven't caught a wave doesn't mean you're a failure."

Grace watched the instructor swim over to give one of the other girls a high five for riding a wave completely to the shore.

"Yes, it does." She let go of the board and pummelled both fists into the water.

"Grace, standing up on the board doesn't define you as a person. Again, you're placing your identity in achieving a goal. I'm trying to teach you to live the journey. The process—not the destination— matters most. Surfing is about feeling the surf."

Grace doubted she could ever do it.

"Feel how weightless you are in the water, the way the wetsuit clings to your body, the way the sun flickers on your face. Be in awe of the wave-eroded cliffs in the distance and delight in the smiles of those who are also in the water with you. Constant, narrow judging will only render you blind to the beauty around you."

She wanted to call it quits, but instead bit her lip and paddled out again. Her shoulders ached and her arms felt very heavy. As she lay quietly on the board she saw the swell of the wave she wanted to catch. With her chest raised off the board, her neck twisted back to watch the approaching wave, she heard the instructor shout across the water, "Paddle, Grace, go! Paddle, paddle, paddle!"

She did as instructed but she almost smacked her head on the board as her hands slipped off the edges and she plummeted under the water, wishing she were anywhere in the world but here.

Her critical inner voice started heckling her immediately. "What's wrong with you? Why can't you get up on the board? Everyone else has, why can't you? You're a total failure. I'm ashamed of you. You're an embarrassment."

When she popped up to the surface, the Wind asked, "Grace, have you heard the saying, 'Everywhere I go, there I am?'"

She ignored both the instructor and the Wind.

"Ignore me," the Wind said, "but I'll still keep talking. Grace, just know this, if you were at home right now you'd be having this same defeatist experience no matter what you were doing. Maybe the cake you decided to bake doesn't resemble anything like the photo in the recipe book when it comes out of the oven and you feel incompetent, or you run late to meet Madison and berate yourself for not leaving the house earlier. This is not about the surfboard. The content isn't the problem—it's always changing. The issue is the structure of your critical mindset."

"Go away!" she shouted.

"Everywhere you turn, your mind will be right there by your side. Learn to live with your thoughts, Grace. You can't run from that which will never leave you."

She sank to the bottom of the ocean, trying to get her feet to touch the wet bed of sand.

Maybe underwater I can escape my thoughts?

～⚬⚬⚬～

The leg rope attached to the board floating above her head forced Grace back to the surface spluttering for air.

"Grace, I know it can sometimes be hard to trust in a higher power when you're at home and stressed out by your homework, but here you're in the ocean. Feel the water cleansing you of all that you think you can't handle," the Wind explained. "You and the water are one; don't see the ocean as separate from you. Feel the water's still vibration. Success means living each breath fully, so enjoy this liminal moment in the water and blend with the ocean's oneness."

Grace instantly knew what to do. She floated with her arms and legs spread out in the shape of a star and submerged her ears underwater to replicate the sensation of being in the womb.

"Fall in love with your life, Grace, there's no other way. Watch the world so small below and rise above the soap opera of your thoughts."

Still attached to the board, she pretended to ride a unicycle as she treaded water.

"Now know this," the Wind said. "You'll have a completely different connection with the ocean when it powers you to stand up on the board. When the natural surge of water pushes you forth, you'll never doubt the divine again. But to get there, Grace, savour where you are now."

"Sometimes I wish I never met you." Grace wasn't angry in her tone—she certainly wasn't screaming—just disenchanted. "I can admit I wasn't particularly happy before I met you, but no offence, none of this self-realisation has made me any wiser. What you're teaching hasn't brought that much more joy to my life, and, in a way, I was quite comfortable with where I was before."

"Was that why you called out to me, Grace? Because your life was so super-fantastic and you were coping with its pressures calmly and confidently?"

"Granted, I wasn't in a good place the night we first met, and yes, I still have my misguided views of how the world works, but now that I'm 'aware'," she took her hands off the board to make the air quotes, "what good does it do me? Absolutely nothing!"

The Wind gave Grace space to vent her frustration.

"I now feel even more of a failure because I know better but don't do better. I'm still trapped. I'd rather have my unexamined life back, thank you very much."

After some time the Wind finally spoke. "There's no way back, Grace. Once the awakening process has begun, there's no path leading backwards. I know it's difficult assimilating this new information and putting it into practice, but you wrongly assume it'd be easier to live your days refusing to acquiesce to the greater designs of the cosmos. Only when you let your soul lead can—and will—change take place. You won't, in a day, be miraculously transformed into an enlightened being; this isn't a day's craft project. It's a venture for the rest of your life."

She was disappointed. Some small part of her crazily believed by year's end she'd have gained complete mastery over her life.

"Grace, earth school is lifetimes long, not a course you take at a community college over a few weeks or months, where on presentation of the graduation certificate you're done. Wisdom is more than knowledge; it's both knowing and doing. This is the classroom of life, and sorry, but school isn't out for summer."

"I have a serious question to ask, Grace," the Wind said, then paused. "Will you be a willing student of life or will woe be your constant companion?"

"Student of life," Grace blurted. She figured she knew woe too well, even for her young years. Besides, she thought this was the perfect opportunity to finally take up her grandmother's advice, "Always choose the option you've never tried before."

The Wind urged her on. "Now, let's get back to it. The ocean will not change. Ever. It's the same water, just in different parts of the world."

Grace wanted a pen and notebook in her hand, not a surfboard.

"Sense missing each and every wave. I really want you to feel being so close, yet so far. When you finally do catch a wave, you'll appreciate the different form the water took to propel you forward. The victory will mean more when you display gratitude for all the steps leading to the triumph. But for now, enjoy the water's form as you're currently experiencing it."

Sitting on the board she leaned forward and placed her right cheek on the foam. The sun tingled the left side of her face as her arms hung down into the sea, wrapped in wet blankets of water.

"It's essential for you to be where your body is, Grace. Enjoy this situation like you purposefully chose it, and if you can't enjoy it, accept it, and if you can't accept it, then surrender to it."

Grace deeply inhaled, paused and exhaled in a way that would make the yoga teacher proud.

"Surrender to the sea. Lay down your arms."

The ocean no longer felt tight; rather it effortlessly supported her in a way she couldn't herself.

"Relinquish the limitations of your body and stop criticising your hands and feet for not going where you think they should."

She sat back up on the board, her legs dangling off the sides.

"Grace, lean into the unfamiliarity of the situation. Soften yourself; the rigidity is what tightens your mind and body, making you brittle. This fierce determination is the very thing that causes you to snap."

Grace loosened her body and shook her hands above her head and kicked her legs back and forth under the water to disperse the static energy inside her. The surf instructor was busy with one of the other girls, but he gave a wave to let her know that he'd be there for her when she was ready.

"Bend, Grace, yield to the water and be gentle with yourself."

She wriggled to the back of the board, flattened her back out and moved her arms into place to catch the next wave.

"Grace, when you forget your divinity and box yourself into your mortality, you support the limitations of what you can't do. Reclaim your greatness by being one with the ebb and flow of the ocean. Be the rhythmic nature of life yourself."

She took a deep breath.

I exist as rhythm.

"Think in terms of the whole, not of yourself as an individual. Cease viewing the ocean as something different and separate from you. It is you, Grace." The Wind stressed the word 'is'. "If you approach surfing from a mind-orientated position, you can't feel the ocean's aliveness. Sense the pulsating energy and express the same nature."

Grace spent what felt like forever watching the waves come towards her and through her: rolling and breaking, rolling and breaking. The waves transformed their form with ease and grace.

"Ride the waves of your moods too; each emotion will come to pass like everything else."

Grace had never considered her moods as passing phenomena before now.

"Don't rush what will develop in its own time, appreciate the lulls and soar with any upsurges. There's a gradual progression to and from the states of minimum and maximum. Trust me, Grace. When you're finally up and surfing, you'll wish you enjoyed the valiant effort that led to the success more. Engage with what you see as a failing moment with gratitude, for soon you'll perceive this moment as essential to your triumph. Failure is a necessary path to any success."

Her confidence was increasing. She kept reading the ocean.

"The saga of catching a wave is no different to the journey of your teenage years. Don't wish this moment away; it's precious beyond belief. Work with the power of the ocean, not against it. Don't attach a limited outcome on your endeavour. Ask the water for guidance and invite its seasoned wisdom in. The way will be shown."

"Are you insane? So it's not enough I'm speaking with you, I now also have to converse with the ocean. You're delusional! What's the water going to tell me?"

"Ask it."

"What?"

"Ask it."

"How?"

"However you need to, but don't sigh before you begin."

Grace caught the heaviness in her chest before the sigh escaped. "Ocean?" She felt stupid. "Ocean," she said, removing some more of the resistance from her voice. "We've never spoken before, but my name's Grace, and . . . um, I feel a bit silly asking you this, and maybe you can't even help, but where do I go from here?"

As easily as the Wind spoke back to her, so did the Ocean.

"It's a pleasure to make your acquaintance, Grace, and I do hope we'll be chatting more in the future. The best advice I can offer at this time is to do whatever feels authentic and returns you to your true nature."

The Ocean's voice sounded similar to the Wind's, with a slightly more weighty tone. Grace was bemused by its answer, but thanked the Ocean anyway.

Grace decided to go swimming so paddled to shore, left the blue board by the red and yellow flags and ran back into the sea. She swam lengths of breaststroke, freestyle and backstroke. She sensed her— and nature's—unbound horizons, feeling in harmony with the water as she bobbed up and down with the ocean's swell. She assumed her favourite starfish position, and it took her to the place where her thoughts didn't undermine her, where there was sound but no sound.

Grace floated wherever the ocean carried her and lost herself in weightlessness.

⁂

"There you go," breathed the Wind. "You asked the Ocean what to do, and it pointed you in the right direction."

"Are you about to give another of your 'If there's only one thing I can impress upon you' speeches?"

"Now that you mention it, Grace, yes I am, and that is: be attached to your soul, but detached from results. The sooner you learn to disengage from personality-oriented outcomes, the greater your sense of internal peace."

Grace languidly swam breaststroke in a circle, liking the coolness of the water passing over her body.

"As you're now aware of the waves arising and passing, recognise how you and the universe are always running back and forth into each other. You're never really apart; you're each merely taking turns leading and following, advancing and retreating. Be in a state of calm receptivity as you feel that dance you enter into with the cosmic, knowing everything arises to pass away."

With each breaststroke, Grace felt her arms come out from her heart and glide through the water in a smooth, circular, sweeping movement, then back again.

"Ask, listen and receive the guidance that directs your life. Ask, listen, receive and question again," the Wind reiterated. "Feel that dance—the equilibrium of that wonderful back and forth—just as the tide brings you out and back in, back out and in again. Witness the harmonious percussion of life and lose yourself in this rhythm and the purity of its wisdom."

Grace was ready to pick up the surfboard and try again, but saw the instructor winding up the lesson and asking the class to head to shore.

"When you leave the water today, Grace, know wherever you are—whether it's in your bedroom, shopping mall or at school—that you can ask the universe for guidance. Be still, wait for the response and know everything that happens after posing your question is the universe's answer."

"I don't understand."

"When sending a loving, soulful prayer to the universe, whatever occurs next is your request being fulfilled. Don't look for a literal response. Know every prayer—without fail—is always answered; often not in the way you expect, but it is heard and acted upon. You don't have to voyage through this life alone."

73 | Meditation

Dylan had said he would pick Grace up from their prearranged meeting point outside the surf lifesaving club at 4 p.m. She'd showered and changed and had got there early. Invigorated by the sea's tranquil touch, she wanted to feel blanketed by the ocean again. In its care, her personality surrendered and gave room for her soul to merge with the divine.

As she waited, she realised she hadn't yet bought her father anything for his forty-seventh birthday next week. "But what do you buy the person who has everything?"

"You offer a shift in perspective," the Wind replied.

Her father arrived, and Grace could tell he was shocked to see her patiently waiting for him.

"How'd you go? Get up on that board this time?" he asked as she got in the car.

"No, even better. I just floated."

"You didn't surf?"

Grace shook her head.

"Then why am I paying for these lessons then?"

"Papa, you just don't get it."

She wound down the window to let the breeze dry her hair as the Wind entered with another message.

"Grace, reconnect with stillness at regular intervals throughout the day and salute the silence that lies beneath all that you do."

She noticed the pine trees in the distance glistening like morning frost in the fading sunlight.

"Be the enduring tranquillity that lies behind the temporary blowing of the pine needles as you go about your day."

"I understand."

Every so often things were fantastically clear with the Wind, but mostly they were hugely ambiguous. In this moment, Grace felt she and the Wind were on the same page. But it didn't last long as it next brought up a topic she knew very little about.

"Grace, on waking, it would be in your best interest to meditate for a few minutes."

"On what? I mean, what exactly is meditation?"

"Meditation is the process by which we notice the thoughts racing around our mind. By being the observer—even if it's only for a few minutes each day—we rest in the universal presence of the divine."

"But I don't have a few minutes in the morning. I can barely get myself to the bus stop in time, let alone analyse my dreams and then meditate on top of that."

"You can't afford not to have the time."

"I really can't spare five minutes in the morning."

"Grace, try to feel the stillness the ocean brought you."

She sunk into her body. "Aha, it was awesome."

"Do you regard tying your shoelaces as a higher priority than this serenity?"

"But . . ."

"No buts here, Grace. First you must connect with your soul. Only from this union can you bring your being to your doing."

"Do you want to stop for a bite to eat?" her father interrupted. "What do you feel like?"

"You choose."

"Grace, you make me laugh. With inconsequential things you're incredibly indecisive, but with big decisions there's never a moment's hesitation," Dylan said.

"Japanese," she shot back to prove her father wrong.

"There, not too difficult was it?"

Dylan turned his attention back to the road, Grace to the Wind.

"There's many ways we can bring meditation into our daily lives," the Wind continued. "When you walk, focus on each step, or as you shower, feel the tiny water droplets on your skin instead of absently lathering soap over yourself. Remember when we spoke about the heartbeat?"

"Kind of."

"How the heart's rhythm is stillness, and by tuning into this beat it's far easier to enjoy all the other rhythms life has to offer?"

"Oh yeah. The divine is the beat that drives all the other beats?"

"Precisely. It's the pulse that beats the whole of life. But it's not enough just to think about stillness; you must live it. We meditate to become a clear channel so that the divine can work through us."

"Now, let's see if we can bring some decisiveness to your menu ordering," Dylan said as he opened the door to the restaurant.

"Papa, I'm not that bad."

"Grace, I love you, but yes you are. There's no right or wrong decision, you just need to make one."

Whoa!

Her father just turned all life coach on her.

"Another thing," Dylan added. "Learn to say no to some things in order to say yes to others."

74 | Forgiveness

Grace sat at one of the canteen's tables that overlooked the clay tennis courts. A few tables in front, Amber-Jane and her gaggle of friends were gossiping about her again. No matter how much she tried to remain detached, Grace still took their comments personally.

Why me?

Part of her wanted to throw a huge, dramatic scene. Thankfully, this commotion now took place in her mind, whereas before she would've physically acted it out.

"Is it really so important they don't want to include you, Grace? Is it worth wasting your energy chasing their approval?"

"I'm well aware I've placed my sense of self-worth in the hands of others yet again," she replied. "I know I'm the one giving my serenity away, but it still affects me."

"Where is the sovereign energy of your psyche? And who's ruling your inner realm? Until you forgive, you'll forever be a victim and never at peace."

"Okay, now you're pushing it. Forgive? Them?"

"Forgiveness is everything."

She threw her head back and groaned.

"Grace, listen to yourself. You're speaking from your personality, not from your soul."

"Excuse me," she said, "but why am I the one that has to forgive? They're the ones who should be begging for my forgiveness."

"Grace, their behaviour didn't hurt you. You hurt you," the Wind said. "Nothing can hurt your soul; it's indestructible. These girls are only chipping away at your personality—where you've placed all your self-esteem—or rather, lack of it. Consider their catty comments as a personal lesson from the universe to help you grow into your truth."

"Please don't go there."

"Have these girls not tested the stamina of your soul? Have they not taught you the virtue of fortitude? Did Gabriel's disinterest not teach you a priceless lesson about love, namely that it can't be forced? Did his non-appreciation of your worth shine a light on how little you valued and respected yourself?"

In this light it was all a blessing.

"You must believe in your own divinity, Grace. Only then can you attract people and situations into your life that endorse and support your majesty. These experiences have all been wonderful healing lessons to encourage you to take the necessary steps to reclaim your true self."

Grace wondered if she'd ever find her place in the world, a special corner carved out exclusively for her.

"Learn the lessons quickly to transform the experience into wisdom so you don't keep repeating them. Don't analyse forgiveness from the personality's point of view, but rather the soul's. You forgive for your own benefit, not the benefit of others. Rise above your circumstances and view the lay of the land from the expanse of the sky. Your school dramas are unravelling perfectly for the highest good of all involved."

"I hate the highest good," Grace moaned. "Why is this my problem?" She craved chocolate and wanted some now.

"This 'problem' came to help you live life at a higher turn of the spiral . . ."

Grace cut the Wind short. "Great! All this spiral stuff again."

". . . and to be the living expression of your inborn luminosity. Witness and worship the 'other' as a manifestation of the divine."

Rather than rejoin the canteen line, Grace pulled out her iPod to listen to her favourite single by The Wolves to drown out the Wind and the giggling of Amber-Jane's clique.

The Wind overrode The Wolves' melodies. "It's not an escape solution for dealing with life you need, Grace, but practice and more practice. Every time you hear these girls gossip and spread lies about you, it's a chance to surrender."

Grace had always equated surrender to falling down defeated in a heap, never realising it could liberate.

"Understand the soul significance of the happenings in your life. Allow what is to arise. Don't believe your personality's interpretation of events. Its version keeps you at a lower vibrational level. We've been over this before; it's not willing yourself to love, but opening yourself to love. Viewing all people and occurrences through the lens of the soul will lead you to the inner poise that's your rightful inheritance."

"But why don't they like me? What is it about me that they find so objectionable? Is this what the rest of my life will look like? Will I forever exist on the outskirts and never feel included?" There was no pause between her words. "Will eternity be the definition of hell, because it's just me, alone with my thoughts, in perpetual torment for the sands of time?"

The Wind allowed her to finish, then said, "There's nothing wrong with you other than the way you perceive yourself and the world. The feelings of unworthiness come when you live in the feeling of your hypercritical thinking and forget who you are. Commune daily with the divine, and this new understanding of self will lead to a greater expression of your true being in the outside world. Support and guidance are constantly waiting in the wings for you," explained the Wind. "Dedicate your thoughts to love not doubt. Act from your heart and the future will take care of itself. And another thing . . ."

Man, did the Wind ever run out of things to say?

"You melt your fears by allowing the divine to flow through you with no concern for how things will turn out. You give up your attachment to outcome. Be a boundless flow of experience and the space for everything to arise. Engage your valour, Grace, and go beyond this school, these girls and your fragile sense of your small self. Consider what other people are going through at this moment."

The notion was lost on her. "Other people?"

"A mother may have lost her newborn child, a wife is holding her husband's hand as he begins a gruelling round of chemotherapy, a father and daughter are sleeping rough on the streets, and you are worrying that a few people—out of the seven something billion in the world—don't like you."

The shame of her self-indulgence felt crushing.

⁂

Later that afternoon in the back garden, Grace stood in the powerful stance of an Amazonian warrior, and declared to the universe, "I'm part of the greater wonder of life, I'll deny this no longer. I'm taking that quantum leap. I'll respond to the longings of my soul, not my debilitating and limiting thoughts. I won't go through the motions of my life in absenteeism anymore."

Grace turned her head to see bunches of torn, dead leaves swirling high off the ground, and her selfishness hit her between the eyes.

Wow! I've never properly thanked the Wind for entering my life and taking me on as a student.

Gratitude was until now a foreign concept to Grace. She had never considered herself lucky to live in a free, democratic country with little pollution, or what a privilege it was to walk the streets safely at all hours, or the good fortune of good health. Grace now understood how truly and utterly blessed she was. She lived a charmed life. Why on earth had she never seen this before? Or appreciated her relationship with the Wind as her saving grace?

No good comes from me living in my head, being controlled by my personality. I have to access the source that exists beyond the barricades that I've erected around me. I will mask my light no longer.

Then Grace did something she'd never considered before. She forgave Gabriel and Amber-Jane for their behaviour and actions. They were doing the best they could from their limited perspective—just as she was doing the best she could. Only later in her life did Grace understand that they were mirror reflections of her own thought vibrations.

"We can only live to the level of our awareness," the Wind said.

She felt compassion flowing through her veins and words appeared signposted in her mind's eye: "At the centre of all love I stand, from here nothing can touch me. I can only give what I am."

The Wind added, "You forgive to free yourself. It's a balm that heals your wounds so you're able to bring more light into the world. Infuse these words you just spoke with meaning to make them come alive, Grace, because we live what we believe."

⁓⁓

The Wind began to impress on Grace another teaching. "Start communicating through myths, symbols and fables so that you can create a narrative tale of your soul's journey. One day the world will want to know how you traversed the terrain of your life. Have you ever wondered about your name, Grace?"

"Other than hating it?"

The Wind ignored her comment. "You may think your parents gave you this name, but your soul chose it before you were born."

"You're off in mumbo jumbo land again."

"Can you move gracefully through this world?"

"I guess, I'm trying, I'm aiming to. No, I mean . . . I will, I am, I must." Grace realised there was no try.

"Can you be gracious in your manner?"

"Oh, I get where you're going."

"You'll soon learn it's not the path *to* grace you seek but rather the path *of* grace you tread," the Wind clarified.

75 | Feeling Good

Another Sunday afternoon and Grace wasn't in the mood to do much of anything, let alone lift her veil to the light. The Wind once said to sit quietly on Sundays to reflect on the previous week's activities—what worked, what didn't—so she'd have an overall sense of the week's energetic flow and gain insight into the coming one. Mostly though, Grace's weeks seemed to just run into each other, into one big mess of a blur.

The Wind suggested getting ready for the week, but Grace wanted to eat a mango.

Anyway, doesn't living in flow mean not making plans?

The Wind explained, "Plans, which give a sense of direction, are still needed but the compass of your soul is what you listen to and act on in the moment."

Grace went down to the kitchen. Her mother was on the phone, her father was watching the 4 p.m. news, and Abel was out. She sliced the mango lengthwise and cut a crosshatch pattern through the pulp to the skin. She carved out the diced pieces and while eating the flesh discovered she didn't do that good a job slicing the fruit. Bits of skin remained on some of the mango cubes making the taste gritty and ruining the juicy flavour.

"Would you serve that mango to guests, Grace?"

"No way! It hasn't been properly prepared."

"So it's okay for you to eat the pieces that still have the skin attached but you'd be embarrassed serving the fruit to visitors?"

"Well, I'm eating it, aren't I?"

"And your attire around the house?" the Wind asked. "You reason that it's okay dressing like a slob—one of your words—because no one sees you?"

"Aha," affirmed Grace as some of the mango juice trickled down her chin.

"But the most important person sees. You."

"Me?"

The juice left a sticky trail down her neck to her chest.

"How you feel impacts how you interact with the world. You and I both know you don't feel that great when you let your appearance, manner and behaviour slide, especially around the house."

"You sound like Mum."

"Well, do you?" the Wind asked.

"No," Grace sheepishly replied.

"You overfill glasses—whether it's with milk, juice or water—as well as your plate. You spill liquids and bits of food on your clothes and rub the stains in rather than wash them off—all under the guise that if nobody sees, it's fine. Enough, Grace! Embrace your divine feminine nature and radiantly wear your invisible crown, even when no one's watching. When you hold yourself to a higher standard of integrity you'll attract a higher vibration of living."

"Oh, it's the magical word 'enough' making an appearance again."

"Correct, Grace. Enough of treating yourself like a second-class citizen. The finer things in life will always elude you until you raise your vibration to match them."

She threw the mango skin into the bin.

"Remember Grace, when you feel good, you engage with people in an undeniably elevated manner, and they with you. To bring this new energy about you must do things differently internally, like surrendering your personal agenda, and externally—even something as simple as changing your hair colour. You'll transform your whole energy field and vibrate at a heightened level. The world changes according to your personal transformation."

Why did she keep sabotaging herself? She didn't need the Wind to tell her. The answer was obvious: low self-esteem. Stable in the knowledge of her true self as a soul, she would make far more nourishing choices that connected her to her heart.

"It's crucial for you to feel at home in your body, Grace; because when you do, you'll make choices more aligned with your soul. When you feel overwhelmed and that the world is against you, your personality is in charge and your shadow choices will betray you. Form a conscious relationship with your shadow to help cross the threshold of your sabotaging patterns. You transform your fragmented being to wholeness by accessing this inmost sacred power. Now that this perception has sunk into your intellect, let it seep into your soul."

76 | Trusting Your Intuition

G race was at a loss with what to do with herself. She typically never had the luxury of spare time—her schedule was always jam-packed with no gaps for downtime, other than her procrastination activities—and now that she finally had some 'empty' time on her hands, there was the quandary of what to do with it.

"Ask your intuition—your compass—to guide your day's rhythm, remembering a state of flow doesn't come from the mind and it's not always logical."

"But don't I need rules, boundaries, timetables, yada yada yada?"

"It's a good idea to have a loose framework, because we need order on some level, but also unstructured moments so organic timing can occur," the Wind said.

"So you're suggesting that I should use my intuition to guide my unstructured time?"

"Correct. Now, part of you considered doing your homework first thing on waking, but then you thought it's Sunday and what a lame way—your words—to spend the morning, so you chose to stay in your pyjamas and—your words again—'veg out' and watch cartoons."

"So I didn't listen to my intuition?"

"Right. You didn't listen but you did receive. Grace, usually you ignore your gut feel. Intuition doesn't visit a doubting mind. You're always divinely guided on the optimum time to do certain things, like how earlier you felt you should make an appointment to see the dentist."

She rubbed her jaw.

"You're continuously receiving guidance, Grace, so be open to it and act on it. Acting on your intuition is what increases its strength."

"Or when I scoffed that bag of potato chips yesterday I knew my body was telling me to slow down and savour the taste. I knew I was eating too quickly to enjoy them."

"Your intuition was dictating the rhythm your body craved," the Wind said.

"I get messages like this all the time, so why don't I act on them?"

"Because your intuition runs at a higher rhythm than your intellect, and you're too used to relying on your literal mind. A lifetime of academic study spent at university can't even begin to compete with the creative wisdom you hold within yourself."

"Why don't more people live by their intuition?" Grace asked.

"Too often it gets hammered out at a very young age and replaced with knowledge that can be quantified. Reason and logic rule in our world today. But we can't reason our way out of our problems, Grace, we need to feel our way through."

The Wind sounds almost human!

"The heart is considered too emotional and unreliable; society has deemed it unfit to rule, regarding it a redundant, useless barometer. Use your intuition to readjust your internal rhythm to join with the universe's cycles. Feel how things in their natural order play out and live life through this truth."

Grace placed her hands over her heart.

"When the sun is out, go and enjoy it—feel its vibrancy. Energise your grace. Notice how the artificial and synthetic can't even compare."

She felt humbled. "I keep forgetting the living earth pulses and is alive."

"Grace, feel the sun on your body and smile in gratitude. That's all that's required of you. This appreciation is your own—and nature's—reward."

Can it really be that simple?

77 | Eternal Perception

It was now Grace's turn to digress. "I know we've been through this, but isn't balance what most people in the Western world strive for? A balanced life—isn't that the ultimate sign of success?"

"How can it be, Grace?" the Wind answered. "The way society uses the word balance implies that it's a static thing and most people's concept of balance comes from their personality when it really takes place within our soul. Anyway, we don't even know what the register of our karmic account is."

Grace cocked her head. "Karmic account?"

"The scales of life could simply be balancing themselves out," the Wind explained. "We mustn't try to superimpose our naïve, incomplete ideas of equilibrium on the magnitude of the universal force."

Wow! This journey really is a dance of interconnecting opposites.

"Have you ever considered how much you learn about yourself when you're out of sync and greatly discombobulated?"

"I've never thought about it that way before."

"Why not deem being out of rhythm as the pathway back in? It'll make you question what's currently deficient—or in excess—in your life and lead you back to your centre within."

Grace asked the Wind to rewind back to its words on intuition.

The Wind gladly obliged. "When you're one with your silence and act immediately on intuitive guidance, life can then change just as quickly. The purpose of intuition is to act on it instantly, today, at this moment—not five years from now—which is what many people do. When they finally do get around to acting on it, they recall when they received the initial flash of insight and berate themselves for ignoring or suppressing it for so long."

Grace wondered how to explain this point to her mother.

"To accurately perceive a situation means looking at it from the angle of perpetuity. When you interpret the situation from a time without end, cosmic truth comes to light—not your finiteness. The infinite grandness of the world presents itself."

"You mean my pettiness dissolves?"

"Precisely. A sense of eternal perception will marry you to the rhythm of all things. Within human cycles and those of the solar system, all elements are faithful to the moment. Individuals, countries, economic systems, nature; they're all playing their necessary part within their discrete cycles, which also overlap and are interrelated to other sequences."

"Wind, I'll miss you." She had no idea where the words came from—or why—but felt compelled to utter them.

"Grace, I'm not going anywhere too far."

"But I had a feeling, a hit of intuition, and the thought appeared in my mind."

The Wind had to confess, "Yes, it's true. I'm not going away per se, but soon our conversations will be less intense because I want you to start living our exchanges and make this wisdom practical."

She felt scared. "How?"

"By going about your daily life as you normally would, but at a higher turn of the spiral."

"Say again?"

"Be calm, grounded, noble, majestic and a beacon of light embodying all I've taught you, Grace. You'll become a living example to others and through your attitude and actions they will gain access to the insights I've shared with you. Think of the impact—on so many levels—that you could have."

"But how do I get others to understand whatever this thing is between us?" Her hands twirled in the empty space.

"When others become open to learning about life in this way, they'll receive the exact same connection. They must first voluntarily reach out for it though, and wake up to their own inner yearning, which acts as the gateway. This lifelong program of study can't be forced on others; they need to want and claim it for themselves. Everyone is at various levels of life experience and understanding, so different pieces of the teachings will resonate. Each will receive precisely what they need to."

"Take what echoes true and let the rest go?"

"Exactly, and the best way to inspire this hunger in others is through the grace-filled presence you radiate. You can't tell them how to live, Grace, only show them the effects that our dialogues have had on you. Remember 'show and tell' in primary school?" the Wind asked.

"Yeah, I loved it. I brought a caterpillar into class once."

"This time, show and don't tell—unless asked. Teach by example, not by instruction."

78 | Repetitive Patterns

It had been a long week and finally it was Friday.
Only one more day to get through.

As she readied her bag for school, everything started to feel like one, long drag. "Wind, where are you? I have a question."

"For you, Grace, I'm only a hair's breadth away. What is it?"

"These stupid, repetitive patterns in my life, my very own *Groundhog Day*—wake, school, homework, dinner, bed—I feel trapped. I feel . . ."

"Grace, you complain far too much," the Wind said. "What do you suppose this whining energy creates in your life?"

She bit her tongue to prevent a cynical reply.

"Continuity has its own gratifying rhythm, it's just that you're not feeling it."

"I didn't call on you for criticism."

"These incessant struggles in your life, Grace, you've made them so. Repetitive patterns don't have to be boring. They can be incredibly pleasing to the senses—wood grains, zebra stripes, the hexagons of honeycomb—all are testament to continuity's gifts."

Frustration was welling up within her. "But why bother observing these patterns?"

"We've been through this before, Grace. When you're aware of them, it's easier to sense the pulse of life. If there's a particular pattern you're rallying against, surrender to it. Don't lose your soul for the complaining—whether it's making your bed each morning or with other chores around the home. Don't let your unconstructive thoughts on these monotonous routines be stronger than you."

A faint light shone through the gloom. "I'm letting my thoughts about my *Groundhog Day* override my peace."

"Configurations of energy are neutral; it's you who puts the negative beliefs, annoyances and irritations on them. Next time a pattern aggravates—and I know for you it'll be sooner rather than later—feel the benefits the repetitious movement brings, not the frustrations. These patterns can ground and comfort you if only you'd let them."

"But I hate school," she whined.

"Grace, school at the moment is a necessary arrangement in your life cycle. As the sun completes its own rotation of rising and setting, school is an equally essential action for you. Don't take this the wrong way, Grace, but isn't complaining your main pattern?"

She didn't want to nod her head, but had to agree.

"Does the complaining lead you to change, to take different actions and re-evaluate your behaviour?" the Wind asked.

Her body tightened.

"We both know the answer's no. Moaning is the end result for you. You don't do it to effect change or resolve anything, but for its own sake."

Grace felt under fire.

"Complaining can be a powerful motivator for change, but not when you fail to do anything active in response. Your whining is a constant, passive feedback loop. Why not seek a new way to exist in the world?"

Grace slumped onto her beanbag and tolerated the lecture.

"You're addicted to playing the victim. When you're so busy feeling persecuted and hard done-by, you're not taking responsibility for what's really occurring in your life."

Of course the Wind was right.

"You are in control of your perception, Grace, always remember this."

"How can I be in control? I'm forced to go to school."

"You are in charge of how you interpret what meaning an event or person has for you."

She let out a deep sigh.

"If you could float up here with me, you'd value all as it is, has been and will be. Rise above your constant complaining. Feel me close and soar high, letting the lower vibratory thoughts pass beneath you."

79 | Progression not Perfection

It was Saturday and Grace was sitting in a café behind the State Library. She didn't like the way her chocolate milkshake tasted and this disturbed her.

I should've gone to Millie's Café instead.

The Wind said, "Grace, it is as it is. Breathe and flow; it really is that simple."

"Enough of the 'breathe and flow' stuff, you're not my yoga teacher," she said biting her lower lip.

"Fine," the Wind replied.

"But the milkshake's not how I like it. There's too much milk in it and you can hardly taste the chocolate. Shouldn't I demand that they remake it?"

"Watch your language, Your Royal Highness of Entitlement."

Grace felt no peace in the pendulum swing of her emotions.

"That's right. Your peace flies straight out the window the minute entitlement marches in. Tell yourself the milkshake tastes as it tastes, and flow with whatever happens from there. Maybe it's not the best milkshake in the world, but does it need to be?"

"Yes." Grace expected everything to be the best, even though she wasn't willing to put in the effort to raise her own standard of living.

"Is this realistic, Grace? Your expectations bring you crashing to your knees. You've taken a milkshake not to your taste as a personal affront to you as a human being. 'Don't they know who I am?' is what you're really thinking."

The truth cut deep. "I don't mean to get so upset about every small thing and take it personally. Honest! But it's as if one thing sets me off and leads to another complaint and another, and before I know it, I've spiralled out of control and am grumbling about everything."

"Why not use your energy to praise instead? Compliment instead of complain?"

She hardly praised anyone; the word didn't even sit well in her throat, catching tight.

"Remember Grace, your complaints are never about what's going on 'out there' but what's going on 'in here'."

She felt a soft, warm breeze in her heart.

"If your heart's frozen, Grace, the world feels like a frosty, callous place. If you have love in your heart, the universe expands to rise and meet you. Your endless whining means all the beauty—yours and the world's—goes to waste."

Grace was annoyed at the Wind for illustrating that her complaining—not the thing or person she found unsatisfactory—was what made life so heavy and unbearable. Her whole worldview came from inside her; joy and love radiated inside out. But this insight was daunting: if life's interpretation was her responsibility, it meant giving up her victim mentality and living consciously. Did she feel empowered enough to make the shift?

The Wind added, "You learn a new language using repetition and practice, right?"

"I guess so."

"You know so through German class, Grace. Now tell me, how will you put this knowledge into practice?"

Grace replied, "I've learned that my thoughts inform my emotions, and my emotions influence my inner reality and create my vibratory state, which is how the universe responds to me. My beliefs also influence my actions and so I'll put this into practice by being present, awake and illusionless."

"Gold star."

"Victory will be mine," Grace said and raised her right hand in the V-sign. She slurped the last drops of her milkshake and used a long spoon to scrape up the chocolate syrup at the bottom of the glass.

"You're making huge progress, Grace," the Wind said, "but the trick is to master this new way of looking at the world as your default modus operandi, not one-off episodes."

I am love, I am love, I am love.

It took her more than a few rounds of chanting to feel the truth of this affirmation.

"Your personality will continue to invent justifications to remain indignant towards all the perceived slights and wrongdoings."

Grace moaned. "The personality can be so controlling."

"This is why meditation helps. It diffuses the feelings of being wronged, of wanting revenge, of trying to rewrite the past," the Wind explained. "It's the personality that gets worked up about these things, not the soul, as it's not something happening to you, but through you, and it's never about the other person or the milkshake—it's about you, Grace. Always. Leave everyone else out of it."

"Look, I'm no yogi and won't be anytime soon."

"Progression—not perfection—Grace. Only as you evolve will more revelations bless you. Turn a little higher on the spiral. A new paradigm exists within you. There is a different way to live."

80 | A State of Grace

One week later, Grace decided to apply the wisdom she acquired over the previous weekend. She decided to go to Bistro Palais by the beach for brunch. She envisaged herself sitting there for hours, sophisticatedly sipping an aromatic medium dark roast coffee in her own good time and nibbling on French toast. She'd bring with her some of the fashion magazines piled up on the floor of her bedroom, look out onto the water, and have both a leisurely and productive morning. There wasn't a queue when she arrived.

So far, so good.

The waiter jumped on Grace for her order as soon as she sat down. Less than thirteen minutes later, the meal arrived. Great service if she were starving and in a rush, but Grace was planning to spend a couple of hours chilling out here. She felt anxious, so she hurriedly scoffed all three pieces of French toast. As soon as she put her knife and fork down, her plate was cleared away.

The waiter asked if she wanted anything else.

Grace replied "no," and he brought the bill. She hadn't even made it past the advertisements to the content of the first magazine, and now there was a queue at the door. She felt she'd been forced into a corner.

Her inner critic returned. Why didn't she ask them to wait twenty minutes before bringing the food, or order a pastry first, or keep half the food on her plate so they wouldn't clear it? Then she could've sat here for longer.

The dream morning she had planned was now effectively over.

The Wind spoke calmly. "Grace, restaurants need to make money.

Only ordering one cup of coffee and some bread over the course of several hours at the most popular place on the waterfront—when there's a queue out the door—is unrealistic. On the other hand, a quiet coffee shop in the suburbs isn't going to mind if you sit on one latte browsing your magazines for hours on end. You need to apply wisdom with discernment."

The waiter returned with the change and asked if Grace enjoyed her meal.

She spitefully replied, "No. I felt too rushed."

He uttered, "Sorry," but it wasn't delivered with any sincerity. In fact, she thought his manner quite rude and she felt incredibly put out.

This whole thing has been a complete disaster.

Grace sighed, catching her emotions. She knew the waiter had little to do with her actual experience of the meal and she now felt remorseful for taking her pettiness out on him.

"Respond, don't react, Grace," the Wind said. "Reaction is your personality expressing its view of what it thinks is right. Be with how the situation actually is, not up in your head writing a script for how you wish it to be."

No matter the Wind's words, Grace still felt wounded by the waiter's behaviour and wanted to rewind the clock.

"Rise to a higher altitude and witness the gifts that exist for your soul in this situation."

Again the trivialities of life undid her. All the amazing things Grace could've thought and experienced this morning—the scrumptious taste of the buttery brioche, the laughter coming from the children building sandcastles on the beach, freedom from the confines of the classroom—all these joyful moments had been lost on her.

"This experience is reminding me to act from a state of grace so I can lay claim to my deepest, truest dignity."

"Precisely. By focusing on what you perceive as wrong, you'll only bring more of what's wrong to you as what you focus on expands.

Seeing everything as not-quite-right only attracts more not-quite-right moments into your life. Stop needing things to go a certain way for you to be happy," the Wind said. "Attempting to control people and experiences will never be the remedy, just as material substances will never fill a longing the way divine love can."

To think she'd been imagining that all would be well in her world if only Gabriel loved her. The absurdity!

"Discard the unnecessary. Was finishing reading these magazines really worth the stress you just put yourself through?"

The question highlighted the scale of misery she'd brought to bear on herself.

"End the insanity and be at ease in your own skin. Your suffering is needless and self-inflicted, but it is functional. It's pushing you to stop reading inspirational quotes in books and instead live the wisdom I'm passing on to you. Pain is the change agent helping you to become your authentic self, Grace. If you feel uncomfortable, or out of your depth, it means you're growing. New energies are forming within and expanding your vessel with light and untold creative possibilities. Be the compass of faith."

She packed the magazines back in her bag and rose gingerly from the table.

"Grace, it's useless posting motivational quotes on your pin board and reciting positive affirmations without rewiring your belief systems and taking practical steps to embrace your divine nature. The universe rises to meet you, but only after you take the first step. Its power responds to yours. Life is calling you, Grace. It's time."

81 | The Art of Waiting

Grace awoke with a tremendous sense of clarity knowing her consciousness had been elsewhere in the night. She plainly saw how fighting life drained and deadened her and how struggling only pushed a sense of freedom even further from her grasp. She wanted to return to the serenity sleep offered, but knew it was time to get up and get moving.

"Allow peace to rise from within; don't force it into being," said the Wind. "This state naturally arises in you. It's a by-product of a stilled mind."

Rather than push, I'll flow. Instead of wanting, I'll allow. I won't look outside myself to get my needs met but instead turn my attention within. The world is in me.

Grace jumped into the shower to find the hair conditioner bottle empty. "Abel!" she screamed.

Grooming and maintenance still didn't mean as much to her as she knew the Wind would like them to mean. She didn't see the point of spending valuable minutes drying herself properly after a shower. So long as she wasn't dripping wet, she just wanted to get the dressing process over and done with.

"Mindfulness is a skill that must be practiced. The personality feeds off distraction."

She hopped out the shower and her wet feet sunk into the hallway carpet as she walked back to her room.

"Grace, living in awareness means deliberately bringing all of yourself to the present moment. It doesn't happen automatically. It requires training and lots of repetition."

"This is about my rushing and inability to pay attention, right? So explain to me how the quality of my life is diminished because I get dressed in a hurry?"

"You believe that taking special care as you dress slows you down, but would you have the same attitude on your wedding day?"

"Er, crappy school uniform versus expensive wedding dress? A bit like comparing apples and oranges, me thinks."

"Exactly the same level of presence is required for each occasion. The grace of presence doesn't distinguish between a boring, run-of-the-mill day and a once-in-a-lifetime event. They are unerringly the same as both are expressions of the only time that exists, the now. Nothing is too small to bring your expanded awareness to."

Grace had already put both socks and shoes on without paying attention. It was amazing how much she did on automatic pilot.

"You'll also be dressed in your wedding outfit that quickly—not even feeling the dress being zipped up—if you don't delight in each and every moment, no matter how dull your personality thinks it is. Grace, you're establishing powerful patterns of behaviour today, which you'll be powerless to change on your wedding day, should they not serve you in this present moment. There is no future, only the now."

This distressed Grace immensely. She always imagined herself lavishing great care over each detail on the day: sensually rolling on her stockings, delicately pulling the garter up, nimbly slipping into the dress. She'd hate to get dressed for her wedding with the same disrespect as she did her school uniform.

"There is no difference between the items of clothing, Grace, only your level of awareness."

Grace now wanted to put her uniform on again, this time with deliberate mindfulness.

"Grace, your mind will meander as it naturally does, so just gently bring it back and restate your intention. Imbue even the smallest gesture with your grace. Feel each item of dress on your skin. Every time you bring your attention back it's a blessing; don't chastise yourself for it."

Grace put her watch on and felt the leather band hug her wrist.

"Sow this level of attention into your day-to-day reality, from how you read a book, walk up the spiral staircase to your bedroom or open the fridge door," said the Wind. "Feel your body and soul in each focused action."

She slipped her arms through the blazer and sensed how the lining rubbed softly against her forearm.

"Grace, why don't you take a second look at yourself in the full-length mirror before leaving the house?" the Wind asked.

It was true. She hardly ever studied the complete expression of her image that she cobbled together before stepping out to face the world, as there was never the time. She was always running late.

"Surely you'd want to take a few minutes to assess how you're presenting yourself for the coming day?"

"I guess."

"When you're older and want a more polished look about you, this is where you'll spend the time. These few minutes will make all the difference to your appearance and mental outlook."

"I know, I know." She was tired of being on the receiving end of yet another lecture.

"While we're on the subject of your morning dress routine, also ask the universe to help align you to the day's rhythms."

"Only today's? Not always?"

"Just this day. It's all anyone can cope with, Grace," the Wind said. "If it's a particularly stressful day, just pray to merge with the rhythm of the moment. Calm your mind and ask, 'What does this moment require from me?' Then respond to your intuition's guidance."

Waiting for the bus, Grace put the Wind's words into practice. She stilled her mind and asked, "What do you require of me in this moment?"

The response came straight away. "You're to wait—not in your mind—but in your body; fully embody the sensation of waiting."

Grace sensed the air thick with all the other morning commuters' haste and blissfully dropped into the space of waiting. When she finally alighted the bus, she felt her body's weight on each step up to the driver. She made eye contact and genuinely wished him, "Good morning."

"Terrific job, Grace! You just learned that waiting is its own necessary chapter within the creative process."

82 | Tips for Living

The next day at school, Amber-Jane and her coterie of followers were yet again making disparaging remarks about Grace, this time on her new hair colour. But as Madison said to her, "Look at Rosemary. I mean, she looks like a horse, is the biggest nerd ever, and man, all that acne. Eugh! But she's not trying to be anything but a dorky computer geek, so they leave her alone. She doesn't want to join Amber-Jane's inner clique, so they give her no grief. You on the other hand . . ."

"Those girls may play mean and hit low, but I've got you by my side and together we'll rise above it," Grace said to the Wind. To Madison, she said, "I'm starting to care less and less about A-J."

Gabriel was on the other side of the cloisters. As they both made their way around the opposite edges he reached the classroom door before her. She was in his line of sight, yet he didn't acknowledge her. But this time Gabriel's impervious neutrality didn't pierce her heart; he wasn't worth wasting her time, energy or attention on. What had the Wind said in the park all those many months ago? "In Gabriel you are seeking what already exists within you."

Grace entered the classroom with her invisible crown firmly fastened. While at one time she wanted his approval, Grace was now steadily on the path of giving it to herself by becoming conscious of the cosmic dance inside her. She had believed that being Gabriel's girlfriend would make her a totally different person and then she'd at long last like herself and feel worthy of belonging. It was another wrong assumption—the external having influence on the internal—which she now knew had been the cause of much of her suffering.

Riding her bike to Ruby's house on the weekend (using all gears to her advantage), Grace cycled past the local cinema advertising its current films, session times and future attractions. On the bottom row were the changeable letters spelling the words:

THERE IS ALWAYS MUSIC IN THE TREES
AND IN THE GARDEN.

But it was only on the ride back home later that afternoon that Grace made out the other corner of the sign where the rest of the letters spelled:

BUT YOUR HEART HAS TO BE QUIET TO HEAR IT.

To Grace, it was a direct experience of going over the same ground from a different perspective. It inspired her to start a notebook of practical family wisdom to pass on to her own daughter in time. She asked Veronika and Carla for assistance and eventually the three generations came up with the following timeless pointers for the yet-to-be-born fourth:

> *Always personalise thank you notes with specific details and before heading to a celebration choose a card—and address and stamp it—so the next day you've only to comment on what made the event uniquely special. Your enthusiasm to express thanks won't then wilt against practicalities and procrastination.*

> *At all times have a well-stocked present drawer in the home for spur-of-the-moment invitations.*

> *Always try to have something home-baked in the kitchen to offer unannounced guests.*

Never drink takeaway coffee without first sitting down and removing the plastic cup's lid, i.e. no drinking on the go.

Same with food—no eating on the move!

And certainly no eating in the car whilst driving.

Keep your right hand free when meeting people at events so you can shake their hand unhindered.

To achieve the natural break in a scone, fold the dough in half onto itself before using the fluted-round cutter.

Develop a repertoire of sweet and savoury dishes that can be cooked at a moment's notice and commit each recipe to memory.

People—not the food and drinks—should be your main focus at parties.

Try to do everything only once. If emails require a response, draft your reply and send immediately. Don't read the same email over and over again without formulating a response.

Never buy what you don't love. If a dress doesn't make you feel absolutely fabulous the minute you put it on, place it back on the rack and walk away.

It doesn't pay to buy cheap.

You don't have to be rich to get the best.

Only keep personal effects that are meaningful, useful or beautiful. Preferably your belongings are all three.

When an enjoyable book's been read, pass it on for others to benefit.

Don't stockpile magazines; instead tear out the pages you wish to keep. Store in a folder and if you don't refer to them often, bin them.

Always carry a pashmina shawl in your bag—it has a multitude of uses.

Pack your suitcase properly. There's nothing worse than getting to your destination and opening the case to find all your items jumbled up in one big mess. That's not the way to begin a holiday.

Pack hair products, beauty lotions and pens in separate plastic bags in case they leak.

From space the earth looks like it has no blocks, boundaries or barriers. All is one. Approach life the same way.

83 | When Sadness Visits

Grace was in English class when there was a knock on the classroom door. The school secretary had a word with the teacher and then called her name.

"Grace, can you step outside with me for a moment please?"

A hush descended over the room as the students all turned to look at her. She walked outside, and the secretary said that she would accompany her to the reception desk to take a call from her mother.

Grace felt uneasy. Something was wrong. "What's going on?" she asked.

The secretary replied in her usual stern tone, "Grace, it's best for your mother to tell you."

They walked the length of the cloister in silence and pushed through the double doors to the school's administration office.

I've never been on this side of the office before. So this is how it looks from the inside.

The cordless phone was waiting on the desk and she raised it to her ear.

"Grace, sweetie, I'm at the hospital," her mother said.

"What? Is Papa okay?"

"He's fine, he's standing right next to me. It's Kosmos. He's had a heart attack."

"So get the doctors to make it better," Grace said. She wrapped her right arm tight around her stomach.

"Darling, I can't. He's gone."

"Gone where?"

"The doctors did all they could. He's no longer with us."

Grace held the phone away from her ear and tried to let the news sink in. The warmth of her grandfather's affection was one of Grace's few securities in life. She gasped, "This can't be taken away from me, I won't let it. Make him breathe again. This can't be happening."

She dropped the phone, pushed past the secretary and sprinted out the building and through the school's main entry gates. She ran and ran, though didn't get very far before getting the stitch, so walked, then sprinted a few more steps, walked, then ran until her legs gave way and collapsed to the ground. She was a few streets from the train station and realised that she had no money to go anywhere. When some air finally returned to her lungs she got up and kicked a nearby wooden fence.

Stupid, stupid, stupid fence.

Grace kept kicking it until she heard the growl of what she imagined to be a large German Shepherd. She ran past the next house, and the next, and the next, until she only wanted to collapse. She reached the dry creek bed near the railway lines and curled up into a ball on the lifeless bank where she sobbed her heart out. Exhaustion descended and her chest felt as if a sledgehammer had smashed it.

Then the words came pouring out. "How dare you! How dare you take one of the people I most love in this world away from me! How do you expect me to survive school now? I have no one. No one. Do you hear me? I don't know what I'm going to do," she howled. Her body quivered and her lower jaw chattered as a gust of air gathered around her feet. "Don't even talk to me!"

"Grace, holding on to your grief will only cause you more pain."

"Holding on? What am I holding on to? There is nothing to hold on to. He's gone!"

"He hasn't gone."

She snapped. "Of course he's gone. Don't rehash your 'I am everywhere and nowhere' routine. If you really are everywhere, Wind, you would've heard Mum tell me on the phone that Kosmos died. Died. He's dead."

"I was with you, Grace."

"Then why didn't you stop it? Isn't that one of your super powers?" she demanded.

"There is a time and season for everything under the sun."

"Stop right there. Leave me alone. Go! Please, please," she begged, "just leave me alone."

"My child, as the cherry blossoms bloom, they must also fall to the ground; as strawberries are picked fresh, they must also eventually rot. Everything in life is fleeting."

She pretended she couldn't hear.

"Grace, please don't turn your back on me. All we have in life are moments. Memorable moments that morph into boring ones, which transform into euphoric occasions that transmute into harsh and painful milliseconds of time. Each is to be prized."

"Oh, I get it. You're about to tell me that this is a joyous moment, and rather than lying on the ground I should be up dancing with a wide smile on my face, right?"

"Life doesn't stay the same forever," the Wind said. "You've read Emily Dickinson's line: 'That it will never come again is what makes life so sweet', haven't you?"

Grace wanted the ground to swallow her up and take her to wherever Kosmos was.

"Moments are fleeting. That's how nature is, living and dying in a continuous cycle of birth, death and rebirth. Fire is a natural part of a forest's regeneration system to invigorate new growth. Nature is a paradoxical process continuously in a state of recycling, like a wave that forms, breaks and disappears back in on itself."

All she wanted to do now was sleep.

"It's a normal human reaction to want moments to be of a different colour and length rather than letting them just be."

"What does any of this have to do with Kosmos?" Just saying his name made the tears well up.

"Moments can't be relived, they're one-offs. You can't have that time with Kosmos again, Grace."

"So why didn't I live my time with him like I could lose him at any moment?"

"What would you have done differently, Grace?" the Wind asked.

"I'd have told him how special he was to me and how I treasured the blanket of comfort his presence gave me. I would've hugged and kissed him more, told him I loved him a million times over." The snivelling started again.

"Grace, it's okay. Cry your pain."

She jumped up and started pacing the creek bed.

"I don't mean to alarm you, Grace, but in time your mother, father, Abel, and Veronika will also be gone. Meaningfully engage with life from your heart, knowing one day all in it will depart."

"Could someone please dislodge this sledgehammer from my heart?" Grace cried to an imaginary audience. "How can he be taken away from me? How can death barge in and remove what's mine, deeming it needs Kosmos more than me? He belongs to me—to life—not death."

"He hasn't been taken away from you, Grace. And he was never yours to begin with."

"Of course he was mine. He was *my* grandfather."

"He was never yours to own—only yours to love, cherish and experience—but never to own, Grace."

"So you're saying everyone I know will eventually die and all I can do is love them in the meantime? Brilliant! Just exactly the comforting words I want to hear at this minute."

"Put simply, yes. And this will help you value all future moments knowing they'll never come again. There'll never be another Kosmos and there'll never be another moment like this one. The pain will only increase if you continue to grasp on so tightly."

Her tears tasted salty and bitter.

"Relinquishing the need to hold on doesn't mean you don't enjoy all of life's experiences. All I ask is that you submit yourself to the impermanence of all things. It's only fear that makes us want to hold on."

"This sucks, sucks, sucks!" she shouted.

"I understand," the Wind said. "So honour how much it hurts and know this pain will pass. Recall what I've taught you. Don't go back to past moments and wish them different, nor place terms and expectations on how future moments should appear."

More tears fell from her eyes.

"Grace, don't fight this moment of wrenching pain. Experience the sensations—without judgment. Smell the trees, touch the dry mud of the creek bed, watch the slow-moving clouds, feel your heart shrivelling with grief and really taste the bitter saltiness of your tears. Can you become one with the moment by folding into it so you don't know where it ends and you begin? Merge with the moment and dissolve all barriers, so only love remains."

Both her resistance and her tears drained her. Grace surrendered. She did it for Kosmos. She stood up and steadied herself on her feet, deeply breathed into her belly and created some space in her mind. She placed her awareness in her feet as she imagined them growing roots and fusing into the mud, grounding her to the landscape. As she did, she felt a sense of oneness rising from the earth's core through the soles of her feet.

The Wind waited for some time in silence before saying, "Grace, view this moment as if it happened to someone else, like Juliet or Ruby. What would you say or do?"

Grace replied, "First I'd hug her and feel my body support hers and let her cry her tears on my shoulder. I'd ask her not to let the hurt and loss she's feeling now cloud the wonder of life."

"So can you feel this also for yourself? Can you perceive this moment from a much higher place than here?"

"I don't want to be here anymore."

"Where do you want to go?"

"I want to see Veronika."

"Let's get home then."

She took a deep breath, kicked the dirt bed one more time and started slowly walking back to the school grounds. Passing through the iron gates, Grace was shocked to see her father in discussion with the school secretary.

"Papa!" she shrieked and ran to him.

He hugged her back and held her tight. "Oh sweetie, oh sweetie, oh sweetie."

Dylan thanked the administrative staff and led Grace to the car park, his left arm around her shoulder, his right hand holding Grace's school bag, which the secretary had picked up from class.

Sitting in the car, Grace felt a mess. She also felt ashamed.

Where did all that time from the phone call go?

A frog lodged in her throat when she asked, "Where are we going now?"

"Home."

"Is Mum cross with me?"

"No."

"Are you?"

"No. Nobody's cross with you, Grace. We're all simply lost," Dylan said. "We've lost our true north."

⁂

As the car turned into their driveway, her mother's hatchback was already there. Her father had barely parked when Grace jumped out and ran inside to hug her mother. She caught sight of Veronika and a wave of enormous guilt swamped her. Her distress had only been about how much she'd miss Kosmos, never once considering Veronika's loss. As childhood sweethearts, she'd known him for almost her entire life.

She went to her. Veronika looked drawn but composed. She pushed Grace's matted hair off her face, kissed her on the crown, and said, "Don't cry, pumpkin. He's gone, but we still have each other."

Grace started to wail again. Veronika held her close, and in her embrace Grace felt her body soften and capitulate. She felt her father staring at them in the kitchen and Grace drew on the Wind's words. "Look at this moment from above; witness the beauty the height gives you." She tightened her arms around her grandmother's petite waist and told her how much she loved her.

Veronika gently released herself from Grace's clasp so she could look into her eyes. "I know, my dear. Kosmos knew how much you loved him too. Never doubt this."

"But I didn't tell him how much," Grace said, ruefully looking down at the floor.

"You didn't need to, Grace, he knew."

With her head hung low, she wanted to know exactly how Kosmos knew but gave up needing proof and decided to trust.

"But where's Abel?"

Her father replied, "We haven't been able to reach him yet. He's not allowed to have his mobile on in class. Soon, though."

84 | Grief and Loss

Grace slept fitfully and woke early. A breeze blew by the tip of her nose.

"Wind, is that you?" It always was the Wind; she asked the question more out of habit. "I was dreaming of circles. If that's not a symbol, then I don't know what is."

"Until the end of time the world will operate in cycles, Grace. You're born, you die, it's summer then it's winter. Life is never a straight line."

Summer was Grace's favourite season. Endless balmy nights with no need for jackets and the smell and sound of good times constantly filling the air.

"Nothing really ends, it merely moves into another form, like you progressing from a teenager to an adult. When we perceive life cyclically it comforts us. If we think in a linear manner all we're confronted with are dead ends," the Wind said.

Grace slowly stretched her body.

"It's human nature to want to get everywhere fast: be an adult before we've completed our teens, achieved success before we've been tested, demand a finished painting before we've even drawn the first line. It's not about anticipating the next part of the cycle, but being one with the phase we're in now. Be with the energetic experience and make peace with the moment."

Grace conceded that she'd be in the cycle of grief for quite a while. "But how can cycles help us on a day-to-day basis?" A sense of embarrassment entered as the question concerned her, not Kosmos.

"Cycles help ground us, bringing much-needed perspective. Seasonal foods, birthdays, anniversaries, solar, lunar and stellar calendars—they all help remind us of the bigger picture."

Grace rubbed her bleary eyes.

"Getting back to Kosmos . . ."

Sharp pain wedged deep into her chest again. This was no ordinary new day. This was the first day without her beloved grandfather in the world.

"Cycles contain growth spurts and stagnation, reminding us life is never stationary. We've been through this before, Grace. Nature teaches us not to get too particularly attached to one phase, as another will soon appear. Nothing is motionless, not even your grief."

"So this pain will disappear?" She phrased it as a question, not a statement of fact.

"Yes, it will. But it could be replaced with more anguish and sorrow."

The changeability of emotions frightened her.

"I really need you to sense where you are in this point of the cycle. Feel this particular grieving phase now—in all its depth—so in later years you won't need to grieve again. Respectfully honour your loss and experience your sorrow."

The last thing Grace wanted to do was dwell on her aching heart; she'd do anything to escape it.

"Look down on this moment from a distance."

As Grace closed her eyes, her nose twitched and the tears started.

"What's going on, Grace? Talk to me."

Her voice was staccato-like and broken. "Something's been shattered inside me. I'm so angry that Kosmos has been taken away from me. Why me?" she wailed.

"You believe bad things shouldn't happen to you?" the Wind gently asked.

"Yes, of course," she said, and sniffled.

"And that difficult life circumstances should only touch other people, but never you?"

"I don't want any tragedies affecting me or anyone I love."

"But to other people, that's fine?"

"Yep."

"Three things, Grace. First, not possible; second, not possible, and in conclusion, it's just not possible. Avoiding 'bad' things is not the sole purpose of your human existence. You believe you're successful if you dodge these bullets, but in doing that you miss the fundamental human experience. To encounter the entire range of emotions through the lens of your soul is the purpose of life." The Wind paused. "I want you to be present in each of the highs—and all of the lows—witnessing their sacredness and accurately perceiving them for what they are, opportunities to give and receive divine love within the dance of creation. Embody presence in all you do and be awakened in action. Now look up above, what do you see?"

Effortlessly, as though he truly was there, Grace declared, "I see Kosmos looking down on me, sending me light. He's sending me all the love that exists in the world to give me the strength to get out of bed and make my way through the day."

"Can you accept this gift he's giving you, Grace? Can you open your heart and receive what he's sending?"

"I can, but I feel so drained."

"Feel his love invigorating you," the Wind instructed. "Visualise his pulsing rays of light energising your grace, and if at any time today you feel you can't cope then call on me, and I will help breathe you from moment to moment. None of us gets through this life on our own, Grace; we all need assistance from the divine."

She felt an incredible resilience emerge within her. She knew she could survive the day with her grandfather's light and the promise of the Wind's breath.

"Granted, physical touch is what you'll miss from Kosmos now that he's gone, but we touch those we love by leaving an imprint on their hearts for eternity. To get through today, make one thing better in your grandmother and mother's lives. Find some way to ease their grief. Veronika has lost her life partner; your mother her father. In helping them deal with their loss, you'll lessen your own. The deepest cuts are healed by grace."

A flash of illumination struck her: This bullet of grief was not one to dodge, but one that had her name engraved on it, and she'd proudly take the hit.

"Always smile to greet the day, Grace—even in difficult circumstances—as with each tender step you take until you shuffle off this mortal coil, you will gain strength, and synchronous events and people will be drawn to your flame as you awaken to your grace and place this sacred awareness into action."

85 | Your Inner Treasure

The house seemed awfully busy when Grace finally rose. Her mother was on the phone to the funeral home and her father was outside mowing the back lawn, even though a slight drizzle had appeared in the air. In a weird way, life was somehow going on as normal, except that she didn't have to attend school today. Grace went to the pantry, grabbed some cereal, a bowl and spoon from the cupboard and almond milk from the fridge.

Her mother put the phone down and kissed her on the back of her head and started detailing the funeral arrangements. Grace wasn't really listening but then remembered what the Wind said to her earlier in bed. She could ease her mother's pain with the gift of her attention, so she placed the spoon down and gave all of herself to her mother's words.

"That's right, Grace. Paying attention so another feels heard is a form of love."

Her mother's stance softened as she felt she was finally being listened to. "I'm so relieved I can talk this through with you," she sighed, then turned Grace's head around to loosely plait her hair. Grace patiently listened to her mother for several minutes until she said, "Now, your brother on the other hand . . ."

"I can go wake him."

With that Grace pushed herself off the stool and headed upstairs to Abel's room to rouse him. Returning downstairs, she told her mother she was going for a walk.

"What? In your nightie?"

She glanced outside. "It's stopped drizzling. I'll bring a jacket."

She put on the tweed duffle coat and only from the shins down could anyone see the bottom frill of the nightie sticking out. Wearing some tatty old sneakers she marched down the driveway, turned right up the street and kept going. "Will I feel sad for a very long time?" she asked the Wind.

"Grace, we need to reassess what it means to heal in our culture today. Some injuries are very obvious, like when you broke your ankle, but there are many slights that happen to us during the course of our days that also need healing."

"Such as?"

"Remember when you thought the waiter at Bistro Palais was rude to you?"

Grace nodded.

"You carried that pain and anguish around with you for most of the next day, and it was completely unnecessary."

"Yeah, I remember."

"The emotional disturbances you don't acknowledge and dissolve the instant they occur, you bring with you to the next moment, thereby tainting a new juncture in time. Try not to carry yesterday's or last year's frustrations with you into today, Grace," the Wind said, "and this will allow you to enter each new moment with a fresh, clean state."

Her sneakers squeaked on the wet footpath.

"As any basketballer who misses a shot knows," the Wind said, "you must let that shot go so you can nail the next one. If you keep replaying the previous failed attempt over and over in your mind, you'll fail to sink the basket currently in front of you."

In light you can't be out of place.

"Now, getting back to emotional disturbances. The waiter's perceived rudeness had nothing to do with you."

"It had everything to do with me," Grace butted in.

The Wind corrected, "No. His rudeness had everything to do with him. You were the one who made it something to do with you. From the soul's perspective, others' reactions to us are just their own expressions of their shadow or their grace. In response to their shadow all you can do is offer compassion. Yes, the waiter's attitude hurt your personality, but the soul thinks—in your words—'whatever' and then displays to him the kindness he can't, in this moment, access within himself."

"Meaning?"

"The waiter was curt to you, but his manner doesn't diminish your soul in any way, shape or form. You accept it and move on; it doesn't cast a cloud on your meal or a thunderstorm over the rest of your day. The reality was that your waiter was impolite—for whatever reason—and that's all you entertain of the fact. Thinking there's something you did to cause his behaviour is a sign that your personality is in control."

Once again, the glaring truth pierced through her heavy veil.

✦

"Grace, remember a few weeks back when you weren't feeling that great and didn't know what was wrong?" Grace nodded. "Well, you could've asked your body what was wrong."

Grace was bemused. "So just as I asked the Ocean for help, I now need to ask my body for advice too?"

"Why do you find this so difficult to take in, Grace? All the wisdom that exists in the world resides in you. It's just that you don't access it as you're habitually looking outside yourself for all manner of things; validation, happiness, security, love."

"But that's what we're taught—to find knowledge in books, happiness in material possessions, security in a blue-chip share portfolio, and love through another's eyes."

"Grace, you go within to seek your treasure."

"But how?"

"For instance, if your shoulders ache, ask them why they ache? What do they need from you to feel better? Also ask them why they're aching now? What is it specifically they're trying to draw your attention to? What cure are they seeking? Be your own healer dispensing your own medicine."

She slowed down to walk at a snail's pace.

"Also Grace, I want you when you're physically ill to create space and time around you to allow your body's own magic to heal itself. When you next have a cold, let it work its way naturally through your system without using cold and flu tablets, which only disguise the symptoms."

"I don't know what Mum would say about that. You know how much she hates people who sniffle."

"I know. She'd want them blowing their noses and not trying to hold it in; we're both in agreement on that."

"But what does any of this have to do with Kosmos?"

"Because the way through this tough time exists within you," the Wind explained. "I want you to be able to discern the rhythm of health as much as sickness, to put joy on par with sorrow and to consider that loss can sometimes be as valuable as victory. Profound healing only occurs through complete acceptance of the current state you're in, and then allowing the emotion to fully express itself in whatever form it needs to take. Do you understand what I'm saying, Grace?"

Her eyes began watering.

"It'll take time to readjust back at school and it'll be even tougher visiting Veronika in their home as you'll expect Kosmos to be there in his chair, his presence filling the room. You'll crave a hug, an encouraging word, and he won't be there to give it."

"I'll never be able to eat with him at Lorenzo's again. There'll be no more bread to share . . ." Her voice trailed off.

"Grace, grief can decimate people, but the first stage of healing is accepting that he's gone."

"But I don't want to."

"The more you resist reality, the more it will break you. If you deem the situation unacceptable then you've pitted yourself against it and turned the present moment into an enemy. You can't argue with what is, Grace. You can't make Kosmos come back to life; it's not in your power."

"But I didn't choose for his time to end."

"No, his soul and the divine did. Commit to memory—and your bones—how little true control you have."

A shiver ran up her spine.

"Can you finally grasp your insignificance in one sense of the word—and world—yet know you're hugely significant in other ways? You can't bring Kosmos back to life, but it was most certainly in your power to love him."

Why didn't the Wind enter my life earlier? Things would've been a whole lot different then.

"Life is exquisitely designed so I entered at precisely the right moment, just as you allowed me in at the accurate time too. Not a second too early, nor a minute too late. Grace, dismember the false self and be guided by the force of this subtle intelligence. Be in sacred relationship with the universe and surrender to life's unfolding. Can you do this?"

With utmost confidence she answered, "Yes." Had she not learned anything from their year together?

She turned the final corner of their block but still didn't feel ready to go back home and deal with the sorrow and angst. The air suddenly stilled and for a moment she thought the Wind had disappeared.

"I'm never away from you, Grace, it only appears so. Exactly as you can call on me, you can also call on Kosmos."

"But he's gone."

"Grace, he's only departed this physical world. Inside he's always there for you. No one ever goes away in essence."

"Really?"

"When you think of him, what impressions come to you?"

"How he devotedly approached life, how much he worshipped Veronika, how his face came alive when listening to classical music, and how he wanted nothing but the best for Abel and me." She choked up and wiped her nose on her sleeve.

"That's all still there, my sweet. These impressions on your heart never go away. If you need him just call out to him, and he'll be there."

Grace really wanted to believe this was true.

"Talk to Kosmos, Grace, and he'll answer back. The divine essence of him never dies, so try not to shut him out. All that's happened is you can no longer see his body like you used to. Likewise, you can't see my form but you can feel my presence, correct?"

A gust of air came up from behind and twigs and leaves floated and danced in Grace's wake.

"It's the same with Kosmos. You'll be aware of him in a tearshaped raindrop clinging to a leaf, you'll smell his zesty aftershave at random moments or hear him in a song on the radio. Grace, you don't think your way to healing, you feel your way through. You've been mentally judging your grief, and now it's time to feel it."

"I am feeling it."

"No, you're not. You're thinking about your loss; how Kosmos won't see you graduate from high school, attend your wedding, or be an influence on your own children, but this is all in your mind. Shift the mental pain to your heart and feel these things you're thinking about—don't keep them as mental constructs in your head."

"So when I think about how much I miss Kosmos, shift the thought instead to my heart and belly and sense how much I'll miss him via the feelings that erupt in my body?"

She figured playing the role of the earnest student could help her through the grief.

"Exactly, but be gentle with yourself. There's no one right way to heal, Grace. Healing is miraculous and occurs in its own divine time—spontaneous or otherwise. People cope with grief in different ways, so let those around you mourn in their own individual way."

Grace subconsciously felt her mother worrying about her. She was almost halfway around the block, but rather than keep in that direction she decided to run back the way she had come. Slowing down as she approached their driveway, she leisurely walked through the front door. Her mother was on the phone again and turned to give her a relieved smile. Her father had finished mowing the lawn and was now absorbed in reading the newspaper.

She headed upstairs to shower. Letting the water caress her body, Grace visualised the liquid droplets washing her grief away, down the drain, to be rejoined with the expanse of the ocean.

86 | Fragrant Blessings

A month had passed since Kosmos's funeral. Grace's favourite season was still in bloom as life strangely returned to normal. The waft of the gardenias in the Botanical Gardens reached her before she spied a couple of them in a corner next to some night-flowering jasmine trees. The intoxicating flowers had always been a favourite of both Veronika and Kosmos, and their scent brought back his memory. She asked the Wind to tell her more about communicating with Kosmos's soul.

The Wind answered, "From your soul call him by name three times. He can then feel and trust that the connection's been established. Send your love to his soul with all your being. In return he'll use his entire soul's strength to guide you in any way you ask."

Grace felt weak today, completely flat, but didn't want to turn to Kosmos and laden him with her troubles. She knew he'd never in a million years feel put upon or burdened, but this Saturday afternoon in the gardens (slowly being overrun with loved-up couples strolling arm-in-arm) she decided to bring splendour to her soul by immersing herself in nature. The heady scent from the flowering gardenias helped enormously.

Alone and sitting on one of the park benches, the alluring, romantic smell of the fragrant flowering shrubs brought her back to the moment. They smelled aloof—but still warm—if that were at all possible. Grace knew it was certainly possible in people.

As the late morning went on and the sun inched towards its crescendo, more people piled into the gardens: children to swing on swings and lovers to kiss on park benches.

"Grace, smell is a great mood shifter," the Wind chimed in, "because the olfactory bulb is part of the brain's limbic system, which is associated with memory. It's why a particular smell can take us back to our childhood in a millisecond . . ."

She didn't want a science lecture now, so she focused instead on Kosmos's love of clean citrus scents.

" . . . though our senses are finite."

She pulled her attention back from the memory of her grand-father to the Wind's words. "Explain what that means?"

"You are infinite but your senses are finite."

"Again?" In the distance she could see patrons sitting outside the botanical café settling down for lunchtime. Grace now felt like ordering some jasmine tea; for some reason just one sip of this sweet and delicate liquid took her to a higher, lighter space.

"Your five senses are a limited way of experiencing the world. When you focus only on the finite world you merely have access to finite power, but when you connect with the infinite, you tap into infinite potential. When you perceive situations from the perspective of infinity, you comprehend what real power is."

"The moon's gravitational force, not Amber-Jane's cool clique at school, right?"

"Correct. Let what you can't see guide you, Grace. Turn your trust to the invisible. Set your gaze on the force field of love that exists in all people and things. Know you can experience life through more than your five physical senses, which don't even begin to compare to the divine riches of your inner world."

"But I can't seem to shake myself from the past."

"Only because you've empowered it with energy. You've over-invested in a sandcastle, and the tide is rising fast."

Grace shook her head, she couldn't take it all in. Instead she asked the Wind to teach her more about fragrances. In this moment the finite world she could cope with; a lesson on eternity she could not.

"Scents impact not only our memory, but also our behaviour."

Grace pondered that point, concurring.

297

"Certain smells make us eat faster or slower, wake us up or slow us down and act as markers of time in our lives."

"That's true. Newborns have that wonderful, innocent smell about them."

Grace got up and meandered to another section of the gardens before heading to the café.

"Inhale and absorb the scents around you. Intensely smell the air and flowers, breathe in their healing energy."

She did as asked.

"Also, get into the habit of smelling your food before tasting it to add to the sensuality of the experience. Aromas are a gift of the finite world, so give thanks when life's bouquet crosses your nose."

"Like the trace of a stranger's leafy green aftershave as they push past you to get off the train?"

"Just as much as the obvious perfumes your mother wears, with the ever-expanding scented layers revealing themselves over time. Try to detect when one layer of aroma evaporates and a new one takes its place. Sense subtlety in the obvious."

Grace was enthused, liking how she could ground this conversation in 'real' time. "I once read in a magazine that the top note of a perfume gives the first impression—it creates the mood. The mid-note," she was amazed she could recall the exact terminology, "is the middle layer—the heart—and gives character to the fragrance. And the base note is its foundation and theme. It's a tale that escalates and plateaus over time."

"Though you do know, Grace, that most perfumes are made of chemicals," the Wind added, "and we have enough synthetics in our lives already."

Grace wasn't prepared to have her sensual image of perfumes equated with chemicals just yet. A thought entered on the boring scent of her bedroom.

"If you don't like the way it smells, change it," the Wind replied. "Every night you're in there slaving over your homework, so diffuse some citrus essential oils in the room to inspire and invigorate you, or bathe with lavender and vetiver oils to relax your body before bed. Feel the underlying rhythm the moment is calling for and bring in a scent to match."

Grace mused on all the distinct odours that appeared via different guises at various times of the day.

"I know you love the smell of rain on freshly mown grass, but tonight, Grace, I want you to attempt to smell dusk. You've probably never thought to inhale the air as day gives way to night, but I want you to try."

"I have," Grace argued back. "It smells of closure."

The Wind expanded further on the topic. "Use your sense of smell as another way to immerse yourself more fully into moments. We can also sniff moods as you rightly suggested—anticipation, excitement, loneliness, fear—as well as the future. For example, smoke often warns of danger."

"I love the smell of Mum frying butter in the kitchen," Grace said. She rested on a bench within the walled English Garden to admire the shapes of the topiaries: balls, cones, pyramids, and obelisks.

"Deeply inhale this nutty, toasty scent and you'll bypass the thinking mind. This way you'll heighten the experience of the short-lived now."

She wished for a patrician's nose, but that wasn't a very 'here and now' thought.

"When you're ready to leave, find the gardenias again and hold your nose close to them," the Wind instructed. "Cup the flowers and allow them to dispense their aroma into your heart. Feel their life force at your core—and in return breathe life back into them through your acknowledgment. Flowers and plants need our recognition as much as we need their beauty. Remember your interdependency, Grace. You're not an island complete unto yourself."

Grace closed her eyes and in her mind drew a heart, feeling herself to be where the two lines met in a V-shape at the bottom.

"Pick a single flower and tuck it behind your ear; don't turn these gifts of nature into mummies in a museum."

She then visualised her own future wedding bouquet of blush-coloured orchids, mauve roses, peonies and gardenias and decided then and there not to have the arrangement pressed, rearranged and framed. The flowers should die as nature intended.

87 | The Current of Life

Grace believed one of the reasons boys didn't fancy her was that she was difficult and asked tough questions.

The Wind replied, "Grace, you're wrong. Boys do like girls who are exacting in their standards and challenge them; who they don't particularly care for are unhappy girls who don't like themselves."

Grace was at Jameson Beach with Veronika, sitting on the benches by the foreshore watching the fishermen set up their tackle. On the sand a group of young boy scouts and their leader attempted to fly a kite emblazoned with a dragon. The picture perfect sky looked as if it were on loan from a movie set, and the salt in the sea breeze cleansed Grace's mind.

"Watch how the fishermen align with the tides," Veronika said as she rubbed some sunscreen on Grace's nose and cheeks. "Ebb and flow. Kosmos really understood this." She rubbed the excess cream into her hands. "The tide goes in, it goes out, and it's never forced."

Grace gazed out to sea.

"If you'll allow an old lady to delve into her past, when I wanted to leave my role as a governess, your grandfather said to me, 'You don't force the change from one state to another, instead you drift out of it into something new.'" Tears formed in the pit of her eyes as she placed her head on her granddaughter's shoulder. "I miss him so, Grace."

The kite arced across the sky as the Wind in a subdued voice whispered, "I'll feed you the words to tell your grandmother."

And so Grace began. "A friend told me just as there are distinctive seasons in life, there are also correlating emotions. We can't only live in the summer of our lives; it's part of the human condition to tough out a harsh and difficult winter too."

Veronika perked up. She straightened her back and delicately placed her right fingers on Grace's shoulder. "That's very true, my pumpkin, and in my life I've had far more summers than winters because I've entrusted my days to the wisdom of something higher." Veronika lifted her hand to point to the sky. "Untold joy befriends you once you surrender to the current of life as it carries you to where you need to be. Work with the current—don't make it an opposing force in your life."

"Let's go get an ice cream," Grace said as she helped her grand-mother up. Linking arms, they strolled to the ice cream parlour.

Veronika continued, "Watch a fast flowing river and imagine trying to swim upstream. Hopeless! But if you move in the direct-ion of the water, it'll effortlessly carry you to the next landing. It doesn't mean abdicating responsibility and drifting through life. People think going with the flow means doing nothing, but more accurately, it implies working with the conditions of your life, not against them."

Grace from experience knew she had to work with the ocean to catch a wave. If she didn't paddle, the sea couldn't propel her for-ward. Mutual energy was required to achieve freedom from effort.

"My friend said the tide takes us out when it needs to and brings us back in one piece too," Grace said. "It'll do the strenuous work for us if we're only light enough to let go and allow ourselves to be carried."

She remembered wading against the current in a shallow stream and how every step on the pebbles felt laborious, but when she turned to amble in the direction of the water, she was able to look up and enjoy the view.

"You have a wise friend, Grace. Hold onto them."

Grace worried that her tutorials with the Wind would soon be coming to a close and that the conditions influencing the river's flow were starting to change.

At the ice cream parlour she chose a single scoop of chocolate ice cream, immersing her awareness in every individual spoonful and imagined herself becoming as rich, creamy and smooth as the tastes on her tongue.

That evening, Grace took her makeup off before bed as a symbolic gesture of leaving the day behind in the past where it belonged.

88 | The Beauty of Holism

It was blowing a gale outside her bedroom window. The Wind was trying to get Grace's attention and tell her something, but what?

Be in time. Exist as the witness. Detach. Pull your energy out of the past. Remain inwardly attentive. Meet the moment with transfiguring grace.

She let out a stifled laugh as she was now giving herself this advice, not the Wind.

After dinner, the Wind pulled Grace outside. "I'll leave a note for you under your pillow this evening," it whispered. "As you prepare for bed, you can meditate on my words."

Grace couldn't wait for the day to end. Lying in bed she practiced the Wind's suggestion of directing different parts of her body to release and relax and to express gratitude for at least five people or events from the day. Her hand then reached under the bottom pillow and the promised note was there. She propped up the goose feather and down pillows and began reading:

> *Holism is not viewing yourself as a discrete unit detached from others or the various disconnected fragments of yourself as separate. I want you to perceive yourself as whole, and integrate all the parts that make up you— your light, shadow and the masses of grey in between. Be conscious of the sum total, not only your pieces, and your wider role in the web of interconnectivity, the net of light.*

The Wind's handwriting was in the old-fashioned cursive style where all the letters of a word ran smoothly into each other.

All is one, and the more you keep labelling this as 'good' for you and that as 'bad', the more harmful it is. Saying you're 'bad' when you do this, but 'good' when you do that only leads to estrangement of thought and actions. Disassociating yourself from the dark shades inside causes fissures and fracturing. You possess both light and dark qualities within yourself. Accept this. Attempting to rid yourself of that which you despise is not the way forward; instead bring the shadows to the light so they can be integrated into the whole.

As a whole and holy being, preserve your humanity by honouring the humanity in others. You were part of a greater whole before you became an individuated spark of the divine here on earth.

Grace placed the beautiful piece of parchment on her knees and recalled how during one self-perpetuated drama the Wind advised her to more deeply attach to humanity than herself. She held that thought in her mind before returning to the letter.

Cultivate a discerning vulnerability as you reclaim your real power. Find your place in the world and fully occupy it, then merge and be one with others. Shadow work births you into compassion, which liberates you. Feel love for every living thing, and this will help you approve of the parts of yourself that you reject.

I'm not saying love at the expense of your family and friends, but don't contain your love. Don't keep it only for your immediate family and forget the larger family of which you're a part. The more you recognise wholeness in others, the easier it'll be for you to accept your shadow tendencies, as well as those in others. Be okay with contradictions, as they'll lead to congruency if you accept them as part of your total self. Holism is not about always and never. It involves observing the patterns intertwining cause and effect, action and reaction and fluidly moving between the mysterious, paradoxical processes of nature. As one of the Mayan oracles states, 'Polarity is the loom on which reality is strung, the magnetic dance of universal forces.'

Thus the letter ended. Just like that. The Wind didn't even sign its name.

Grace pulled the pillows down, tucked the letter back underneath and promptly fell asleep to explore the symbols behind the Wind's words in her dreams. In the morning there was another note lying on top of her bedside table.

Missed opportunities don't exist. If the opportunity is vital for your soul's growth it'll come around again, only the next time wearing a different costume. You will experience all you were meant to in this lifetime. Never doubt this. What's rightfully yours will never pass you by. Fret not, now give thanks for your breath and greet this new day with love in your heart.

89 | Invisible Changes

Grace couldn't see her 'heightened awareness' making a noticeable impact on her daily life. It was as frustrating as cutting sugar out of her diet, and religiously working out at the gym, and at the end of a fortnight still being the exact same weight. She thought she'd be gliding through life by now.

Shouldn't my world be problem-free and flowing perfectly?

"Is that what you still think the meaning of life is?" the Wind asked. "A comfortable stroll through the woods?"

"I just want . . ."

"I know what you want. You want everything to go your way and, Grace, that is just not going to happen."

"But it should." The petulant teenager reappeared.

"Regarding your progress, isn't it enough for you to feel the sea changes within yourself?"

"Er, no." Why couldn't the Wind remember she was only a teenager? Of course she needed external validation of her growth by others, especially her peer group.

"It's not only teenagers, Grace, most adults also need validation."

At least she didn't feel so alone.

"All change first happens inside. Outside changes will follow soon enough, as the external becomes the mirror to the internal. Keep the focus on developing your interior life, Grace. It all starts and ends there."

"I guess it's the only thing within my sphere I can control too."

"Attune yourself to what's required from you in each moment, and divine timing will take care of the rest."

"Instead of trying to make things happen, let them happen," Grace pronounced.

"And to achieve this attitudinal metamorphosis some aspect of us needs to die. Not literally," the Wind explained, "but there's a part of ourselves we must release. The caterpillar can't accompany us on the journey of transforming into a butterfly."

"It's impossible." Grace knew this for sure.

"To transcend, we must dismantle the blocks in our lives holding us back. Consider how nature only uses what's necessary; the unnecessary is forsaken as a drain on resources. To transform your life ask, 'What's depleting my reserves?' Is it a person, an attitude or an outdated belief system?"

Grace looked inside and asked, "What's preventing my metamorphosis?" Then it came to her in a flash. "I believe I'm not deserving of this transformation."

"When it's time to give up the limiting beliefs that aren't working for you they'll instantly melt out of your life. It's all perfectly orchestrated, so trust when it's right for the butterfly to emerge from its cocoon into new circumstances—it will. Grace, you are that butterfly."

But she was still human. "I'm tired of trusting, Wind. Can't I have some cold, hard proof?"

"Transformation is all around you, Grace. It may appear as if nothing's happening, but know a tremendous creative force is at work—and play—in the dark. Hold onto this knowledge instead of looking for results."

"This is the 'Trust that the mountain exists behind the fog' speech, right?"

"The metamorphosis only comes when you trust the universe's schedule over your personality's timetable," the Wind affirmed.

"Invisible changes are occurring," Grace confirmed to herself.

90 | Reaching for the Stars

That evening Grace was at a farm an hour from the city owned by one of the partners at her father's firm. Both she and Abel were bored beyond belief. It was an annual event, and their father really didn't ask for any of their social time throughout the year save for showing up at this one work event. This was the extent of their social obligations to him.

"I'm so bored," Grace complained to her mother.

"And ya think I'm not?" Abel added. "These people are office drones."

Carla immediately leapt to Dylan's defence. "These drones make up a large part of your father's world. Remember, you're not here for yourselves and your own amusement, but for him. You are a reflection of your father this evening—and if you cared anything for him, you'd know that. Now, go be jovial!"

Abel usually fulfilled his family duties with as little effort as possible but tonight said, "Sis, I guess we should go put our small talk skills to use."

They decided to start with a couple younger than their parents, who were walking with piled-high plates filled with meats and vegetables from the barbecue.

"Hi there. Struggling with those plates, I see?"

"Yes, well, we want to try a bit of everything," replied the lady.

"Let me introduce ourselves. I'm Abel and this is my sister, Grace. We're Dylan Rose's kids."

Abel transformed his usual slang into eloquent sentences when he felt that the moment called for it.

"Oh, so you're Dylan's offspring," the guy answered back. "He talks about you two non-stop. I'm Geoff and this is my wife, Sasha. My office is next to your father's. It's great to match the faces with the names and accomplishments."

What's this guy talking about?

Geoff turned to his wife and said, "Abel is doing a science degree at Blacks University, and Grace is moving into eleventh grade at Hamilton High, and both are doing incredibly well in their studies. Abel's also interested in herbal medicine, and Grace hopes to pursue some sort of creative study when she finishes school."

Neither of them could speak. Was it themselves he just described?

"You are the apples of your father's eye," Geoff continued.

"Well, it was a pleasure meeting you," Abel interrupted, "but if you'll please excuse us, I've just remembered a message I forgot to pass on to our mother."

"Of course. Lovely meeting you both," Geoff and Sasha chimed together and turned their attention back to the buffet on their plates.

They ambled across the manicured pasture and paddock to go find their mother.

"Now that was spooky."

"I know! Papa almost sounds proud of us."

The Wind interjected, "Your father is eternally proud of you, Grace. He's just not that great at showing it."

"Wait! Why are we going to find Mum?"

"To tell her how weird that was."

"It wasn't all that strange, Abe. I guess we don't see the way Papa feels about us when we're not around. I mean, we're usually either screaming at him to leave us alone or asking for money."

Abel stopped in his tracks. "I can't remember when in the last year I asked him about his job and actually listened to what he said back."

Grace urgently grabbed Abel's hand. "It's Papa we need to go find."

They found him with a group of other senior partners standing around the barbecue.

310

"Papa, can we speak to you for a sec?" Grace interrupted.

Dylan excused himself. "What's up, kids?"

Grace didn't know where to start. Their father did so much for them, which they never really acknowledged. "Well, Papa, it's your generosity, love and protection of us, the ability to enjoy the small things that bring you great happiness and . . ."

Dylan cut in. "Am I dead, Grace? It sounds as if you're reading a eulogy."

"What she's saying, Dad, is you're the one who's helped provide us with all of our opportunities. All the good fortune we've experienced in our lives comes from the love and support you've shown us."

Grace touched her father's hand and expressed from her soul, "Papa, we, well certainly I, aren't mature enough to appreciate your silent actions as loud declarations of your love."

"Or be adequately appreciative of all the sacrifices you've made for this family," Abel added.

Dylan stared at the ground to compose himself before calmly adding, "All I want is for you kids to enjoy your lives, find contentment in small pleasures and love those dear to you."

"We will."

Grace very rarely felt those special moments people write about in books, but knew this was exactly the type of moment they spoke of: an understanding that went beyond words, a deepening of a bond that even death couldn't prise away. They'd never shared a group hug before, but this seemed like the ideal time. As soon as they relaxed their embrace the company director barged in to steal their father away. Dylan looked back and nodded that he also sensed something extraordinary pass between then.

The night closed in and the stars took their rightful place in the supernal sky to form a luminous blanket. Grace couldn't keep her neck horizontal long enough to enjoy the scene. She was mesmerised.

"Because we're out of the city and away from the pollution, that's why they appear way brighter," Abel said.

"Your brother's right, Grace, but the reason you're also looking in wonder and awe at the stars is because most of your evenings are confined by a ceiling," the Wind added. "The stars remind us how beautiful life is when we keep our focus elevated. Appreciating the scenery in the universe and our relationship to it requires discipline, perseverance and alternating between the territories of the magical and the everyday."

Her brother said, "We're way too dependent on artificial lightin'."

"Abel's right again," the Wind agreed. "When we revere the wondrous light show happening in the skies each evening, the grandeur highlights our own insignificance. Paradoxically, the stars also shine to mirror our mighty and significant brilliance, but how often do we acknowledge them?"

"A little like our father," Grace admitted.

"The constellations convey the world's vastness," the Wind continued, "the larger rhythms of existence and our unity with the divine. We're so caught up in trying to acquire external power . . ."

She knew how this sentence ended. " . . . but is it us that make the stars light up on demand?"

"These celestial bodies exist for us to wish upon and to view our highest selves through their radiance. These small, bright points of illumination hold the real power in the world, not electricity towers, politicians or celebrities. Grace, let the stars in the sky guide you through the ages of time, let them share with you their stories of fate and destiny."

Then Abel divulged some words that made Grace's throat close up. "I just want to be a good man." But no sooner had the words left his mouth, opening the path for deeper sentiments to be expressed between them, that his typical outlook returned. "From what looked like a pretty sucky night, it kinda turned out okay in the end, hey Sis?"

"Aha." She'd learned to align her field of consciousness with divine timing.

"Grace, don't limit yourself to the ceiling," the Wind said. "Operate from the level of the stars. You and they are made of the very same fabric, so go out there and shine!"

Facing Abel, Grace declared, "I'm so grateful you're my brother."

"Ditto, with sister on the end."

They embraced and felt the undulating of each other's breath.

91 | Expressions of Creation

On waking the next morning Grace felt alive—tingling and pulsing with life even. An imaginary door had opened and she felt a shift of attitude. She prayed to be in a state of appreciation for all the coming day would bring. She pondered on how a butterfly can only emerge from its cocoon when it's ready to fly, and when the outside world can support the first flapping of its wings.

Both the inner and outer must align themselves in willingness.

"Grace, I can only teach you as many of the universal laws as you're open to."

"I'm ready for them all."

The Wind said with a chuckle, "I'm not saying this to offend you, Grace, but in years to come you will laugh at your own folly in believing that you could receive the universe's wisdom in one instant download. It's too intense, and you're not yet strong or light enough. Anyway, this wisdom gets passed to you over lifetimes, plural. Anything of true worth comes over time and requires a display of disciplined dedication, stamina and patience. Grace, doing anything properly takes perseverance and devotion."

Don't I know it!

The Wind continued. "Working in the right attitude, rather than with muscle, is what brings forth the higher vibration. Your personality's effort is nothing but the caboose. Unfortunately it mistakenly thinks it's leading the train."

Walking to the bus stop, Grace examined a withered, lifeless flower resting on a concrete driveway causing her to think of the wrinkled raisins she sprinkled on her porridge this morning.

"Remind me again, Wind, if nature is about constant creation, why is it necessary to observe the dying forms?"

"Creation is ordered by rhythms and cycles, and there is order to all creation," the Wind explained. "Withering is still an expression of creation, Grace. It's newness though that you and your generation are preoccupied with: this week's latest fad, the hottest fashion trends and cutting-edge technology gadgets. There is enormous validity in the old and the aged. In all processes—including dying expressions—there rests and breathes great beauty so allow your-self to be destroyed and remade. And ask yourself, 'What are you so busy racing towards?' It's a long journey out there, Grace. Pace yourself."

What, or who, am I sprinting to? And where?

The Wind changed tack. "You could also argue that the blossom isn't truly resplendent, as it hasn't lived yet. It hasn't begun to express its full magnificence to the world."

"You'd be going against mainstream society then."

"I'm not so sure about that, Grace. You yourself may change your mind when you're a bit older," the Wind said. "Nature is constant reinvention. Whether it's presently born—or a step away from death—each element of the cycle contains expanding perfection. Recognise these regenerative patterns, whether it's in relation to the seasons, crops or phases of human life."

Grace admired the Wind's abundant energy.

"We fail to value the completeness of life when we focus only on one part, a solitary element of the whole. The fading away signifies the completion of an entire life. Open your eyes beyond the decline to witness the birth that exists there too."

Grace crossed the road to wait for the bus.

"When you're with Veronika you view her as a seventy-three-year-old lady. You forget that she was once your age, a single woman before marrying your grandfather, a mother raising your own moth-er, then working as a governess. Veronika isn't only a grandmother. She has much more experience and wisdom in her than this one role you've locked her into."

"Veronika was my age once?" It was as though the thought had never crossed the naïve Grace's mind.

"You appear surprised by this notion."

"I just, I don't know. I never thought about it or imagined it."

Blighted by her ignorance, Grace felt humbled. She recalled a few years back Veronika saying to her, "I've been in your shoes," but Grace didn't take it literally.

"Tap into the vast, indescribable wisdom that exists inside her. Veronika adds much to your life as a grandmother, but brings even more depth and intensity when you embrace all she's been before."

The bus arrived and Grace sat at the front on her own, engrossed in conversation with the Wind.

"Both the blossoming, unrefined beauty of a teenager and an elderly lady's deeply wrinkled face teach us to appreciate each stage of the cycle."

"What do you mean?" asked Grace, hoping nobody would sit next to her.

"There's nothing sadder than an older lady envying youth's fairness or the teenager sacrificing her innocence before her time. Cherry blossoms in full bloom are dazzling, but they're equally stunning when they've blown off the trees and lay broken and trampled on the ground. The blossoms are in different stages of their beauty, of their growth and decline. Their essential gloriousness isn't altered whether they're being admired up high on branches or resting on the soil below, ignored."

92 | Awkward Awakenings

When the bus eventually made it to school, Grace ran to the bathroom stalls and locked herself in to secure some peace. She had never craved privacy more.

"Okay, keep going, Wind."

"Nature is always involved in an active expansion process—like us in our interior lives—and the skill is accepting which part of the growth cycle we're in and not resisting it. There is as much cheer in the first daffodils of spring as in a rose in the frost clinging to its vanishing life. It's necessary for us to celebrate both the fading and that yet to flourish."

Grace lay back on the toilet bowl to rest her back.

"But don't mistake me," the Wind added, "it's not always a smooth process. As we're developing there are growth spurts mixed with plenty of stops and starts along the way. It's important not to get disheartened."

"But the awakening process can be so ugly," she whined.

"Awakening and the teenage years are never easy, Grace, as the growth is intense, awkward and mysterious, but it's still a beautiful journey."

Grace decided to now view everything happening in her sixteenth year as messy, but necessary.

"As we mature, we might choose to live life at a slower pace and what we once valued in our youth may no longer hold any relevance for us. We unreservedly accept any changes that develop and appear in our attitudes or physical limitations."

"Similar to Kosmos with his cane." Grace bit her lip.

Since his death it appeared life carried on in some shape or form for the Rose family, even though at times grief sunk each of them to great depths of despair.

"Don't ever feel like life's ground to a standstill," said the Wind. "Remember the constantly changing equilibrium at play. The degree of personal contentment you feel will rise as you make peace with both the positive and negative aspects of each state and integrate them as a whole into your being. At your age, Grace, you have lots of energy to experiment and try new things, but with no business acumen, style or aplomb, because you're still finding your feet. By the time you reach Veronika's age, you would've found the way, but might not have the audacity to be as bold or 'out there' as you are now in your approach."

The image of Kosmos's cane kept flashing up in her mind. "So not all aspects of me are simultaneously coming into flower then? Some are actually ripening?"

"Grace, all things begin and end at their appropriate time— from love affairs to work contracts to leisure pursuits. While you're in the school system you assume this is all there is; you can't yet imagine the breadth of life that exists beyond these school gates. High school is not your forever, Grace, but it is your present."

Boy, ain't that the truth!

93 | Living in the Mystery

Grace was sitting at the breakfast bar one Friday morning in March, gazing out the window onto the garden trying to discern the difference between a flash of inspiration and a distraction.

"Let me explain the distinction," the Wind said. "Imagine you're completing your homework and recall an email you forgot to send to a friend. Write the email, follow through on that guidance, but don't get distracted and spend another hour emailing all your other friends. It requires discipline, and a focus on being effective instead of busy."

Grace sensed an air of sentimentality from the Wind.

"I know you have a lot on with school commitments, but keep feeling me around you, Grace. Keep our union constant."

It was the consistency Grace struggled with, but when out of touch she gently brought herself back by evoking the energies of the ocean's ebb and flow and remembering that everything in life operates in cycles of time.

A vast improvement on telling myself how much I suck.

"Each day is precious, Grace. The more you experience this truth—not just as a saying on a fridge magnet or a bumper sticker—the less you'll berate yourself. You'll be driven to live life from a higher rhythm. Treat these twenty-four hours with the respect they deserve for they won't come again. So what's on the cards for today?"

"I want to taste the multitude of exotic spices in my chai tea as I sip it, hear the baby blackbirds chirping in the trees, smell all the possibilities the coming day will bring, witness the divine in the weeds and tap into my own grace-filled presence." She spoke with stops and starts, looking up to the ceiling and around the room, so she didn't completely sound like a robot regurgitating pre-programmed answers.

"Single-mindedly focus on one action at a time and we'll be in dialogue throughout the day. Don't let your mind wander too much!"

"Unfortunately it has a life of its own," she joked back, then said seriously, "I know I'd like to spend the day relaxing at the beach, but I can't cut classes so I'll learn as much as I can at school and then ask Abel if he wants to go for a drive down the coast later and watch the sunset." Grace was dreading school before this chat but she'd somehow now turned the rigmarole of the coming day into a pleasurable event.

If that's not a 180° change in attitude then I don't know what is!

"And I'll focus only on what's essential."

"And how will you know what's essential?" the Wind asked.

"By remaining in dialogue with you and bringing my being to all my doing. And remembering that all I have is this moment and that I get to choose the meaning which I attach to it."

"Yes, Grace, it's you who provides all the meaning, so trust in the perfection of the moment."

"All that matters is my state of consciousness in the now, the only time that ever exists, so I won't invest undue energy in building a mentally constructed image of a false self in situations that don't even exist."

"And?" the Wind prompted.

"I won't look back. Nothing good exists there. Rear-view mirror living only leads to accidents."

"Marvellous, Grace! Keep awakening to love. Plant those seeds. Life's blessings don't miraculously appear. Occasionally they do—but more often than not they come from kernels planted long ago. Time must be spent tending the garden. You can't plant a seed and expect it to blossom the very next day."

Grace's usual response would've been, "Why not?" It was almost comical that she once believed her whims to be more powerful than the universe's. Thankfully, her evolving self was now open and curious to all. "Explain why, Wind."

"You wouldn't appreciate the flower as you've not grown with it. When you're only focused on the flower—the result, the end goal—you've ignored the growth process, where life occurs and the divine resides. Remember, to all creation there is a visible and invisible gestation period. The hidden magic takes time to reveal itself. Imposing your own timing schedule on the flower's birth is an impossibility."

Grace finally understood how delusional her previous ways of operating in the world were.

"Everything presents itself in its own good time when both you and the universe are ready. Picture the seed again. It has its own predetermined growth pattern, but your devotion and attention can enhance it. It'll grow quicker if regularly watered with love—as much as water—and planted in an opportune place, at a fortuitous time and given adequate support. Grace, prune away the dead parts of your life to create space for the buds to bloom."

An incredible sadness now descended on her. She had the feeling she'd soon have to be teaching this wisdom to herself.

"You'll thrive, my love. Through the divine you'll accurately perceive the truth of any given situation."

"I don't think I'm ready."

"Readiness has nothing to do with it. The only time you have is now," the Wind gently explained. "And I'm always here for you, Grace, I just won't be so hands-on. The intense immersion tutorials are over for now. It's time for you to fly, to expand your understanding, express your compassion and be of loving service to the world. See beyond the lens of your personality to symbolically perceive the universal truth behind all events and situations. Be the living expression of your soul."

Grace was silent for a moment and then confidently ventured forth. "The personality is far more concerned with its own image than with serving others, so embodying my soul and being the observer—acting from the height of the stars—is how I choose to live. This is the next step of my transformation. The seed has been planted. Wind, you've shown me the way. It's now time for me reclaim my throne, embody my regality and wear my grace like a crown."

"Grace, with every thought, feeling and action you'll teach yourself and inspire those whose lives you're privileged to touch."

The flowers on the frangipani tree beside the kitchen window gently swayed and then took on a tranquil stillness.

ABOUT THE AUTHOR

Kristina Dryža is a futurist living in Adelaide, Australia. *Grace and the Wind* is her first novel. For more information please visit her website at www.kristinadryza.com.

www.ingramcontent.com/pod-product-compliance
Lightning Source LLC
Chambersburg PA
CBHW051137030726
47504CB00004B/915

* 9 7 8 0 9 9 2 4 4 7 3 3 5 *